FROM
HELL TO
MIDNIGHT

**Center Point
Large Print**

**This Large Print Book carries the
Seal of Approval of N.A.V.H.**

FROM HELL TO MIDNIGHT

RICHARD S. WHEELER

CENTER POINT PUBLISHING
THORNDIKE, MAINE

This Center Point Large Print edition
is published in the year 2006 by arrangement with
Pinnacle, an imprint of Kensington Publishing Corp.

The text of this Large Print edition is unabridged. In other
aspects, this book may vary from the original edition. Printed in
Thailand. Set in 16-point Times New Roman type.

ISBN 1-58547-809-1

Cataloging-in-Publication data is available from the Library of Congress.

Chapter 1

It was too quiet. The old mine perched on a flat far above, its weathered boards blending into the arid mountainside. The harsh sun had bleached the works almost white except for the corrugated metal roof, which remained gray and rust-streaked.

Nothing stirred, not even the air. It was as if this mine, this place, had been caught in amber long ago, and now stood well preserved up there.

Hannibal Jones saw not even a bird. He had been climbing this ancient trail for two days, leading two pack mules laden with his gear. He had pushed higher and higher into these strange and dead mountains east of Ely, through silent canyons with scarcely any vegetation, over rock that showed no sign of being shaped by water. Once he had passed a small snake, the only living thing he had seen, though he knew that even this forbidding land had its complement of creatures, most of them nocturnal, able to feed when the fierce sun had given them respite from heat.

It was as if this whole country was dead, or nearly so. He had rounded a promontory and spotted the mine at once. It was the Alice, and only a few years ago it had been yielding a bonanza for its owner, the horrible Harold Haggarty. But that was the mystery. Why was it suddenly abandoned? Had it run out of ore? Had they hit water that had flooded the drifts? A cave-in? Heat? Noxious gases? Had the Alice Mine run into one of the array of financial troubles that plague most mines? Ore that couldn't be reduced? Changes in transportation? A strike? Unhappy stock-holders?

No one knew.

Hannibal tugged the lead lines and continued up the steep grade, feeling the strain on his muscles as he worked his way up the precarious, rock-strewn trail, which obviously had not been used in many years. At several points he had been forced to lever slide rock off the trail to permit the passage of his mules.

The Alice was reputed to be haunted. That was fine with Hannibal; it kept the superstitious away. He had come across occasional references to it in Nevada papers; the haunted mine east of Ely, where no one escaped alive, where prospectors vanished, where mysterious rock slides terrified the intruder.

He did keep a sharp eye on the vaulting slopes above. Sun and wind and frost were always loosening surface rock, and sometimes the slightest disruption of the rhythms of nature sent it roaring down some slope. Often, in the course of his business, he had seen small avalanches tumble down desert grades, seemingly triggered by nothing at all. But of course Hannibal knew that something started them; maybe even the slow, steady clop of his mules.

He took pride in his big mules, carefully chosen and carefully shod for this remote desert world. These two could make a living on brush that would starve a horse, negotiate narrow trails that would panic a horse, stay calm where a horse would blow up and pitch its load, and probably itself, off a ledge.

There were no such things as haunted mines except in the rich folklore of his calling. Hannibal Jones was no prospector, and took pains to separate himself from the sourdoughs that roamed these remote and perilous corners of the Great Basin. He was both a mining engineer and a geologist, and his unusual business was the revival of old mines, a calling that had taken him into some of the loneliest fastnesses of the West.

Armed with a pair of degrees from the Columbia School of Mines and solid field experience, he had researched the life and death of hundreds of abandoned mining properties in the West, and had then examined them one by one, looking for what the owners had missed. It had been lucrative, but sometimes an irregular income when he hit a dry patch. But he was far from poor, and the game was exciting to him.

There were dozens of ways in which a mine might fail to give up the wealth it possessed. The most common was simply inefficiency. He had found heaps of tailings so rich in mineral that they could be mined again. Sometimes he came across mountains of low-grade ore, stockpiled against the time when it would be economic to ship it to a distant railroad. Sometimes he discovered flooding that had overwhelmed the pumps and forced the mine to close. Then he had to devise a way to drain the mine. Sometimes the owners had missed a seam, or failed to see how a fault had displaced the seam. In such cases they had imagined the ore had run out, when in fact a hundred yards or three hundred or maybe only fifty feet off the seam, the ore continued on its way.

That was his business. And it was a good one. He actually liked the quiet, lonely life outdoors, when he could probe a mine at his leisure. His work always began in offices and archives and libraries and newspaper morgues, where he studied the legal documents, noted the annual yield, read assay reports, followed the mine's life in the local newspapers, all of which gave him a fine background on any property long before he headed out to look it over.

Once he had discovered mineral wealth, he filed claims if he could, or bought the property for a song, and soon converted his property into a small bonanza. It varied. Most often, he negotiated a deal with the owners. For a price he would show them what they had missed and how to mine it. Each mine had a different history, a different set of owners, or in some cases no owners at all.

Now Hannibal made his slow way up the grade toward the Alice. He did not dress like a prospector, but always wore what he supposed were professional clothes, suitable to his unique trade. These included high-top lace-up boots made for walking and ankle support, strong canvas trousers, a blue shirt, a tweedy jacket, and a red polka-dot bow tie. The tie was important. It separated him from the ruffians who roamed the wilds of Nevada and other lonely places. Perched on his nose were wire-rimmed spectacles that corrected his nearsighted vision, and on his head he wore a good white pith helmet in heat, and a broad-brimmed felt in cold weather. With this sturdy attire he lived in complete comfort and ease, and fully in accord with his learned profession.

Of course he shaved daily, scraping off the chin whiskers with a fine steel straight-edge. Each morning he would undertake that ritual, no matter how hot or cold, hanging a small mirror on his tent or some convenient spot, lathering up with a bar of yellow soap, stropping the razor, and then scraping away until his cheeks were as smooth as a baby's. Thus he always presented himself as a man of parts, a man with gravity and dignity, a man unlike the usual ruffians who called themselves prospectors.

In a way, his clothing also reflected his nature. He was a serious, thoughtful man comfortable with himself, practical, gifted at wilderness living, proud of his achievements. And his dress proudly reflected all of that. The leather of his high-top boots helped him resist sprains and was thick enough to ward off the strike of a pit viper. His packs were as meticulously planned and maintained as the rest of him. One mule's burden largely consisted of a small field laboratory and some prospecting tools, hammers, pry bar, shovel, and pick. He was capable of assaying most any mineralized rock right on the spot. That mule also carried a cask of water, which he husbanded carefully.

The other mule carried his clothing and toiletry,

food, a shelter, and a small canvas tent. All in all, he could survive for two weeks with this outfit, longer if he found water and food.

He topped a hillside and ended up on a plateau where the old Alice stood mutely in an amphitheater, a sort of frown emanating from it as if he were a trespasser, which, in a way, he was. It stood perhaps three quarters up the mountain, and from this aerie he could gaze into a white haze and discern, just barely, the dry flats of Nevada thousands of feet below.

The mine itself seemed ordinary in appearance even if it had been the richest gold bonanza in the world through the eighteen-eighties. It had made its gaudy owner, Lucky Haggarty, as Harold came to be called, a multimillionaire. Shortly after Lucky's death the mine had closed, and no one had ever figured out why. And now no one knew who owned the Alice. Certainly not Lucky's several wives, or his progeny, the product of these bigamous marriages, or his legendary mistress.

The shaft was not vertical, but inclined downward into the mountainside, and there was a hoist works at the head that could draw a skip, a pivoted ore car, up the incline from below. The hoist works had been powered by a small boiler, long since dismantled and sold off.

A barracks had housed the single miners. It must have been difficult to keep them at this isolated place. A few gray cottages were scattered about the flat, homes for administrators, married people, and foremen. Heaps of tailings had been dumped off the edge of the plateau, but certain heaps of rock remained on the bench, and these interested Hannibal. They were probably low-grade ore, uneconomic to ship. Everything on this remote mountain plateau had arrived or departed by animal muscle, including the ore.

He eyed the sunbaked flat, barely five acres in size, and hunted first for water. Somewhere there had to be water. He always made water his first order of business. Without it, he would have to turn back before completing his work. A mine employing twenty or thirty men who lived in a barracks would require plenty of water for men and mine animals. He eyed the silent barracks, whose glassless windows formed black teeth along the weary wall of sun-bleached wood.

The usual debris cluttered the mine head: cable, old pulleys, twisted rail, ancient casks, a rusting ore car. He spotted a hand pump below the cliff, and tried pumping it. It emitted a squeak, then a howl, and yielded nothing. He didn't expect it to; its leathers would be dry and unable to suck water up. But at the base of the cliff west of the mine head, he spotted a tiny pipe leaking a faint trickle of water that formed a brown stain down the rock and vanished into the rubble below it.

Water, then, if it was potable. He would test it. He always did, using his field kit to look for heavy metals. He was not inclined to drink arsenic or cadmium. He spotted no skeletons or dead insects where the water briefly pooled in the rock before vanishing. That was a good sign.

The roar caught him by surprise. One moment an eerie silence on a sunbaked bench; the next a thunder rising from the bowels of the mountain, booming and rattling. He peered up and froze, for above him a hundred yards was an avalanche of red rock, tumbling, rolling, shattering, careening, bouncing. And it was about to land on his head.

Chapter 2

Hannibal jammed himself against the cliff, hoping the velocity of the slide would carry it over his head. Rock sailed over him, dust boiled around him, bits and pieces clattered by, bouncing on the flat. A massive rock the size of a horse thundered by, hit the flat, and shivered the mountain. Several bits of sharp rock hit his pith helmet, knocking it askew. Dust choked him and he buried his nose in the tweed of his sleeve.

Then, suddenly, it stopped, save for a small rattle or two as the last stray rock bounced down the grade. The dust boiled up, obscuring his vision. He was covered with grit. A lazy breeze slowly carried the orange dust away and things came into view. His mules had panicked and retreated to the lip of the flat, but seemed to be okay.

He stepped warily away from the cliff where he had plastered himself to the rock, keeping a wary eye on the slope above. Nothing moved. He studied the talus. It matched the reddish color of the uppermost rimrock above. He pulled a blue bandanna from his pocket and slowly wiped his face and neck and ears, scraping away the grit until he felt whole again. Then he dipped it in the trickle dropping from the pipe and wiped the cold water over his face and neck. He felt better.

He removed his wire-rimmed glasses and carefully washed the lenses, dried them, and restored them to his nose. He studied the cliff above, seeing only blank blue sky and anonymous walls of weathered rock. No wonder the place had a reputation for being haunted.

Still, the scientist in him required answers. He would unload his mules and then see about that slide. It was his nature to put things in good order, so he unloaded his pack mules, watered and picketed them in some brush where they could scrounge a living, made camp as far from the brooding cliffs as he could get, and then studied the amphitheater for some trail that would take him up those precipitous slopes to the landslide area. He didn't believe in ghosts. He did believe in the possibility of human mischief.

He remembered to take a small camp ax with him. There wasn't a stick of firewood near the mine, and he hoped to boil some tea for dinner. As an afterthought, he slipped a small revolver out of his camp gear and slung the holster from his belt.

The best way up was roundabout, so he hiked left until he found a dry wash and then began ascending it, climbing over huge sharp boulders. The grade was steep, sometimes fifty degrees, but he persevered even when his pulse was rocketing and his lungs were howling. But in half an hour marked by moments of sheer terror, he reached the red-stained rimrock and worked his way to the slide area.

A segment of the cliff maybe ten yards wide had loosened and fallen. Far below, postage-stamp size, lay the mine buildings. Above, the arid brown mountain climbed to the bold blue sky, with nothing but desert weeds to vegetate it. Bristlecone pine and juniper dotted higher slopes. Hannibal paced the area, finding nothing obvious. No footprints in that wind-blown rock, no tools left behind, no sign of human life, or any sort of life.

Along the newly sheared edge were some light crumbling spots in the sandstone. Hannibal hit the edge with his camp ax and the percussion left similar marks. But that didn't mean anything. He might sooner believe in ghosts than in someone bent on killing him. He widened his search, looking for trails from this place, and found a couple, trending upward. The trails had very little dirt on them and the obscure smudges on those pathways translated into nothing. It was possible someone had been here and unloosed that avalanche of rock. It was possible that sun and wind and frost had prepared that avalanche, and it took only the arrival of a man and two mules to trigger it.

But one thing he knew: It was not the work of ghosts. He studied the brooding mountains, empty and secretive, and found no sign of life. In this corner of the world, all life struggled. He observed the sun sliding toward its appointment with the western horizon, and hurried down the trail, using his camp ax to brake his descent. By late afternoon, just as a chill rolled in, he reached his campsite.

The mules had wandered. He had picketed them. He remembered it clearly. But now there was no sign of them. He headed downslope and found them a hundred yards below the Alice Mine, busily gnawing rabbitbrush and greasewood, which were supposedly inedible. At least inedible to anything but his mules.

He gathered the picket lines and then felt a prickle. The lines had not pulled loose from the stakes he had pounded in the ground, but had been neatly cut. He refused to believe that at first; the mules had simply untied themselves from the picket pins.

He gathered the mules, examined them for injury and found none, and slowly walked his way up to the flat. The picket pins were where he had driven them into the clay. And attached to each was a short piece of rope, neatly sliced.

Someone was stalking him.

He saw no one. There was little to hide anyone. Only rock. No trees, no brush concealed anything from his vision. There were no footprints in the earth. Not so much as the dent of a boot heel. It was time to search the buildings, which he did one by one, wary of scorpions and snakes as well as two-legged desert creatures. He kicked in each door, his revolver in hand, and found only deep silence. He probed through the forlorn miners' barracks, pushed into the hollow, stained cottages, explored what had once been the whitewashed company office, kicked open toolsheds, pried open a powder magazine. He did not quit until he had examined every structure, every outbuilding, including a large latrine that had probably served the whole mining camp. And everywhere he found only deep silence, dust, a faint acrid smell of decay, and loneliness.

He faced the silent and brooding slopes.

"Whoever you are," he said in a voice that carried, "I mean you no harm. I have come in peace. I invite you to join me."

He addressed the cliffs in other directions in much the same way, and bought only silence from his investment in friendship. Yet someone, or something, had been there in his camp while he was scrambling up the grades. Not ghosts.

He faced the forthcoming night uneasily, debated pulling back from the flat, perhaps moving down a few hundred yards. He wouldn't want to fall asleep there, where someone was stalking. But if someone was stalking him on the flat, then that someone would also stalk him below. Better to confront the shadowy person. Or was it a person at all? Could a creature be the cause of all this?

He headed for a decaying shed and hacked the plank walls. The arid wood fell apart under each blow, and soon he had enough fuel for a hot supper. He ate simply in the wilds, often oatmeal gruel with raisins added, which was filling and required nothing but some water and a fire. That would suffice this evening. Oatmeal was not only a food that was easily carried, but emergency animal fodder as well. He had brought thirty pounds of it.

He built his fire in twilight, wondering if he was playing the fool, highlighting himself in the flickering light. He searched the darkness uneasily, looking for the twin glow of staring eyes in the murk. But he saw nothing. He boiled his gruel, added salt, and ate it slowly. It offered little pleasure, but that didn't matter. He favored practical foods. His mission was to find mineral wealth, not to live sumptuously in an isolated desert camp.

The fire swiftly decayed into a glowing orange heap of coals, and darkness crept closer. Nothing broke the eerie silence, and he persuaded himself that he was utterly alone. There might be a mountain lion or a desert mule deer or a dozen other creatures about, but he saw nothing. Only the looming black timbers of the mine works poking the bright-lit heavens.

Tomorrow would be fruitful. He would run several tests on the tailings that had been dumped over the edge of the flat, and several more tests on the low-grade ore stockpiled in gray heaps near the mine shaft. Maybe, if the timbers were sound, he would explore the mine itself. A jackknife jammed into the mine timbers always revealed what he needed to know. Good wood resisted the blade. Rotted wood did not. Some samples taken from the various faces far below would prove valuable, and he hoped to take several.

He would not leave without examining the geology, and sometimes that was the hardest of his tasks. But it was often the most rewarding. He had acquired, somehow, almost a sixth sense about the way the veins ran, and the faults that disrupted them. And when the geology baffled him, he threw himself at it with a fevered need to conquer it. Much could be read from the surface. His trained eye could locate faults, upthrusts, lateral movements. Sometimes from reading the vegetation he could locate water or seeps. By the time he finished with the Alice, he would have an excellent idea of its potential.

Often, in the course of his work, he would conclude that an old mine was truly defunct; that there was no more ore to be gotten from it, that its owners had cannily exploited it every way that modern technology could manage; that nothing remained in the tailings worth a reworking. That was true of nine out of ten, he figured. It was the tenth mine, the one mismanaged or abandoned, that excited him. This was one of those.

No one had ever fathomed why the Alice was abruptly closed. Why the miners were laid off one shocking day. Why one month of 1889 the ore reserves were splendid; why the next month of 1889 the mine lay silent and forlorn. Hannibal had searched relentlessly through the records of the Nevada mining bureau, through old newspapers, through milling and smelting records.

The Alice was still owned. Taxes were being paid by a shadowy company in San Francisco named Western Holdings. A letter to that address, seeking permission to examine the works, had gone unanswered. A visit to the Market Street offices revealed only a locked pebbled-glass door. Inquiries among the mining fraternity yielded nothing by way of names. When Lucky Haggarty died, so did his fortune.

Hannibal had calculated the risks and decided to examine the Alice anyway. If there was gold, he would find it. If there were problems that made mining uneconomic, he would find those too. If his finds were promising, he would track down the mysterious owners of the moribund mine and make an offer.

He waited for the orange coals to diminish, then shoveled gritty soil over them so that they would not be a beacon, and sat in utter darkness under the carpet of stars, wondering whether he was truly alone.

Chapter 3

The mules stirred, restless on their pickets. One snorted. One squealed. Hannibal woke with a start, grasped his revolver, listened a moment, and then slipped out into the cold clear night, his weapon in hand. The icy mountain air smacked him. Above, a pale sliver of moon cast cold light over a gloomy landscape. He saw nothing. The night was as quiet and bleak as the mountains.

Twice more that long night the mules awakened

him, snorting and dancing, tugging on their pickets. Each time, Hannibal could find no sign of trouble. The old mine buildings rose out of deep shadow, the lunar light glinting on their corrugated metal roofs.

The third time, Hannibal stood in the dark, feeling the cold penetrate his long underwear, and again addressed the shadows.

"Whoever you are, I mean you no harm. If you would like to make yourself known, just step up, out of the darkness. You'll be safe. We'll build a little fire and talk."

But not even the sighing wind responded. It wasn't ghosts. The mine might have that reputation, but Hannibal Jones was a scientist, and scientists looked for rational reasons, things that could be proven, things that obeyed the laws of physics. Animals, then. Some creature prowled this place, its prints invisible on the hard rock. But Hannibal was uneasy with that. There was enough clay and dirt to reveal the print of a bear or any smaller mammal.

He pulled his bedroll out of the tent, wrapped the two blankets around him, and settled to the ground outside, determined to catch or see or frighten away whatever was troubling the lonely site of the Alice Mine. He sat patiently, cross-legged, huddled deep in his blankets against the chill, dozing now and then, his hand always on the sidearm.

But nothing more happened. A faint light caught the serrated northeastern mountaintops, then a band of light that drew color as it brightened, eventually turning blue. And at last, the dawn of a new day. The sliver of moon faded, a ghost in the dawn sky, and Hannibal decided to begin his day, tired as he was. He performed his ritual shave, enjoying the comfort of the keen straight-edge as it scraped away his whiskers. When he was done, his cheeks were smooth.

He headed for his kit, and discovered that his household goods had been scattered. His mess kit, pots, cotton sacks of grain and meal, were spread over a wide area. Animals, then. He collected everything, found nothing amiss, nothing eaten. That troubled him more than the scattering of his goods. Animals ate what they could. It sure was a puzzle.

After frying some johnnycakes, he set to work. He would put in a couple of busy days here, maybe more. He would need to run tests on the tailings to see whether valuable minerals were being overlooked; he would need to do the same with the heaps of low-grade ore. He would need to estimate the volume of low-grade material, and if the tailings proved valuable, the amount of cubic yards of that as well. He would need assay samples, carefully selected from the various types of rock he found, each labeled and put in a special compartmented bag. He had a small lab with him, but not a proper assay furnace that would reduce ore and provide exact descriptions of the minerals and their percentages.

After all that, he would explore the mine shaft if it was safe to do so, attempt to take samples from the faces far below, study the geology and estimate reserves, if any, and all the while make copious notes in his journal. Only by meticulous record-keeping could he turn these dead mines into profitable ones.

The sun swiftly warmed the slopes and brightened the day, and his weariness left him as he began his lonely work. He would have a yarn or two to spread back in Ely, and a dozen other western mining towns when he returned to the cities.

Ghosts indeed. The bland blue sky, the silent bluffs, the occasional green or silver vegetation making a grim living in a hostile land, all were natural things he knew well. The only question was the nature of the clever animal that had scattered his gear and frightened his mules.

He collected his samples bag, a pick hammer, and a magnifying glass and set off for the tailings, which had been dumped down a grade to the north and stretched a quarter of a mile. That was a lot of rock torn out of the Alice. And he spotted plenty of quartz glistening in the early sunlight. Each promising egg-sized piece he licked clean, studied with his powerful magnifying glass for particles of free-floating gold or a blue streak indicating gold sulfurets, and dropped into his bag. The human tongue is, he knew, the prospector's finest instrument and he used it relentlessly.

He eased down the slope, careful not to sprain an ankle on loose rock, and collected six two-ounce samples of likely and unlikely rock, some of it quartz but most of it the country rock, granite, that had been pierced by the Alice Mine. Were they throwing out gold at the Alice? Or any other valuable mineral? He would soon know. He pulled and clawed his way up-slope, topped out on the flat, which actually wasn't very flat, and set to work. He set up an alcohol burner, a small brass scale with balance weights, a mortar and pestle, a horn spoon, a matrass or test tube, a blow-pipe, some blocks of charcoal, salt, a flask of mercury, and flasks of hydrochloric and nitric acid.

Little by little, he reduced a two-ounce sample of the quartz tailings to rubble, and then to powder, vigor-ously grinding it in his iron pestle. The simplest test of all is simply to wash some powder carefully in a horn spoon, and if gold is present it will remain on the bottom of the spoon while the debris is washed away. Hannibal applied the water in tiny amounts and found only a few microscopic grains of gold in the residue.

There were various other tests to conduct with the remaining powder, and these involved heat and acid. First he boiled the powdered rock with salt and mer-cury, hoping for an amalgam that could be heated until the mercury was driven off, leaving spongy gold residue. Then he smelted various rock powders in hollowed-out charcoal blocks, using his spirit lamp and a blowpipe, but the results were disappointing. He dropped the spongy material into his matrass and added salt and nitric acid, looking for silver. If silver had been present as he heated the sample, it would have precipitated as silver chloride, a cloudy liquid, and swiftly turned purple-black.

He found a little gold in the quartz, but nothing in

the country rock. Of silver he found nothing at all. But there were traces of copper and lead in some of the samples. That was disappointing. Silver and gold often were found in the same ore. Thus he toiled through the morning, oblivious of the surrounding world. If a ghost sailed by, he would not know it.

He nooned on hardtack and a tin of tomatoes, not needing anything else. He wished only to rest his body for a few minutes and then begin further explorations. The mine works rose silently above him, a dark scowl of timbers jabbing a hollow sky. He downed his chow and made notes in his ledger, each experiment carefully recorded with his L.E. Waterman fountain pen, an invention he considered a godsend. At one point something shadowed his page, but when he glanced up, he saw nothing: no cloud, no animal. But when he again glanced at his ledger, a blot was obscuring his last written word.

"Ghosts!" he said, and laughed.

He devoted a hot afternoon to studying the mountain of low-grade ore, which he estimated to run seventy thousand tons or so. The ore averaged three ounces of gold and a half ounce of silver to the ton, with traces of lead and copper. He did some quick calculations, assuming a rail spur from Ely would run half a million dollars a mile in that rough country, and concluded that the mine operators were entirely right: The ore could not profitably be shipped, and could only be stockpiled in the hope of better days or more efficient ways to mill it.

But all that could change. The mine might yield hundreds of thousands of tons of additional ore. Or so much high-grade that a spur would be worthwhile. Or maybe, as often happened, one type of ore would give way to another; what began as a gold mine might end up a silver mine or a giant copper deposit. He had analyzed several such mines and made a tidy sum from them. But it was most likely that the Alice would not be a very good bet after all, even assuming he could ever discover who owned it or why it had been shut down.

He finished his examination of the tailings and stockpiled ore by late afternoon, but he was far from done with his study of the Alice. This mine, like most, was surrounded by a patchwork of claims filed by others who hoped to horn in on the bonanza. Usually they didn't. But Hannibal knew geology, and knew things that eluded most prospectors and treasure-seekers. He knew a rich ore stratum might outcrop miles away, and at an entirely different altitude; that there was more to locating ore than filing claims adjacent to the existing mines. Before he was done, he would have a rich understanding of the geology of a wide area, and he would see whether other places, over the ridge and out of sight, might prove to be just as productive as the Alice.

But that would occupy him tomorrow, and maybe the next day too. For now, he would begin his probe down the shaft, and see what might be seen.

He armed himself with a pick, a geologist's hammer,

a well-filled carbide lamp, an emergency candle, a jackknife, a samples bag, a canteen, a pad of paper and pencil, and a coil of rope.

He first studied the mine head, especially what lay above it. Anything that might produce an avalanche would have to be removed before he entered. He had no intention of sealing himself in. Nothing but massive gray granite guarded the mine head, but it was capped by five hundred feet of red sandstone rimrock. The shaft descended along a gradient he estimated at thirty percent; its rails were intact. He probed the overhead timbers with his jackknife and found them hard and solid. This was not wet country and he expected nothing else. He worked his way down the slope for fifty yards or so, pausing frequently to test the timbers.

And then he came to the slide. The shaft was blocked by a huge cave-in that piled country rock wall to wall, from the rails to the timbering. He turned his carbide lamp on that massive heap of rock. There was nothing he could do. He was about to leave when something tickled his curiosity. He threw the lamplight toward the top and discovered no cave-in at all. Nothing had dropped down into the shaft as far as he could see. The rock had been put there by human agency. He climbed up the heap and held his hand at the point where the rubble met the roof, and felt the movement of cool air.

The barrier was deliberate.

Chapter 4

Air. Moving steadily up the incline toward daylight. Hannibal held his hand to the top of the shaft to make sure. Air, all right. He needed a closer look, so he carefully clambered up the rubble, keeping his carbide lamp ahead of him. He was ascending country rock, granite rubble similar to the rock from which the shaft was hewn. He climbed as high as he could and felt the cool air moving over his face.

He trained his lamp at the point where the rubble met the roof of the shaft. He saw no cave-in, no black dome that had emptied itself into the shaft; nor did the rubble ascend higher. Instead, there was a slit of darkness, barely an inch or two, from which the cool air issued. But he could see nothing even when he trained the reflector upon that slit. This heap of rock was there by human design, not by an accident of nature. He eyed the square-set timbering that paraded back to the mouth of the shaft, and noted there was no lagging, planks atop the timbering to keep loose rock from tumbling into the shaft. The granite was so hard and solid it had needed no support. That was further evidence that this heap of rubble had been built there by human agency. And one other thought intrigued him. That air came from somewhere, some vent or adit, or maybe even a natural fissure somewhere. The Alice kept her secrets.

He would need other equipment, a pry bar and pick

and shovel, to hollow out a passage through the rubble barrier. He carefully lowered himself to the floor of the shaft, taking pains not to sprain an ankle, and considered the matter. The blocked shaft suggested that there was still ore in the Alice and someone wanted to keep it there or at least prevent its discovery. But who was that someone? And why? He suspected that other explorers or prospectors had wandered in, discovered the air, and sought to gain entry. And yet the rubble was not disturbed. It was as if the ghosts of the mine had carefully piled the rubble back in place whenever someone had disturbed it, and so it had remained for years.

He knew he ought to be careful, not of ghosts but of the phantom mortal who was silently guarding the mine. As if to punctuate the thought, a cascade of rock careened down the bluff and peppered the area around the mine head. Fearful of being trapped, Hannibal raced up the steep grade, peered sharply about, noted a cubic yard or so of red sandstone from high above scattered wantonly about, and listened for the sound of another avalanche. But he saw nothing.

He extinguished his carbide lamp and stepped into the bright light, which blinded him. He dodged sideways along the cliff, but nothing more happened. It was as if nothing had happened, and he doubted that anything could be made of it. Each and every day, sun, frost, wind, and roots sent rock careening down cliffs everywhere. He squinted up the bluff to the red sandstone stratum, seeing nothing amiss. Yet that rock was what had tumbled down around the mine head.

His red bow tie was askew, so he straightened it.

He checked on his mules. Both were unharmed and on their picket lines. They were staring toward a side canyon upslope, their ears cupped forward. Hannibal could see nothing there; it was a place of silence and solitude. He checked himself. Next thing he would be believing the mine was haunted if he was not careful with his thoughts. He drew a shovel, pick, and pry bar from his tools and took them to the shaft. He hunted through the debris, looking for an abandoned pipe, which he intended to place in the mine head for air, should there be a major avalanche, but could find none. A man could dig his way out of big trouble with air and water and maybe a bag of raisins.

The day was waning and he wondered whether to tackle the rubble then or in the morning. He decided that was a decision he didn't have to make. He eased down the steep grade of the shaft, hauling his heavy tools, and then lit his carbide lamp at the rubble that blocked passage. He was soon prying large chunks of rock off the top and tumbling them down to the floor of the shaft. But when he had a foot or so cleared, he found that the rubble continued on the other side for as far as he could see, within the mine. It would be no small task to carve a crawlway into the mysterious Alice Mine.

Light was fading. He could see, by looking up the grade to the mine head, that twilight was descending. He would call it a day. Tomorrow would be an eventful one if he could burrow through the rubble and into the mine.

He reached the surface without trouble, remembering to bring his heavy tools with him, and immediately felt the dry and pleasant air and the radiant heat of sun-warmed rock. It was time to care for his faithful beasts. He stepped down off that sloping plateau, and discovered no mules where he had picketed them. He repressed anger. Probably a lion had panicked them and they had yanked up their pickets and taken off. In the soft light he saw little, certainly no sign of his mules.

This Alice Mine was going to be one of the tough ones, but he had dealt with those before. Some mines seemed almost alive, resentful of any probing and poking, while other mines welcomed him and seemed delighted to have him examining their treasures. The Alice, so hard to reach, so distant from any other mortal, was shaping up to be the worst.

"Sam! Esther! Where are you hiding?" he yelled.

Was that a small snort? He walked into the gloaming, down a rocky slope, and into a pocket far below, where the mules stood quietly.

"I didn't think you'd go far," he said. "Good grass. No wonder."

He collected the lines and froze. Both mules were picketed, the pickets driven neatly into that rocky soil. He peered about fearfully. Had he done this almost without thinking, out of old habit? No. He had never been there. He stared uneasily into the half-light, saw nothing, and came to a decision. The mules were on good feed. He would leave them and bring water.

If someone was going to steal his mules, Sam and Esther would be long gone.

He turned to the slopes and addressed the phantom.

"Thank you for putting the mules on grass," he said. "I take it for a sign of friendship. I'll be camping near the mine, and look forward to your company."

His words did not echo. He heard only the sighing of deep wilderness. Back in his camp he chopped more firewood out of the decaying shed, boiled up some oatmeal with raisins and salt, and spooned the dreary mix into his mouth. He cared about food, but the effort to generate delicious meals while out in the field only wasted time and energy. Better to put his resources to good use finding out what he needed to know.

He didn't worry about the fire, at least not much. If anyone meant him harm, he would have long since suffered it. But that made him restless and he was having second thoughts. Someone had tried to kill him with an avalanche or two. Intuitively, he backed away from the flame. He washed the pot and then inventoried his equipment and larder. This was no place to be caught without something he needed. But everything was all right, including his water reserve. Whatever had moved his mules had not touched the water. He smiled. He should have said *whoever,* not whatever. The place irritated him.

He lit his spirit lamp and pawed through papers in

the portfolio until he found what he wanted. It was a carefully wrought copy of a diagram of the Alice Mine he had found in the Nevada Bureau of Mines archives. If he was going to penetrate the mine tomorrow, dig past that lengthy barrier, he wanted to know where he was going.

The inclined shaft penetrated some thousand feet, following a seam of quartz gold, and was paralleled by two lower strata of quartz, all of the three strata gold-bearing. There were drifts to either side at all three levels. This was awkward mining, everything on a grade, nothing level. He found no sign of an adit or a vent, which made the source of that moving air all the more mysterious. The highest, or original, shaft had been richest, with gold running five thousand dollars to a ton of quartz ore, but the lowest of the three levels rivaled that, with gold values running three and four thousand.

He suspected flooding had halted mining at that level, and he thought there might be an adit running from that level to the mountainside far below the mine head. And yet none was indicated. He dismissed the idea. He would have found the tailings from the adit, a bright blot upon the soft dun slopes down there. But the air came from somewhere, rose through the mine, and out of the shaft he was probing.

He packed away his papers in oilskin, and slid into his bedroll, not neglecting to position his revolver beside him. He hurt. Not even his relative youth and athletic life kept him from hurting. No one who probed mines or worked around mines escaped the hurt they did upon the human body.

As he lay there in the soft silence, one last ploy occurred to him. He arose, wrapped a thick blanket about him, stood in the chill night under a bowl of flinty stars, and addressed the hollow world.

"Mr. Ghost, one last word," he said in a conversational voice that he knew would carry. "I'm here without permission. I tried to get it. I sent my request to the only place I could, but my requests were never answered, and whoever functions behind that glass door in San Francisco never opened to me. You, out there. I would like your permission. I find no signs anywhere forbidding trespassing. If you don't want me here, nail one up in the night. But I hope you won't. I want to talk with you about the Alice."

He heard a boulder bounce from on high, clop, thump, rattle, bump, thud, and then it landed near the mine head.

"I suppose that's a No Trespassing sign," he said, "but I don't know. You're going to have to do better."

But only silence greeted him. He was certainly in the quietest place he had ever been. The wind never came, and the breeze was a whisper.

He peered into that bowl of heaven, seeing some infinity away, seeing galaxies and stars and a hundred thousand pricks of light, and wondered what he believed. Had it all been the work of God or Nature or somehow both? Was he seeing only the tiniest corner of the universe? He didn't know.

But he knew that no ghost haunted the Alice Mine. Someone was guarding it from people like himself.

Chapter 5

The thud awakened Hannibal instantly. It rose out of the earth, echoed through the night, and ebbed. His ear, attuned to such sounds even as he slept, registered the thump even as his body registered the shock that rattled the earth.

Even before he was fully awake he knew what it was.

He arose, cast aside his blanket and let the icy air finish the job of awakening him, and fumbled for his carbide lamp. In a bit he lit it and had the light he needed. He slipped into his camp moccasins, wrapped the blanket over his union suit, and headed for the Alice. Stars, brittle chips of ice a vast distance away, vanished where the mountains rose to meet them.

A whiff of cordite hung in the air. He expected something like that. The shaft was full of whirling grit that irritated his nose. He should have tied his bandanna over his face. He pressed down the slope, reached the blocked area, and found a great deal more rock. And his efforts to open the sealed shaft had vanished in a new heap of rubble. The blast had dropped tons of rock from the roof of the shaft.

He backed out swiftly before he could hurt his lungs further, and sucked in fresh night air. He knew he had damaged his lungs and regretted it.

Ghosts indeed. Someone was floating around, keeping him out of there, shutting off the Alice from scientific examination.

It was quiet again, except for the occasional rattle of a pebble loosened by the blast.

"You've sealed it up," he said, hoping his voice would project. "That's too bad. I'm a geologist and engineer, looking for ways to bring dead mines to life. Most owners are grateful. A few have rewarded me for my efforts. I've given them something of value. If you would like to talk to me, come in now, or join me for coffee in the morning."

There was only the silence. Somehow he knew he should expect only quiet and mystery. He headed back to his camp, extinguished the lamp, and crawled into his bedroll. But he could not sleep. He clutched the revolver, finding no comfort in it. His adversary was human, not supernatural, but he wondered why he had seen no boot print, heard no breathing, experienced no voice. If this was the work of a human, that human seemed to float on air and make no noise.

Well, he could find meaning in what he had experienced during the past two days: an avalanche that might have killed him; animal tethers neatly sliced; a second rain of rock; and now a blast that sealed the shaft. Someone wanted him to leave; leave or die. That someone probably didn't want to kill him, and was trying not to—for the moment.

He found no answers in the stars, but he knew he would not sleep the rest of the night. An occasional pebble rattling down from on high, jarred loose by the blast in the bowels of the mountain, kept him wide awake.

He could attempt to work through the rubble and enter the shaft, in spite of the warnings, or he could back off for now. There were two mines near Wickenburg, Arizona Territory, that he intended to look at, and another near Globe, and a third near Brodie, California. And he had twenty other prospects. There were more mines than he could explore in a lifetime.

He put off the decision and decided to see how things looked in the morning.

The earliest dawn light, a rim of blue over the mountains to the east, was enough to pull him out of his bedroll. He chopped more firewood out of the abandoned shack, started a fire, and set his speckled blue coffeepot over it. Then he began his morning ritual, which was very like a prayer. He lathered his face with the shaving brush, stropped his straight-edge razor, peered into the pocket mirror he hung from the door frame of the ancient barracks, and gradually scraped away yesterday's beard until his face felt silky to his touch. He cleaned his shaving gear and packed it. Then he pulled a blue chambray shirt over his long underwear, tied his red polka-dot bow tie, pulled up his canvas mining britches, tied his high-top boot laces, settled his pith helmet on his head, and faced the quickening world.

"Mr. Ghost," he said, "coffee's on."

That amused him.

"If you're a spirit, then I'll get to see the coffee go down your hatch and disappear."

He laughed. He sipped, felt the Java stir his body to life, and watched the light brighten beyond the eastern ridges.

The world remained silent and cool. Like most deserts, this one could be sharply cold at night and roasting hot by mid-afternoon. A man needed clothing for every occasion.

It was time to water the mules. He headed off the plateau to the patch of grass below, and found no mules. No mules, no picket pins, no rope. But the tracks were clear enough. They headed downhill and angled right in a straight line.

Ghosts again. Meandering livestock rarely followed a straight trajectory. This one took him through chaparral, some of it loaded with barbs and thorns, but that is why he wore canvas britches and high-top boots. There were hoofprints in the clay, and daylight enough to follow them, and what more did he need, other than some cooperation from the irksome ghost who was telling him to vamoose? He was puzzled. No sign of human passage accompanied the hoofprints. One would expect a boot heel to show up, at the very least.

The trail continued down a sharp grade, through cactus-choked gulches, dropping steadily until he was three or four hundred feet below the Alice mine head. Then it dropped precipitously into a tiny gulch, hardly fifty feet wide, a streak of green in the arid land. And there were the mules, picketed beside a rivulet barely a foot wide, which trickled slowly down the tiny paradise. It was cool there. Piñon pine and juniper crowded its slopes. Grass choked its bottoms. He found an occasional willow whose roots drank from the tiny stream.

He sighed. The ghost was a prankster. His mules were watered and well fed, having razed any standing grass within the circle of their pickets.

"Mr. Ghost," he said, "thank you for seeing to my mules."

He slipped and skidded down to the intimate bottoms, inspected the cheerful mules, worked his way upward to find the source of the flowage, and stopped suddenly. There was a grave with a gray marble marker. It was back from the creek and on higher ground. A grave? He circled it. Plainly a grave, with black wrought-iron fencing around it, and a marble marker that said—what? Both sides of the marker were blank. No name, no date. Now that was an odd thing.

He proceeded another fifty yards and stopped before what at first he imagined was a spring. But it wasn't. It was the masonry head of a tunnel of some sort. The water was discharging from within. And barring the way was a simple door of iron rods and strap iron, resting on rusty hinges. He studied it, astonished. A grave with no name, and now a tunnel discharging water, a tunnel that looked very like a mine adit, intended to drain a works from below.

Stepping carefully, he tugged on the door. It squealed open. Nothing barred his passage. He couldn't see far in the dull dawn light, but could see enough to know it ran straight-arrow into the mountain in the direction of the Alice, far above. This adit, if that's what it was, had not appeared on the diagram of the mine, but here it was. And here was the source of the air that rose through the Alice and was vented out its main shaft.

He resisted the temptation to enter. One swing of that iron grilled door, one lock, and he would be jailed in there forever. He sighed. First the ghost chased him out of the Alice, and now the ghost was inviting him in through the back door. He could make no sense of it.

"Mr. Ghost," he said loudly. "I don't know your design. First you chase me off, then you invite me in and feed and water my mules too. I suppose I'd better stay for another day or two and see what else you have in mind."

He was greeted by a vast and uncaring silence. He doubted his sanity, talking that way to whatever phantom was playing pranks on him.

He picketed his mules on fresh grass, hiked up to the flat, found a hacksaw among his tools, collected a carbide lamp and the rest of his gear for exploring a mine, and returned to the adit. The hacksaw would keep him from being imprisoned in there if that grilled door slammed shut behind him.

The whole business baffled him, but he set it aside.

He was a mining geologist and he would do what he always did, which was to recover value from dead mines. He slipped into the tunnel, walking beside the purling flow of water. It narrowed swiftly and showed no signs of being man-made. Indeed, the little stream had cut its way along a fault here. It was a narrowing cave, not a mine works. Indeed, less than fifty yards in, it pinched to a width of a few inches, and that was as far as a human could go. It wasn't on the mine diagram because it wasn't an adit. He lit a candle and watched the flame and smoke, which was drawn steadily into the dark crack in the rock. This was probably the source of the air that was exiting the mine far above, in the Alice works. Lucky Haggarty had been lucky indeed, to have a mine that ventilated itself. By all accounts, the Alice had been unusually economic to run, which had simply added to its fabulous value, and the legend that cloaked it. Lucky Haggarty had had more than a bonanza; he had had a piece of paradise.

Dead end. Hannibal retreated into the sunlight, paused again at the mysterious, unmarked grave, and a thought occurred to him. If the marker was blank, it meant that no one was buried there, but someone would be someday.

He knelt at the grave, trying to discern what it was all about. But it remained a mystery. He wondered whether there were other graves at the Alice. Mines cost lives. Somewhere around the Alice, he probably would find half a dozen. Maybe one of those graves would be the source of the ghost.

"Ghost indeed," he said aloud. And laughed.

"Mr. Ghost, the only question is what you have on your feet. Not boots, I'll wager," he said. "There's not a print of a shoe or a boot or a bare foot anywhere around, except for my own. You are probably wearing moccasins."

But he received only silence as a response. That made him uneasy. Some mines had legends attached to them. Some mines had curses. But this mine had a live ghost.

Chapter 6

Hannibal nooned on the flat, bringing his journal up to date. He kept meticulous notes, and these sometimes gave him clues he needed. He recorded the discovery of the fissure draining water from the bowels of the mountain, and then, hesitantly, he recorded the mysterious mishaps and near misses and annoyances that would add up to a ghost except he didn't for an instant believe nonsense like that. Maybe it was time to find the cemetery, always a valuable source of information about a mine he was studying.

The journal done, he decided to devote the rest of the day to the geology of the mountains that contained the Alice Mine. He wanted to know what happened over aeons of time; why gold had collected here; why the quartz strata were tilted at about a thirty-degree angle, and why there were at least three of them. He suspected a batholith, an upthrust of magma that had lifted the stratified sandstone above it, and tilted it. Maybe three batholithic episodes.

But he especially wanted to find the faults, for those were places where miners suddenly met blank walls and the end of a fruitful vein. Sometimes he could measure the offset from surface evidence, and conclude that the seam would pick up again at a certain distance. Refreshed by his nooning, he ventured down to the tailings pile, hoping to find three types of country rock, pulled from the three levels of the mine. While he was down there, a hundred yards below the flat, he hunted for a cemetery. Rarely was anyone buried above a mountain mining operation; almost always the burial grounds were well below.

He hiked down an arid gulch, the world about him parched and dun, with nothing but silvery chaparral to vegetate it. This was a natural and easy grade from the mining flat, and when he rounded a bend he found what he was looking for. A few headboards, sun-bleached and gray, stood in a row, all of them tilted in some crazy way. There were no stone markers. And only five headboards in all. All were standing, none lying on the clay. Most of them had lost the painted names and dates that once signaled whose grave it might be. The sun and wind had done their work.

Plainly, most of those who died had been carried away and buried elsewhere. These were probably the graves of men without families, loners, men who had been buried by their fellow miners. Hannibal studied the weathered boards for names, and found some, even after years of weathering and decay.

Roman Gart, birth date obscure, death 1887. Milward Donavan, dates obscure. Gardner Gear, 1830, 1888, probably the last of the graves because the Alice had shut down about 1889 as far as anyone knew. There were two other boards whose paint had flecked away, though Hannibal thought that a man with a pencil and tissue paper could draw outlines of letters just by putting borders on the flecked areas.

He recorded the known names and dates in his pocket journal with a pencil. If there were names, there might be relatives, and information.

He stood, listening to the deep silence. The sun was burning in now, as the desert heat built.

"If any of you are my ghost, come shake my hand," he said.

No ghost shook his hand.

With some fresh samples of the tailings in hand, he did a systematic study of the whole area, which occupied the rest of that day. He found nothing unusual. The geology was not even complex.

He returned to the flat, took another look at the main shaft of the Alice, knew he would need some equipment and a crew to dig through the rubble, and felt frustrated.

"All right, Mr. Ghost," he said. "I'm going back for more information. This mine was often in the news. It was once the pride of Nevada. Now, if you'll oblige me by moving my mules to fresh grass, I am going to fix a dinner. But beforehand, I'm going to pull out my flask of good bourbon and have a drink. If you care to join me, I'll pour two. That ice water will be a perfect splash. If you don't care to join me, then I'll see you in a while, because I'll be back."

Of course that met only with silence. He studied the vaulting slopes, dry dun rock, red strata, spotty vegetation, lifeless dirt and rock stretching to the horizons.

"No place to live, even for a ghost," he said.

He refused to concede defeat. But this mine was going to take some additional research. He could not unravel its secrets until he knew why it had closed, and that was not something he would discover here.

He grabbed a cook pot to collect some icy water from that flowage below, trekked down the arid slope to the hidden glade, filled his pot with cold water, and checked the mules.

They had been moved another notch down the slope. A red rose dangled from the bridle of one. He plucked up the rose, not quite believing it.

He adjusted his bow tie and polished his wire-rimmed glasses. He tried mightily to think of something to say to the ghost, and gave up.

A female ghost.

He clambered slowly up the hill, wearied by his long and frustrating day, found a tin cup, poured a generous dollop of Tennessee's best into it, added a splash of cold water, and settled down for the social hour.

He lifted the cup. "Here's to all ghosts, including the flesh-and-blood variety."

The response was a rattle of red rock from the cliff

above the mine head, which clattered and snapped and snarled its way down, and hit the ground near the mine like a mortar barrage.

Hannibal smiled and nodded. That bourbon was as fine as any he had tasted, and the cold water rendered it perfect. A pity that no ghost showed up for a good visit.

It was maddening. Where did the red rose come from? Was this not the Shell Creek Range, a band of upthrust tree-topped rock in eastern Nevada? Was there not twenty-five or thirty miles between him and Ely, the nearest town? And were there not desolate wastes, uninhabited by any mortal, the entire distance?

A joke, perhaps. He had been the butt of jokes all his life because he took his calling too seriously. He had no answer, and the bourbon and cold water tasted fine, so he whiled away his last hours at the Alice Mine in perfect peace, except for the red rose that refused to depart from his thoughts. Tomorrow he would begin the long trip to Ely, followed by a longer one to Carson City, where he would probe records, and then to San Francisco. He was not done with the Alice, but he confessed to himself, as the bourbon warmed his belly and softened his thoughts, that this might be a mine that he couldn't crack open.

At twilight, he addressed the ghost.

"Thank you for the rose," he said. "Tomorrow I'll depart, but I am not done here."

A skinny moon hung over the horizon, casting white light upon the slopes. High, silver-edged clouds raced across its face, suggesting a change in the weather. He sat in the quiet, letting the night and its rhythms speak to him. Sometimes he thought he saw ghostly shapes patrolling the distant ridges, but they were only moon-shadows.

Who was playing ghost, and why?

The person playing ghost was not male, but a woman who wore moccasins or some similar soft slipper that would leave no mark at all upon the hard clay or the brutal rock. A man's boots would swiftly reveal him. Hannibal knew the print of his own high-top boots as well as his camp moccasins.

A woman, then. But who, and why?

He could not answer it. The night-world was bright in the moonlight, and then dark, and filled with motion as shadows raced across the empty mountains.

He turned to his gear, found the lamp, carefully dropped some calcium carbide into the reservoir, and added water. The gas, acetylene, would burn brightly and with intense heat. He didn't want the heat; he wanted the light. He struck a lucifer to the jet and it caught. He adjusted the vent to conserve the carbide, and hung the bright-glowing lamp from a post. In his kit he found a pad of paper, his fountain pen, and a clipboard to write on.

Dear Ghost, he wrote, and was not happy with it.

Dear Alice, he wrote. *I am going to name you Alice after the mine. If you are the guardian of the mine, I can understand some of what has happened to me, but other things remain a mystery.*

46

I am Hannibal Jones, a mining geologist among other professions, and my business is to revive dead and abandoned mines by discovering whether ore exists, what went wrong, and what remedies might be employed. That is why I am studying the Alice.

I think perhaps it remains a rich mine, though I cannot discover the reasons it was abruptly closed in the late eighties. I look for reasons: flooding, low-grade ore, poisonous gases, labor trouble, depressions, falling prices for precious metals. Things of that sort. But none of them seem to apply to the Alice, which is why I am asking your help.

I am here without permission, but I sought it repeatedly, and if I discover the means to make the mine profitable, I intend to give the owners full value for their property. Potentially, this remains a superb property, able to bring comfort to its owners and to employ many people at a good wage.

I cannot fathom your purposes, sometimes threatening, other times helpful. I am going to do more research about the Alice, and return. And when I do, I will bring two wineglasses, set a table for two, and open a bottle of Bordeaux if you should care to share it with me.

Sincerely, Hannibal Jones.

He read it, not satisfied with it at all, but he was a geologist, not Shakespeare. He folded it, slipped it into the sole envelope he had with him, addressed the envelope to Alice, hiked to the mine head, placed his letter on rock just inside the shaft, and pinned it down

47

with another rock. That was all he could do.

He returned to his camp, extinguished the acetylene lamp, and settled into his bedroll, enjoying the white moonlight that spilled over the brooding mountains. He hoped Alice was a beautiful and warm-blooded woman, and that she did not object to anyone named Hannibal.

Chapter 7

Ely was bustling. Hannibal counted three horseless carriages as he hiked in leading his burdened mules. Copper had done it. There were mines in most every direction, many of them copper, with gold and silver as a valuable byproduct. But in the early seventies, when the Alice was first put into operation, Ely didn't exist and the nearest artery to civilization was a heart-breaking 170 miles away, at Cobre, on the Western Pacific Railroad.

Hannibal hiked along Aultman Street, past a curious mixture of slapdash buildings and stately permanent ones. He was hunting for the assay laboratory of Garth Broome, legendary wizard of mining chemistry. Leave the samples first; then settle the mules at the livery barn and find some civilized comforts himself.

Broome's nondescript board-and-batten building loomed ahead. Hannibal tied his mules to the hitch rail just as a chattering horseless carriage sputtered by, a gentleman in a silk hat driving while his lady clutched a pink straw broad-brimmed chapeau to her head. The mules tugged violently at their tethers, and then sub-sided.

Hannibal dug into a pannier and extracted a small heavy bag, and entered.

The acrid smell of furnace heat greeted him. The doorbell jangled, and soon Broome emerged from the rear room and peered at his customer from rimless half-glasses.

"You, is it?"

"Me. I want assays on each of these. Mind the labels; they mean something to me."

Broome squinted. "Scavenging again, Jones? What kind of life is that, scavenging dead mines?"

"To make a living, Garth."

Broome laughed nastily, baring rotten yellow teeth. He extracted the samples, one by one, each with a number inked on it.

He set them all in a row on the counter, picked up each, and chuckled. "I've done so many assays of that low-grade at the Alice you hardly need a new one."

"There's some from the tailings too."

"So I noticed. I can tell you now, Jones, it's still not economic to ship that low-grade out of there. The cost from there to the mill here would eat up your profit. But I'll assay these if you want."

"I do, and record each by its number, and pay attention to the byproduct metals."

Broome peered cheerfully from above his half-lenses. "You buy into it?"

Hannibal was reluctant to say he was poking around

49

uninvited, so he just smiled.

"Serves me right," Broome said. "I haven't heard that she's selling."

Hannibal's pulse jumped, but he could play this game too. "I haven't heard that she is either."

"Well, she'll grow tired of it sooner or later," Broome said.

"How long will this take?" Hannibal asked.

"Got a dozen ahead of you. Maybe two, three days."

That was the maddening thing about Broome. He was rarely busy but he liked for people to think it. He was the best assayer in the state, and one could bet a fortune on his findings and feel right about it, but in the meantime he'd abuse his customers as much as he could manage.

"I need the results faster," Hannibal said, slowly picking up his samples and restoring them to the sack.

Broome smiled and let him. They both knew that the other assayer in Ely, Dirk Winsom, was erratic, drunk, and unreliable. You would not want to buy a mine on his results.

Broome frowned.

Hannibal bagged the last of his assay samples and turned to leave. "I'm heading for Carson City anyway," he said.

Broome glared. "Maybe I could give you a little priority."

Hannibal shrugged. "You've already told me what I needed to know, Garth, so I guess I'll just pass. All these would do is confirm my fieldwork anyway."

Broome nodded curtly.

Hannibal noted that one of the two assay furnaces in the rear room was cold. But over the years he'd had his fill of Broome's games, and decided it was time to draw the line. He picked up the heavy canvas bag and started out.

"Say," Broome said, "don't you want to know who owns it?"

"You already told me," Hannibal said. He smiled broadly and stepped through the clanging door. Like most every shop in Ely, this one had jangle-bells announcing the arrival of a customer.

His mules stood with necks lowered. He dropped the ore sack into the pannier and buckled the flap.

Broome had let on more than he realized, and Hannibal smiled at the whole encounter. Ely was in the throes of a boom, copper everywhere, and the streets were crowded with pedestrians, carts, ore wagons, and one or two rackety horseless carriages that drove dray horses wild and started stampedes.

When Lucky Haggarty bought the Alice from a prospector for a thousand dollars back about 1870, there was no Ely and no town within two hundred miles. Everyone thought it was a fool's purchase, a mine so remote that it would be impossible to freight out ore, keep help on the premises, and freight in life's necessities. But Haggarty was nobody's fool. He raised enough cash to build a small mill and an amalgamation works, operated by the sparse pine on the higher slopes. He paid his help an extra dollar a day and put them on six-week shifts, with two weeks off. The help beelined for the wicked town of Elko up on the railroad, and most always returned broke and happy, ready for six more. A stage line ran the gold to the railroad and shuttled miners back and forth. It worked. The remote mine swiftly turned a profit and soon made a fortune. Other mines in the White Pine district blossomed, Ely was born, and soon Haggarty's bachelor miners patronized twenty saloons, a vast collection of loose women, a tonsorial parlor, three billiard parlors, two bathhouses, a dime-a-dance hall, and found a lot of comforts just thirty miles away from the remote, austere Alice. And best of all, they still got a dollar a day more than the going wage, just for living out there.

Lucky Haggarty began life as Harold, an accountant and factotum for mining companies, but he proved to be smarter and luckier than his employers. Whatever he touched turned to gold, and pretty soon he was no longer Harold, he was Lucky, and that was an exact and perfect name for the man.

Hannibal remembered all of that as he led his two mules to the White Pine Livery Barn. There he negotiated with the hostler, stowed his panniers in the office, and extracted his hotel satchel. He might as well stay a day or two and find out what he could. This town had memories of the Alice, and there were men living there who had mined it. He would talk to each one, if he could.

He rented a one-dollar single at the Copper Queen,

washed up in the lavatory at the end of the hall, put on a fresh shirt, and set out to discover what he could. He left some dirty laundry at the front desk for the Chinamen, and headed into a hot dry day. His first stop would be the Haggarty mansion on Campton Street. Once Ely had rooted itself, Haggarty had built a fine, two-story yellow clapboard with white gingerbread, and moved in with his wife Faye and their sons Maxwell and Mordecai. Hannibal heard that both sons had died, one of yellow fever in Central America, the other by provoking a grizzly sow with two cubs. But Faye . . . Who could say? Broome could.

Hannibal found the place easily enough in the seven-hundred block. It was obviously empty. Its windows blinked bleakly at him. No curtains graced them. The lawn and shrubbery were carelessly maintained by someone paid to look after them. Its yellow paint was peeling, and so was the white on the shutters, but not badly; there was no fatal neglect there, as far as Hannibal could see. There was a pump jack in the backyard, and a brick privy in the corner of the lot. Some neglected lilac bushes added rough grace. A carriage shed on the alley wore a padlock. Hannibal headed for the alley, found a rear window, and peered into the dim shed, discovering an ebony Victoria covered with thick white dust.

The place hadn't been sold. Maybe Broome was right. The mine was Faye's. Hannibal returned to the street, satisfied that no one lived there and that the place was at least rudely maintained. This was where

53

Harold Haggarty became Lucky Haggarty; where the owner of one bonanza found himself the owner of half a dozen. Haggarty had bought stakes in surrounding mines, did so without even knowing the geology or potentials, made his bets as if he were putting chips on a roulette number. And they all came up winners. Lucky Haggarty was soon so rich he hardly knew what to do with his money.

Faye knew. Give it to their Anglican church. And they did. There in Ely was a brick church, almost of cathedral proportions, the gift of Lucky and Faye Haggarty, and in the vestibule was a discreet plaque saying so. Faye was in favor of doing nothing with the mountains of money; Lucky had no lack of ideas for spending it, and soon owned some of the best thoroughbred horseflesh on the continent, California orange groves, forests of Costa Rican mahogany, two San Francisco hotels, a steam yacht anchored in the San Francisco Bay . . . and a mistress. Maybe several. But one of consequence, a lush mistress he called Baby, and treated better than one would treat a royal princess.

Her name was Belle, and he lived openly with her in San Francisco. She accompanied him to the theater, to the opera, to the great restaurants, to the horse track. She was his guest and companion aboard the *Alice*, as he named his twin-screw steam yacht. And all the while Lucky was living his adventuresome life, Faye was living in chaste austerity, watching over the yellow clapboard home in Ely, absorbing rumors about Lucky and his life and his woman, or women. And even as the Alice coughed out an unending stream of pure gold, and silver byproduct, her heart was growing cold and a storm was rising in her virtuous soul. And when Faye could no longer bear it, she tore their world apart.

Chapter 8

Hannibal found the headquarters of the Nevada Miners Federation in East Ely. It was little more than a shack of rough planks, with a potbellied stove and a desk and chair within. Hanging on the wall behind was a cloth banner, red cotton with a white-felt pick and shovel and a fist. A Currier and Ives calendar hung from the rear wall. A battered file cabinet hugged one side of the plank desk. A rust-pitted shotgun stood on its heel in a corner. Along with vast quantities of copper, labor unions had arrived in Ely. This one was an independent local.

A beefy and half-bald gent with oddly short arms sat in the chair, eyeing Hannibal suspiciously. The man's gaze focused on Hannibal's polka-dot red bow tie and the baggy tweed coat.

"I'm looking for some old-timers," Hannibal said. "Thought you could help me."

"What for?" the man asked, his tone guarded.

"To talk about an old mine, the Alice, and why it shut down long ago."

"Never heard of it."

"The Alice was the first mine in the area, and it ran from the seventies until about eighteen-eighty-eight, give or take a year."

"So?"

"I want to know why it closed. I'm a mining geologist."

"I don't let out the names of our members."

"I'm looking for men who are probably retired."

The man stared at Hannibal from hooded eyes that smouldered, weighing him, assessing him, studying his clothing. "No," he said.

"I'm not working for anyone but myself, if that's bothering you. I'm hoping to find out why a good mine suddenly closed its doors."

"No," the man said, and in a voice that told Hannibal the decision had been made, it was irrevocable, and there were walls between himself and the man in the chair.

"All right. But if you think of someone, I'll be at the Copper Queen for a day or two. Hannibal Jones; here's my card. I'd like to talk with anyone who worked that mine."

"Let me tell you something, Bow Tie. Them mines, they hire snitches down in the pits, and the snitches tell the bosses who we are. We find a snitch, it ain't comfortable for him down there anymore. We don't tell anyone who we are. Along you come, right through the door, and want to know who we are, fancy coat, bow tie, and all."

"I don't work for anyone but myself."

"You got manager written all over you."

"I'm a geologist and mining engineer, and my speciality is finding value in exhausted mines. That's all there is to it. If you know the names of some early miners here, I'd like to have a little visit."

The burly man sighed, and suddenly grinned. "Lotsa luck," he said. He gestured toward the door.

"If the Alice could be reopened, there'd be good jobs," Hannibal said.

"There's no such thing as good jobs. There's only work in black hellholes, deep underground, full of poison gases and dust that wrecks lungs. And for slave wages so fat-bottomed people like you can get rich."

That was plain enough. Hannibal wanted to argue. He wanted to say that iron and copper and lead and tin as well as precious metals all made life better, that the iron of the potbellied stove that warmed this man in winters had been mined, and so were a hundred other metal products this man used daily. Every trumpet and trombone in the world had been mined. Every door lock, every stagecoach tire, every screw and nail, every copper electrical wire had been mined.

"Send me some old-timers, my friend," Hannibal said.

"Friend he calls me," the man said, and laughed cynically.

Hannibal stepped out, and into a hot day. He wondered what the future would bring to mining in the West. Large companies, large unions, large trouble.

That left the miners' saloons. There were plenty of

those. Most would no more welcome him than the union organizer, but that couldn't be helped. Actually, he admired miners. It took courage and skill and muscle to work in the pits, never seeing the sun, month after month. It was relatively well-paid work, but the risks and conditions outweighed whatever they took home. Some died in accidents; some died of silicosis, or miner's lung. Some went sour living in a hole so much of the time. Most didn't live a full life span, and few liked what they were doing or really wanted to work in the pits.

Hannibal had been belowground hundreds of times, maybe thousands, and never liked it, never felt at home there. But that wouldn't make him a brother of these men who filled the saloons after each shift.

He tried the Mint, the Copper City, the Miner's Rest, the Combination, wandering into each, surveying the customers, discovering young and weary men nursing a beer to dull the pain of their day. Sometimes he ordered a beer on tap, sipped a few suds, and walked away. There wasn't a gray-haired miner in Ely, he thought. Anyone working a mine that had started in the seventies and closed in eighty-eight would show some gray, some balding, some lines in the face.

Maybe it wasn't a bright idea, touring the saloons. Maybe he should stop at the newspaper, talk to an editor. Those gents knew everything worth knowing. All Hannibal needed was a few names.

He paused for some chili and cornbread at the Nevada Café on Murry Street, and found himself eavesdropping on some old-timers playing pinochle at a rear table. At least Hannibal thought it was pinochle. He could scarcely tell poker from whist. Five old men. He felt the chili warm his stomach while he caught a word or two issuing from the geezers. Mostly they were complaining about the high cost of laundresses and Chinamen.

"Used to be cheaper when I was swinging a pick," one said.

Hannibal dabbed some chili off his lips and walked over to the table.

"Mind if I interrupt the cards a moment?" he asked.

"You got it bashward, stranger. The shards smugger the talk."

That was from a toothless one, and Hannibal could barely make out the slurred words.

"I'm a mining geologist," he began.

"I knew it had to be something that bad," one said.

"I'm looking for anyone who worked in the Alice."

"The Alice, eh? I ain't that old," said another.

"Alice is hard work, all right," said a third, and smirked.

"Meeeow did," said the toothless one.

"You want to talk about it?"

"You whoof to lissen? When I start talking, I drive everyone outa the place."

"Sure, I'll listen."

"Lemme get my molars. I shmug the things."

The skinny old bird rose and vanished through a rear door. Hannibal caught a glimpse of a rear apartment, and realized the man was the proprietor of the café.

"Anyone else work the Alice?" he asked.

"Don't get him started on the Alice," one responded. "We'll just shut down the game and vamoose. His teeth rattle my brain."

The proprietor returned, this time sporting some ivory teeth that formed two uniform rows.

"Things don't fit," he muttered. "Hear this?" He flapped his jaw and was rewarded with sharp clicks. "That's (click) why I hate (click) the things. This here's African elephant ivory (click) but it don't rest light on my gums."

"I'm Hannibal Jones."

"Walt Cube . . . (click)."

"Cube?"

"Can't say it right."

"Cuban," volunteered another.

They offered Hannibal a seat. He wished he might take notes, but sensed it would be intimidating.

"When were you at the Alice?"

"Long as it was open, I guess. What do you want to know for?"

"I'm thinking maybe it's a valuable mine still."

"Valuable! It's got a curse on it. Anyone (click) two cents of gold outa there, he'll be (click) sorry."

"Were you there when it shut down?"

"Was I there! I was last man out and I feared they'd (click) the lift before they took me up to grass."

"What level?"

"Bottom. Best level of all, (click) gold quartz seam so thick it was like picking candy."

"High grade?"

Cuban cackled, clacking his store teeth. "Wanna see?"

Without waiting for a response, he ducked into his apartment and appeared moments later with a small egg-shaped hunk of quartz. "(Click) here I smuggled out day before she shut down. Took her out in my tailpipe, since they (click) the lunch buckets."

Hannibal smiled. Rectal gold. That was how plenty of miners fattened their pay envelopes.

This piece of milky tan quartz had visible gold specks running through it.

"(Click) ounce to the ton," Cuban said.

It was a very handsome specimen. Hannibal studied it with a practiced eye.

"So (click) every one-ton skip reaching grass had (click) thousand dollars in it."

"Any sign it was running out?" Hannibal said, returning the specimen.

"(Click. Click!) No."

"What about the upper levels?"

"What about 'em? (Click.) Can't wear these teeth; they torture my gums. Gotta quit."

Cuban sprang up, vanished into the apartment, and emerged again smiling and toothless.

"Muff bettah," he said.

"Why'd they shut down?" Hannibal asked.

That was the whole question. That's what he needed to know. That would unlock the mystery, and maybe even explain the alleged ghosts.

"Muff yaough," Cuban replied.

"Can you answer yes or no?"

"Meaggh."

Hannibal sighed. The Alice was still eluding him.

Chapter 9

In spite of the difficulties, the interview with Cuban went better than Hannibal expected and yielded some valuable stuff. From him, Hannibal learned that water did not threaten the mine, nor were there ventilation problems; that miraculous fissure in the mountain shot air through the entire works and drained off water. Lucky Haggarty was lucky in more ways than one.

Cuban also cleared up something else. The press had reported that the mine closed in October of 1888, which was true enough, but the mill continued to process stockpiled ore for another eight months and then was dismantled and shipped out, along with the mine boilers. Operations didn't cease until the summer of 1889.

Still, the closure of a bonanza mine in good times when gold prices remained high and stable was a mystery of unfathomable proportions, and Hannibal couldn't imagine the reasons—if any. Court records in San Francisco, Carson City, and Ely had offered no clues. There was no legal wrangle over ownership.

"Mr. Cuban, who's in that grave with the unmarked headstone below, where the water runs out of the mountain?"

"Smeach ell grave? Mieu don't know of it."

"You've never seen it?"

"Beeanno."

"Is the mine haunted?"

Cuban grew excited. "Meau thinks maybe a mighty cursh lame on that meeno."

"Ghosts?"

"Hobgoblins, meeoina. Tommyknockers."

Tommyknockers, the gremlins of the pits, always causing trouble underground.

"Ghosts. Anyone haunting it?"

"Beeanno."

"Hey, let's play pinochle," someone said. "The Alice, she croaked and ain't coming back."

"Shut up and deal," said another.

Hannibal thought he'd gotten what he could.

"I'll buy you a sarsaparilla," he said to the old-timers. They grinned.

On his way out, he paid a waitress to deliver.

Cuban only deepened the mystery. The mine had been shut down cold at the peak of its life, without a cloud on the horizon, without water or air trouble, without legal entanglements, without any decline in the price of precious metals, without any visible indication that ore was running out or reserves were waning. Someone closed the door. And someone was doing a very good imitation of a ghost, and threatening any wandering soul who happened upon the decaying old works.

Hannibal had heard about the curse, a violent one

that threatened death and grief upon anyone who ventured there, but he could never pin it down. Whose curse was it? And when? And why? It was probably nothing but the sort of rumor that often floated around old mines, often as an explanation of bad luck, tragedy, suicide, cave-ins, and other sorts of grief. The silent buildings did seem to brood there on that lonely flat, and Hannibal had been struck by his own uneasiness when he poked through the old sheds, barracks, offices, and work yards. It was not a friendly place and those weren't friendly mountains. They were harsh to the eye, and seemed to brood silently in deep isolation. There were scarcely more remote mountains in the United States.

The only problem was, he didn't believe in ghosts or in sinister mountains or in spirits, curses, gremlins, or the deranged souls of people who had suffered during their lives. Absolutely not, and nothing could persuade him otherwise. He lived in a universe governed by rational laws of physics, mathematics, chemistry, electricity, and so on; not a place haunted by witches and warlocks. He was also certain that with some patient digging, he would get to the bottom of it, and when he did he might well be able to reopen the Alice and share in some of its bounty.

He stood on the sunbaked street, wondering what to do next, and decided that the offices of the *Ely Miner* would be profitable. He located the newspaper building on B Street next to the red-light district, which was the typical locale of most papers and rightly so. Journalism was one of the less reputable professions. Reporters could be bought with a drink. He wandered in, jangling the doorbells. The jangle-bells seemed to be the current rage in Ely, and did have the virtue of announcing a visitor.

A cadaverous gent with muttonchops appeared, wiping his hands on an inky towel.

"I'd like to look at the files of the *White Pine Evangel*," he said, knowing the *Miner* didn't exist until after the Alice had shut down, and had acquired the files of the earlier weekly.

"Sure, what ya looking for?"

"Old mining news, around eighteen-eighty-eight or nine. I'm a mining geologist."

The editor shrugged and pointed. "Wipe the ink off the seat or you'll stain those trousers."

"Thanks."

The earlier weekly was preserved in bound annual editions, each covered with sober gray buckram with a date stamped into the spine. Hannibal pulled 1888 and 1889 off a shelf, eyed the ink-stained wooden chair dubiously, could find no rag to improve it, and finally eased himself down anyway, knowing he would leave with a blackened bottom on his britches.

He opened the 1888 edition and turned to October, the month when the Alice folded. The first issue was full of news from outlying mines, monthly production, and some water rights problems. There were stories about new construction and shops, and a legal dispute over an easement. The second issue was missing its front page. Torn clear out. No mention of the Alice. The next issue was also missing its front page, and so was the next. But the November issues were intact. In the months previous to the closing of the Alice, there were casual references to the mine's production, injuries, personnel changes, and so on. But no large story and nothing at all about a forthcoming closing.

Frowning, Hannibal pulled the 1889 bound set from the shelf, and hunted for any stories about the Alice. He found only one, saying that eleven people remained at the mine and mill site. Then he came across another issue missing its front page, this one in June. But the Alice had virtually disappeared from public attention.

He tried 1887, spreading the buckram cover on a desk and examining the pages of the weekly. There were frequent references to the Alice here, occasional production stories, but no regular data about ore being processed. Visits to the Alice from prominent mining men. And various mentions of Lucky Haggarty, its owner, who came frequently to the mine to monitor operations. One story mentioned its manager, C.J. Lowry, who was investing in new lift equipment and other improvements. Then Hannibal discovered a November edition with its front page missing. That awakened his interest: November eleventh, 1887, was the date when Haggarty died, and the missing page was from the newspaper of the following week. That was the first year the *White Pine Evangel* had started publishing.

So the Alice, and Haggarty, had been expunged

from the files in Ely. He wondered if that was so elsewhere. And why. Satisfied that he could garner no more from the old record, he pushed the heavy bound volumes back into their nesting place and headed for the door.

"Find what you want?" asked the proprietor, who was sitting at a linotype.

"Anyone been here looking through the old *Evangel*?"

"Not for years."

"There's a few missing pages, all front pages."

"Beats me why people steal the only original we got rather than make a fair copy."

"What's missing is news of the Alice Mine and its owner."

"Never heard of it."

"It was shut down in 1888."

"What were you looking for?"

"I don't quite know. I'm a geologist, and I'm always looking into the life and death of mines."

"Well, I guess someone wanted the stories badly enough to rip them out."

"But not since you've been here?"

"How could I know that for sure?"

"You ever hear of Lucky Haggarty?"

"Who hasn't?"

"He owned the Alice. This was his first big pile, and it never quit him."

"Is there a story in this?"

Hannibal shrugged. "Might be someday; not now."

In truth, he didn't want the editor poking around, asking questions. "It's history now, seventeen years gone, and hardly anyone alive remembers it."

"Joel Hartwig's who I am. I edit this when I'm not selling ads and delivering it to everyone's doorstep. And you are?"

"Hannibal Jones." He handed Hartwig a card. "If you come across some old issues of the *Evangel*, especially 1888 and 1889, I'd like to have a look."

"How do I reach you?"

"For a day or so at the Copper Queen. After that, San Francisco. The address on the card."

Hannibal stepped into the bright day. The visit to the newspaper had yielded nothing. Or maybe it had. Was the missing material just a lazy person's way of avoiding the task of transcribing a story? Or was it a deliberate effort to obscure the Alice and its closing, for reasons unknown?

He suspected it was exactly that. Someone had been attempting to wipe away the very memory of the Alice Mine from the records. Someone wanted a bonanza mine to vanish from history. He thought it would be worth his time to stop at Carson City and see what was present, and what was missing, from the local paper, *The Nevada Appeal*. And from the records of the state's mining bureau. If the same material was missing there, he might draw some inferences from it. Missing material was almost as good a clue as untouched material.

The Alice had a busy ghost, he thought wryly.

Chapter 10

Hannibal adjusted his polka-dot bow tie and rang the chimes. He wondered what sort of reception he would get, and was braced for a swift rejection.

Faye Haggarty's handsome new clapboard home nestled in the foothills due west of the Nevada state capital. It had a well-manicured lawn and fresh iron-gray paint with white trim.

A maid in black answered, swinging open the door cautiously. She looked him over, obviously deciding whether he was a tradesman, but he intervened.

"I would like to speak to Mrs. Haggarty," he said. "I'm Hannibal Jones, a mining geologist, and I wish to discuss the Alice Mine with her."

He handed her his card.

She stared at it, at him, and silently vanished. When she returned she bore a message: "Mrs. Haggarty no longer owns the mine nor is she interested in discussing it."

"Well, I can understand that. I'm interested in its history, and her recollections of it. Would you ask her whether she might be willing to discuss those matters?"

The maid eyed him from her rimless spectacles and vanished again. After a moment he noticed someone discreetly examining him from within the dim interior, and then the maid returned.

"Mrs. Haggarty will see you in the sunroom briefly," she said.

Hannibal was elated. That was more than he had expected. He followed her through a dim foyer and parlor, and suddenly found himself in a bright, glassed, cream-enameled room where Mrs. Haggarty awaited.

He was stunned. She was in her fifties, erect, blond-haired, but still such a glowing beauty as he had never seen before. She held out a small and pale hand while he gazed into an unearthly face, so perfect in form he could not find so much as an eyelash out of place.

"I am Faye Haggarty," she said. "Do sit down there," she said, waving that hand indolently toward a love seat upholstered in ivory silk.

He held her hand briefly. "I'm Hannibal Jones, madam, and most grateful for your interest."

"I should warn you, Mr. Jones, that I will hold you strictly to my recollections; the mine is long dead, not in my possession, and I hope it stays that way. Which is my way of saying that if you are here on mining business, we must conclude our visit at once."

She settled in a settee across from him, and he marveled anew. She was dressed in a sky-blue velvet suit with a creamy silk blouse and a jabot at her throat.

"I'm very glad you could see me," he said, a little anxiously. She had that effect on him. "If you don't own the mine, then I am not here on business, though I should tell you straight off that my business is finding value in old mines, ones considered exhausted or unprofitable."

Her face was a mask.

"The Alice fascinates me. Of all the mines I've looked at, it has the richest history."

"It has no history, Mr. Jones. Except for what it did to people."

"I am sure you have been there many times, and can recollect what it was like when it was operating," he said.

"Only once, Mr. Jones."

"Was that when it was new and isolated, or later?"

"The day it closed."

"Later, then."

"I was there to make sure it was closed and would never again reopen."

"You did not want it to continue?"

"The Alice Mine, sir, brought me nothing but grief."

"Did you own it then, when it was closed?"

"No. My husband—Mr. Haggarty—made some deathbed . . . changes in his estate."

He sensed she was choosing words carefully. She sat sternly, as if all this was against her will and nothing but an act of great courtesy. She had offered him nothing, not even tea though this was teatime.

"He was a remarkable man, Mrs. Haggarty."

"We will not discuss him. I fear I have nothing to offer, Mr. Jones. I saw the mine only once even though it was our principal asset. It required a difficult trip through desert wilderness and I saw no reason to go there."

She was plainly fixing to dismiss him.

"I am told there is a ghost. And a curse."

"I don't know about the ghost, but the curse is my own, sir. I myself placed it upon the Alice the one day I was there. I lifted my arms to heaven, that day, and begged a most merciful God to curse anyone who sought the wealth of the Alice. I asked that the mine be damned, that trespassers be swallowed up, that whoever extracts a dime's worth of wealth from the Alice be plunged into misery the rest of his days."

The vehemence in her voice shocked Hannibal. She was no longer the discreet, demure beauty, but a woman almost savage.

"The mine did that to you?"

"Do you know what evil is, sir?"

"I scarcely know how to respond to that."

"Evil is the means to live without the fetters that virtue imposes on all of us. Evil, sir, is what resulted when my Harold acquired the Alice Mine. You can have no idea of how my man began his downward descent, and how my life was indelibly changed for the worse. From the very first day that gold was milled and cast into ingots, my family, my life, my dreams, my hopes spiraled downward into Hades. That's the polite form. Into hell, sir, into damnation. So it is my curse, spoken within the listening of a hundred ears, that now lies upon the Alice Mine. And may it always remain. If you should attempt to reopen it, may it fall upon you."

Her vehemence shocked him. Still, shouting curses and imploring God to punish trespassers didn't really alarm him very much. He didn't believe in such things or such powers. But the curse had obviously been enough to scare off most people, and maybe that was to his advantage.

"Why?" he asked.

"That's not part of the history of the mine, Mr. Jones."

"Yes, I believe it is. How a rich mine affects its owners surely is a part of its history, which is what I came here to learn about if you're willing."

"Is that really why you came here?"

"I was hoping you might still own the mine."

"I never did. It was always Harold's until he got rid of it, a month or so before he died."

"How did he get rid of it, and why, Mrs. Haggarty?"

She peered into the sunlit yard, past the lush ferns hanging from the ceiling of the sunroom. He knew she was debating whether to talk or not. But then she smiled. The first smile she had bestowed on him, but a smile without joy in it. A ritual smile.

"He flipped a coin," she said. "He decided things that way; years of dissolute life had reduced him to letting coins make his decisions for him. The man you call Lucky Haggarty had no will of his own, but surrendered it to the head and the tail of a quarter."

Hannibal listened closely. The reluctant widow was finally talking a little, though he feared she might suddenly halt.

"He was dying of heart failure. Too much food, too many spiritous drinks, too many cigars . . . Too many women. Too much gold."

She waited for him to respond to that amazing list, but he kept silent.

"So," she said, "you pretend not to hear me."

"It was because I feared you would not continue with your story, madam."

"I like you," she said, as if this were a revelation. He knew he had won her by not dissembling.

"A toss of the coin?"

"He acquired that habit early. One day he was a dutiful employee of a mining company, with a wife and two sons. The next, he owned the Alice and it was a bonanza. The next, he was flipping coins. Poker, monte, horse racing, speculations. He won and lost the Alice several times, and once got it back with a double-or-nothing wager on the turn of a card. Mr. Jones, he turned the three of clubs. His opponent turned the two of spades. From that moment he was no longer Harold. He had a new name, one his wife barely understood."

"He had several rich mines, did he not?"

"Depending on the cards, Mr. Jones, always depending on the cards. If he had a dozen mines one week, he might have only the Alice the next. But somehow the Alice survived."

"It must have been hard on you."

"Oh, not at first. I lived in great comfort. Our older son grew up with all the advantages, and we shipped him off to Dartmouth. But always, Mr. Jones, our world was changing, even if I barely saw it and didn't understand it."

She gazed into that sunlit side yard, seeing things she probably would not share. And yet, Hannibal found her candor surprising, if not shocking.

"Lucky's most famous bet, Mr. Jones, is the one that is whispered about. For years I pretended it was otherwise. The story makes sense only if you understand that I enjoyed a certain reputation. It was flattering to learn that I was regarded as the most handsome woman on the continent. But one reaches a certain age when all that counts is truth. Harold got into a poker game with several people at the Reno Club, and began losing steadily. Soon the others reached their limits and bowed out, but continued to sit at the table to see how it all worked out. They were men whose names you would instantly recognize. His opponent, Rockwell Flyers, owner of the Russian Mine in Virginia City, soon possessed all of Harold's lesser mines, and then Harold offered a bet. On the turn of a card, he would get his mines back if he won; if he lost, Rockwell Flyers would enjoy one night with me. Harold Haggarty lost."

Chapter 11

It was as if an anarchist's bomb had exploded in that sun parlor. Hannibal sat rigidly, unable to process what he had heard, and doubting that he had heard it.

She smiled thinly.

"Mr. Jones, I see you are discreet enough to remain silent when a lady confesses a scandalous indiscretion. But I am certain your mind teems with thoughts. Did she go willingly? Did she enjoy it? What happened when she met the man? Where did it happen? How did that night play out?"

She had caught him at his own thinking, and he found himself reddening, even through the heavy tan he had acquired from an outdoor life.

"I'm a semi-lady, so I'll give you a semi-answer, and you'll have to make do with it," she said. "The truth of it is that I found the arrangement very flattering. After all, it was me versus a few hundred thousand dollars. What lady wouldn't find a certain satisfaction in it? Poor Harold didn't get his mines back, but he still had the Alice, and he could lend me out for an evening." She gazed blandly at Hannibal. "Have I shocked you?"

He thought suddenly of the Episcopal church in Ely, endowed by Faye Haggarty.

"A thought crossed your mind," she said. "I could almost read it. Come now, fess up."

"Ah, I was thinking of the church you endowed in Ely."

She laughed, a tinkling, chiming waterfall of mirth. "Oh, that. Episcopalians make their own rules, my dear."

"Is this why you cursed the Alice?"

"Oh, heavens, no. I emerged from that as a woman of reputation. I was lionized at social events. I could scarcely have had a more entertaining time. Lucky Haggarty's blue chip." She laughed easily. "Or maybe his blue chippie."

"Then why?"

"It's a long story and it'll bore you."

"I'm up to it."

"I'm not sure you are. I think you teem with all those virtues that make life a bore."

He didn't know how to answer that one either.

She shifted in her love seat. He was amazed at her beauty, the porcelain complexion, the soft eyelashes, the direct gaze that made him swim in a turquoise sea.

"Harold always believed in all those dreary virtues," she began. "You know. Hard work. Thrift. Honesty. Mastery of a skill or profession. Savings for a rainy day. Independence of mind. Education. He was such a dear bore. But we did well, you know. By the time I first conceived, he was off to a good start in business, pleasing to his employers, you know, all of that sort of thing. If life was dull, it was also secure and respectable, and the sun shone down upon the young couple, Harold and Faye. Ah, but who would have suspected what lay within his bosom? His wife certainly hadn't an inkling, Mr. Jones."

"He began gambling, I take it."

"Oh, that's a simple way to look at it. What happened, after he had bought the Alice for a song, is that he got lucky. And the luckier he got, the more he abandoned all those dreary virtues. No longer did industry and skill net him a fortune. That was for chumps. No longer did integrity and modesty earn him respect. No longer did long hours, shrewdness, saving, sacrifice, moderation in all things win him a dime. All those

Protestant virtues simply crumbled, Mr. Jones, and he came to believe in Fate. With a turn of the card he won or lost a mine. Or a yacht, or a mistress. Belle, you know. The other woman, shall we say, was won at a card game. So why believe in all those New England virtues?"

"But surely things went bad; he lost bets. Fate dealt him cruel blows."

"That's the point, Mr. Jones. Fate dealt him cruel blows. It wasn't his incompetence or laziness or any failing. It was Fate. The goddess of luck ruled his life. And once she did, why, Mr. Jones, nothing else had meaning! What was wealth? Fate! What was gold? Fate! What was a loving wife? Fate! What was a horse race? Fate! What was a child? Fate. Once you have surrendered all things to luck, you also surrender life itself to luck. Why are you alive? Fate. Why didn't you die in that train wreck? Fate. Why are you healthy? Or sick? Why do you own stock in a hundred companies? Fate, Mr. Jones. The spin of the roulette wheel of life. And that's the door that Lucky Haggarty opened and went through."

Hannibal listened, wondering why this virtual stranger was suddenly unburdening herself, openly discussing intimate details of her life, referring to her husband's mistress, casually discussing her own liaison with a strange man, the result of a turn of the card. And what did it have to do with the Alice Mine, cursed and haunted?

"I see I'm boring you," she said.

"Not at all. But the thread to the Alice Mine is sometimes lost to me."

"Ah, the Alice. The legendary mine. Even that was lucky, you know. What other mine had a natural drainage system, and a crevice that carried fresh air into the works? Miners told Harold it was the best mine they ever worked, dry, comfortable, safe, no gases or trouble. And that made them work harder. And it was all luck, you know. As if God had given Lucky Haggarty the perfect mine."

"Well, it wasn't perfect. It was located far from everything."

"Ah, Mr. Jones, Lucky didn't see it that way. He saw forests up above the mine that would fire boilers that would run stamp mills and reduce the ore right there."

"Well . . . I believe there is a mountain of ore that is lying there and unprofitable."

"You've been there."

"I have just come from there. Since there was no one to ask, and its ownership is guarded, I took the liberty of examining it. If you know who the owner is, I will send my apologies and I will seek permission to explore further."

"You want the gold."

"It is my business to bring dead mines to life."

"Lucky would have pulled out a deck and asked you to cut it, and would have given you the Alice if you won."

"I'm afraid I doubt that."

"That's what I like about you," she said.

"Do you own the Alice?"

She smiled, that thin compressed smile. "I don't need to. I inherited all the assets that a woman could want."

He started to say she hadn't responded to his question, and let it pass. This wasn't a cross-examination. "Who does own it?"

"Well, there could be two other people, couldn't there? My son's widow—he died years ago, you know. Or Belle."

"Or none of those."

That faintly displeased her.

"What happened to the Alice, Mrs. Haggarty?"

"Oh, I don't quite know."

He sensed he was on tender ground, and simply waited for her to pick up the thread.

"He had congestive heart failure, you know. The end was coming. He couldn't breathe very well. He believed in luck. Only luck. He didn't believe that anyone should inherit anything except by luck. So he brought his lawyer to witness a coin toss, announced that heads, the mine would stay open, tails, it would be shut down within days of his death and stay shut down. It was tails, and the lawyer was instructed to do it. Then he flipped the quarter again. Heads, Belle got the mine, tails, I would. Heads came up and his mistress got the mine. But you see, the first toss resulted in closing it. The second toss gave it to Belle. So it was worthless."

"So Belle owns the mine?"

"But she doesn't. She didn't want a mine that could never be opened again. So Lucky took it back."

"That's very strange. Didn't she fight it in court?"

"Nothing. No legal actions. The title's worthless, you know. Lucky wanted it that way."

"This doesn't make sense."

"To Lucky, it made sense. He died two weeks later, the mine was shut down according to his wish, and after that I lost interest."

"Where's he buried?"

"That was another toss of his coin, Mr. Jones. Heads, his widow was to bury him. Tails, his lover was to bury him."

"And who won?"

"I don't know. I was never told."

"Why did he do that?"

She smiled again, her lips pursed. "We try to make our lives orderly, Mr. Jones. But not Lucky Haggarty. Do you know what really inspired him? After he adopted luck as his guiding star, he adopted chaos. If nothing meant anything because it was all the result of luck, then the ultimate joke upon others would be chaos. The more chaos he could create, the happier he was. He probably died laughing, thinking of all the maddened, frustrated, anguished, bewildered people he had plunged into chaos."

That was astonishing. A rich man with a rich mine fell into living a life of chance, and when that wearied him, fell into creating all the chaos he could manage.

He eyed Faye Haggarty and saw, at last, some rue on

her lips. She had to live with chaos. She didn't even know where her wandering husband lay buried.

But Hannibal thought maybe he did.

"What about that grave below the mine? Is he buried there?"

"Grave, Mr. Jones?"

"The one with the blank headstone, polished gray marble without a word on it."

She fussed a little. He watched her hands flutter and then settle.

"There couldn't possibly be anyone there," she said.

"An empty grave?"

"Maybe the grave of the ghost," she said.

Something had changed. She stared at him without warmth, her unspoken wish plain.

"It's time for me to go," he said. "Thank you for the interview."

"It's not an interview you'll forget," she said. "A curse and a ghost and an empty grave and luck and chaos."

"And a gracious woman," he said.

She smiled. "Flattery won't remove the curse," she said.

Chapter 12

Hannibal retreated from Faye Haggarty's house scarcely knowing what to think. He was a mining geologist and engineer, and now he was trying to cope with scandal, family secrets, subterranean feuds, and maybe madness.

She had sketched a man who had plunged from sober virtue into a life so bizarre it could not be decently published. A man whose vision of living had gone from the virtues to luck to chaos. The latter fascinated Hannibal. He could understand believing in Fate, in chance, in luck. But if what Faye had said was true, Lucky Haggarty had plunged over the brink and into a world of malice, finding his amusement in making life miserable for others, his ghost licking its chops at the sight of heirs and maybe others—like a certain Hannibal Jones—wrestling with a fortune that still lay untouched in the rocky slopes east of Ely.

But all was not chaos. Someone, some entity, regularly paid taxes. The mine was patented. There had to be a will filed somewhere, in some probate jurisdiction. If there had been a legal struggle among heirs, it would show up. If the mining bureau kept production records and other data, those would be available. And surely some of all this would still reside in lawyers' files, newspapers, cemeteries, and even living memories, if he could find the right people and ask the right questions.

Still, he was a geologist, not a detective. The whole chaotic business repelled him. He believed in an orderly world and an orderly nature. If Lucky Haggarty had, indeed, spread chaos and frustration as a sort of final joke, then Hannibal detested the man. What decent mortal would do that?

He thought maybe he should abandon his pursuit of the Alice, a mine with such perverse owners and history that it might just be best to quit, to head for other promising properties that might be brought back to life. And yet, the Alice fascinated him. Faye fascinated him. And the looming ghost of Lucky Haggarty fascinated him.

Never in his life had he heard a woman talk the way Faye had. It was odd. What lay shrouded in silence in other women was openly discussed by Faye. It disconcerted him, hearing her talk of an indiscretion, of her husband's mistress, of living with a philanderer. He scarcely knew what to make of it. He could plumb the secrets of a piece of quartz, but not the secrets of a beautiful woman.

He sighed. Faye Haggarty would make a marvelous wife for any man. He had been attracted though she was half a generation older. He had made his choice long ago: The outdoor world, long periods of isolation, the pursuit of valuable minerals, all triumphed over dull domesticity, and he had simply abandoned marriage as a goal. Not that he didn't suffer the usual pangs, but he told himself that he had more absorbing things to do with his life than sire children. Women were a bother, especially the bossy type. Maybe someday after he was rich, he would look twice at one.

He hiked back to the Nevada capitol buildings located on a pleasant campus in the heart of the small town. In the dry heat of a summer afternoon, he probed the mining bureau records. The name of H.C. Haggarty showed up frequently, and vanished frequently. Haggarty had won and lost mines as if they were poker chips. But the Alice was different. Haggarty owned it and kept it, and no record revealed that he had won and lost that one a few times at the poker table.

Hannibal headed for the clerk of court, wondering whether any suits involving the Alice or Haggarty had reached the state's supreme court, but the clerk came up with nothing. Hannibal sought probate information, wondering about Haggarty's will, and found nothing. Had the man disposed of all his earthly property without a will? And why hadn't anyone fought it?

He tried the state revenue bureau, looking for tax payments on mines, and found the clerks uncooperative.

"Taxes are confidential, Jones," one announced.

"Well, tell me this: Are the taxes on the Alice Mine in White Pine County paid up and current?"

"You'd have to ask the county clerk," the functionary replied.

"I'll do that," Hannibal said. He had spent an afternoon probing through state records and had no more solid information about the Alice than when he started. But there was still Faye's amazing story of a life gone astray, of a man turned mad by his own gold mine.

He headed into the early afternoon looking for a lunch, and finally settled on La Grande Maison de Florentine. It lived up to Carson City's reputation as the Bad Food Capital of the World, surpassing even

Tulsa. He spent a half hour attempting to digest what he presumed was hog-bristle gravy on rutabaga, and then headed for the offices of *The Nevada Appeal.* Surely Haggarty would show up frequently in those pages. Was he not the most celebrated Nevada mining magnate of the 1880s? Was not Nevada the fount of the liveliest journalism in the country?

A functionary ushered him to an ink-stained corner where the usual buckram-bound annual editions stood in orderly rows. He paged through several years of the late 1880s and did find a few mentions: Haggarty feted at Odd Fellows Banquet. Haggarty donates a thousand dollars to the Millicent Greathouse Home for Troubled Girls. Haggarty pinched for disorderly conduct; charge dismissed. He had, it seemed, insulted a saloon bouncer.

It didn't come to much. Given the man's notoriety and the fact that he had spent a good chunk of his life there, Carson City's newspapers and records didn't yield much.

Hannibal returned to the Carson House facing a decision: quit or continue. He had a business to run and the Alice Mine wasn't really business. Not unless he could deal with its owners.

He made his decision in the Carson House Saloon, a polished mahogany corner filled with comfort, padded-leather seating, and quiet cheer. Nevadans didn't know about food, but they were expert at drinking. He adjusted his bow tie, set aside his pith helmet, and settled down to some Kentucky bourbon and branch, served over High Sierra ice. He always made his best decisions in just such circumstances.

The more he sipped, the more he was inclined to pursue the Alice Mine just to satisfy his curiosity. He could postpone other, more promising projects. Bisbee could wait. So could Wickenburg. So could Douglas. They were merely mines. The Alice was an adventure. He smiled at his own folly. The Alice was a seductress and he was willing to be seduced. And the Jack Daniel's tasted just fine. A pox on the prohibitionists.

The Alice it would be. That decision made, he continued to imbibe, hoping to settle his bad lunch, but all he did was get sleepy, and he finally retreated to his room up three flights of stairs. It occurred to him that he was a loner. He had just spent over three hours in a convivial saloon, surrounded by gents in bowlers, and he had not addressed a one of them and had discouraged all social commerce.

He placed his pith helmet on the shelf. He hung his jacket on a hanger. He sat on the edge of the bed and untied his shoes. He untied his bow tie and tugged it out of his collar. It was a fine, discreet red bow tie. Then he thought of Faye. Indeed, he had thought of little else all evening, though he didn't want to admit it to himself. The most beautiful woman he had ever seen, all the more so in her fifties than younger. It was crazy. He thought and thought about Faye Haggarty, who made her own rules. Maybe she would tell him more about the mine.

He tied his shoes. He stood before the mirror, tugged his bow tie around his neck, and expertly tied it in a crisp bow. He donned his tweed coat. He clapped his pith helmet over his head, though the sun had long vanished. He descended three flights, down a grand stairway with a polished banister in the middle of the Carson House, and soon plunged into the night. It was a fine, fresh eve, not yet late, though Carson was already quiet. What a sober little town it was, with no entertainment other than bad food and corrupt politics. He headed west in the starlight, guided by a sliver of moon. He set aside misgivings and boldly approached the elegant home of Faye Haggarty, widow and heir of the great mining magnate. He was not too late. A light glowed in one upstairs room. He wondered about the maid, and hoped she was day help and had long since abandoned her mistress to the comforts of solitude.

He paused, gathered his courage, and marched to the massive door. He swore he could smell magnolias in the night breeze, but knew it for a nasal mirage. He doffed his pith helmet, paused, and then rang the chimes.

A vast silence ensued. He felt the cold breezes eddying down from the Sierras. And finally a voice:

"Who is it?"

"It's Hannibal Jones, Mrs. Haggarty."

She opened. In the dim light he beheld a woman in a soft white robe, hair down and loose, face a mask. He thought she was beautiful, with the gentle light enhancing her porcelain face.

"I thought we might have a drink. Talk about the Alice," he said.

"A drink? A drink, Mr. Jones?"

"Why, I found myself thinking how much I enjoyed our visit. How gracious you are. How marvelously honest. How you make your own rules. How you took in a stranger and made a friend . . ."

"Just a minute," she said. "Now you stand right there. Don't move an inch."

That was promising. She vanished into the dark interior, perhaps to light a light. He twirled his pith helmet as he waited, glad that he had worked up the courage to visit this magnificent woman who made her own rules and talked candidly about them.

She returned at last, carrying something, and he discovered it was a large goblet.

At the door she lifted the goblet and splashed its contents, cold water, in Hannibal's face.

"There's your drink, Mr. Jones. Good night."

The door swung shut and clicked gently. He felt water dribble down his cheeks into his collar. He put a hand to his bow tie and found it was soaked. His shirtfront was soaked too. She had not missed.

He felt chagrined. What had inspired him to do such a thing? Call upon a woman obviously preparing to retire? A woman older than himself?

He knew what had inspired him, and it wasn't the Alice. He turned away, seeing a side of himself he hadn't known existed, and not liking himself at all.

Chapter 13

Well, he thought, she made her own rules, all right. He had just encountered the upper class and discovered that they are different from other people.

He felt the cold water soak its way down his shirt. He returned the pith helmet to his head, wondering why he wore it at night, and headed through the quiet lane toward his hotel. The farther he walked, the funnier it seemed. Here he was, a geologist and mining engineer poking into high society, about which he knew nothing. He was very good at field-testing rock, but knew little about field-testing the rich. In fact, he knew nothing much about people at all, having buried his nose in technical books since reaching maturity.

Lucky Haggarty's friends and heirs fascinated him. They lived in a world he had scarcely fancied, but now suddenly he wished to meet them all. He hiked back to the hotel in an increasingly exuberant mood, not knowing why and not caring why. He entered the hotel and passed the desk clerk, hoping the clerk would take notice of the dark wet splotch on his shirt. He hoped the clerk would say, "What happened to your shirt, Mr. Jones?" so he could reply that a rich lady had dashed cold water upon his amorous intentions. That was mirth enough to carry him up the flights of stairs to his room. Now he was a man of the world. He had never before attempted to seduce a woman, but now that it had happened, he counted it a delicious experience, give or take a little ice water.

He went to bed a changed man. He would no longer mine rock; he would plumb the rich for their secrets. As he rid himself of the cold and soggy attire, he hoped that Faye Haggarty was lying abed brimming with regret, pining away for him, thinking about sending a tender note in the morning redolent with invitation.

The next morning he awoke in a new world. He felt pure energy flow through his veins. His red polka-dot bow tie was all dried out. He scraped off his whiskers seeing a new man in the mirror. He knew exactly what to do: He would go to San Francisco, where Lucky Haggarty had made a home for himself. The richer he'd gotten, the more he'd enjoyed the sybaritic metropolis on the bay. They all remembered Lucky in San Francisco. Hannibal knew he would have no trouble tracking down the man who owned the Alice and hung on to it almost to his last breath. With a little luck he might find out who owned it now.

He devoured two helpings of cantaloupe and French toast, paid for his room, and headed for the railroad depot. A spur would take him to Reno, and there he would catch the Central Pacific's California Express. At the ticket window he hesitated suddenly, tempted by something that had never before tempted him. This time he didn't resist. He bought a first-class ticket all the way to the coast. Always before, he had traveled coach-fare. He was a businessman, after all. Business succeeded by economizing on expenses, such as rail travel. But this time . . .

He plunked down eighty-seven dollars cash and got a lengthy yellow ticket that entitled him to first-class passage in a chair car to Reno, a Pullman berth and chair-car passage to Oakland, and ferry passage to the white city on the ocean. It was a marvel, first-class passage. Why on earth had he never done it before?

By late afternoon, he was aboard the maroon lacquered cars of the Express, and found his reserved seat. He pulled off his pith helmet and adjusted his red polka-dot bow tie. The Pullmans were always at the rear, coaches up front. The car behind his was the diner, and the car behind that the observation, or club, car, with a fine view of the receding silvery rails as the train wended its way west.

A porter swiftly stowed his luggage in the overhead bins, and he settled down to read his mining journals as the Express huffed and chuffed up the steep grade out of Reno and into the pine-clad Sierras. Ah, this was living! He imagined Lucky Haggarty himself settling into just such a car as this, unless he had his own railcar decorated to his own tastes. Hannibal imagined that someday he himself might own such a private car, and take a bevy of voluptuous women on a trip around the country, off to New York and New Orleans, his private porter feeding them oysters and caviar and champagne. He thought he would like a brunette and blonde and redhead, each to complement his moods.

But for now, he was content just to experience first-class travel on a crack train, and rub shoulders with the people of his own privileged class. It certainly beat wandering around arid mountains with a pick hammer hacking out bits of rock to examine. His vocation had won him a comfortable living, even some reserves, but plainly there were better ways to live. It occurred to him that he could easily snatch the Alice from whoever was abusing it, and could soon turn himself into a modern version of Lucky Haggarty. Lucky Jones. That name appealed to him. Lucky Hannibal.

As the train toiled slowly up the awesome slopes of the Sierras, Hannibal headed toward the observation car, found a comfortable swivel chair, turned it to observe his fellow travelers, a bespectacled businessman on one side, a thin, dour matron on the other.

"Ah, porter, a gin and bitters, please, on ice."

The beverage was swiftly produced, and Hannibal sipped a first-rate, well-made, generous dollop of spirits. It was a daring drink. No one but British exiles ever ordered one, but the attendant had produced it instantly. Hannibal smiled. This was living!

After a few splendid sips he wheeled around to observe his comely neighbor, who was wrapped in pink silk with a floral hat perched on dishwater blond hair.

"Madam, the scenery is splendid, isn't it?"

She nodded.

"And where are you headed?" he asked.

"To Nob Hill," she said. "I'm going to shoot my husband."

The response thrilled Hannibal. Truly he was among

the rich, who made their own rules and didn't care what anyone else thought.

"That sounds like an excellent idea," he said.

"He gave me a disease I can't get rid of," she replied.

Hannibal's ardor for a night with her in his Pullman bed swiftly evaporated. "I think you've got the right idea," he said.

"No, it isn't. I could get the electric chair. But I wouldn't mind turning him into a soprano."

"That would be just."

"Why are you always agreeing with me?" She studied him lazily. "You seem to be a clerk," she said.

"Ah, that's not quite it. I'm a mining geologist."

"It's the bow tie. Tradesmen all wear bow ties."

It was plain to Hannibal that he would need to improve his attire in San Francisco. He decided he would study the gentlemen of that town and buy some ready-mades that would get him by. The woman had returned to her gazing and yawning.

She settled into her reading. He waited for the chance to see what absorbed her, and finally found out it was *Vanity Fair* magazine. He surveyed the others in the club car. Twilight had settled over the Sierras, and he caught the wink of early stars and snowy peaks and a vast black forest. A whiff of coal smoke eddied through the car; a downdraft must have sent the smoke from the doubled-up Pacific engines dragging the Express up the grade.

It was time for dinner, but he really wasn't ready for

that. What he hoped he might find was an attractive single woman, well coiffed, with a big diamond on her finger, who might enjoy sampling a night in a Pullman bunk with a rogue named Jones. If need be, of course, being a man of the world, he would seek out the conductor and trade the Pullman bunk for a compartment.

He spotted one couple sitting at the very rear, watching the silvery rails vanish into the gloom, but they seemed to be attached. The rest were businessmen looking bored, or imbibing ritually in a pre-dinner drinking ceremony. Hannibal sighed. He truly wished to find a rich lady who would enjoy a Pullman night with a mining geologist. But it was not to be.

He hastily downed another gin and bitters, tipped the handsome, smiling steward generously, and headed forward to the diner. It was still filled with people, and he had to wait, but finally the dining car steward seated him at a table with three striking young women. He could hardly believe his luck. These were probably coach passengers; they were not so elegantly attired, but who knows? Maybe the lower classes were less inhibited than the upper. And not a one of them wore a ring of any sort.

He smiled amiably at them. They were all dark-haired beauties, improved by two gins and bitters. The menu this evening offered beef stew, porterhouse steak, chicken à la king, Brussels sprouts, candied yams, creamed broccoli, spinach salad, and raspberry tarts or ice cream.

The black waiter swiftly took his order for the

chicken à la king, yams, and broccoli. Hannibal also ordered another gin and bitters, and smiled affably at his companions at table.

The three young ladies had finished their main course and were awaiting dessert. They smiled shyly at him.

"It's a fine evening," he said.

None of them replied.

"One can see the snowy peaks in the moonlight."

They looked blank.

Finally, one of them spoke to the others, and in a tongue Hannibal could not comprehend. He could not even fathom the language. Spanish? No. French? No. German? No. Portuguese? Not a chance. Hungarian? Romanian? Slovenian? Sighing, he concluded that he would not spend the night with anyone other than his lonesome self.

"I would enjoy buying you an aperitif after dinner," he ventured. "My old friend Blake, the steward in the club car, knows just how to pour magic."

They smiled.

"What nationality?" he asked.

The older one shook her head.

So much for seductions, he thought.

The women paid, smiled shyly at him, and left. He watched them head forward into his own Pullman car, and for a moment he thought that maybe they would discover he was bunked right next to them, and they would enjoy the company of an ardent swain with professional credentials. But when he finished his meal and headed into the silent Pullman, he saw only walls of heavy blue curtains. He paused at the washroom, and then headed toward his own rolling nest.

Moments later he climbed into his own lower bunk, which had been opened by the steward, and reminded himself, sadly, he was a mining geologist and his purpose was to resurrect the Alice.

Chapter 14

When the ferry docked at the foot of Market Street, Hannibal gathered his bags and caught a hansom. He knew exactly where he would go this time: the St. Francis Hotel on Union Square. It might strain his resources, but so what? He was weary of penny-pinching. If he was going to pursue the upper class, he might as well pursue them in comfort.

Ah, San Francisco! Sybaritic city! Some of its vast wealth had sprung from the Alice Mine, located on a remote slope of eastern Nevada. He negotiated a corner suite, wanting windows in two directions, one overlooking the bustling square. He ascended in an Otis elevator operated by a little monkey in a pillbox cap, and soon was settled in his rooms. He arranged his shaving gear on a glass shelf above the running-water sink, lined up his shoes in a neat row in the closet, hung his clothing up so the wrinkles would vanish, and eyed himself in the stately mirror.

The red bow tie seemed inappropriate. For that matter, so did the baggy tweed jacket and mismatched trousers and high-top shoes. And so did the pith helmet. Well, then, his first stop would be a clothier's. He would have to buy ready-mades because there would be no time for him to put a tailor to work. Yes, a new pin-striped suit, a bowler of the finest beaver, a pair of cravats (in case one got soup-stained), a box of white shirts with removable collars for starching, and black oxfords for his feet. And oh, yes, calf-high black hosiery and the garters to hold them up.

He headed into a bright cold day. San Francisco specialized in chill, and he was soon walking briskly to warm himself. It was a far cry from the climate near Ely. By the end of that fine day, after visiting several lordly clothiers and haberdasheries, he wore plumage guaranteed to give him access to the toniest salons in town. His old clothing, discreetly wrapped, was sent by messenger boy to his room. Hannibal tipped him a quarter. He ventured out upon the boulevards dressed in a pin-striped black suit, snowy-white shirt with French cuffs, a regiment-striped red tie, black derby, and black gloves. Plainly, Hannibal Jones was a man of parts. Why, he was better dressed than San Franciscans!

His first stop was that tall anonymous building on Market Street. He ascended one flight of stairs and again found himself before the pebbled-glass door with the black-painted title on it, WESTERN HOLDINGS. It remained as silent and locked as last time. He withdrew one of his cards and his Waterman fountain pen, asked for an appointment, and slid it under the door.

He really hadn't expected anyone to be there, but it was obviously the first place to stop.

The Alice still eluded him, but he was confident that Lucky Haggarty would not. This was his lair, and here, in bits and pieces, would lie the remnants of his bizarre life.

The hour was late, but there still might be time to examine the files of one of the daily papers. He chose the *San Francisco Exchange*, an afternoon business paper that specialized in mining news. He reached its offices on Sutter a little before the dinner hour, and was lucky to discover a bewhiskered gent in a green eyeshade and arm garters leaning deep into his chair and smoking a foul yellow cigarillo.

"I'm looking for some mining information. Too late?" Hannibal asked. The ink-stained old gent eyed Hannibal's out-of-the-box attire and snorted.

"I'm Hannibal Jones, mining geologist."

The name was obviously familiar to the old coot. His rheumy eyes lit up slightly.

"I'm looking for anything I can find in issues going back through the eighties."

"Sit your ass down and we'll talk," the man replied. "You won't want to dig through old bound volumes alone in here after dark. We have cleaning ladies who are ax murderers, window washers who were pickpockets. But maybe I can steer you. I've been with the paper since Adam and Eve ate the apple."

Hannibal doffed his unfamiliar bowler, which rested stiffly on his weathered brow, and settled into a ratty chair. "The Alice Mine," he said. "I want to know whatever there is to know. It was once the richest mine in the West. I have some ideas about what might be done with it. That's my trade."

"I know who you are," the man said. "Romney, here. Constantine Romney. Editor longer than I can remember. Now what's this about the Alice?"

"I'm trying to locate owners and heirs."

Romney sniffled slightly, and ran a purple tongue over yellow lips. "No heirs. No owners. That's one of the things I'd like answered. I'd give my left nut for a good story on the Alice that names the names and untangles that web." He eyed Hannibal. "Now first, Jones, what do you know?"

"I know that someone's paying the taxes, someone's hanging around the old mine trying to scare off people and maybe generate a few ghost legends. And I know Mrs. Haggarty, who's still going strong in Carson City, doesn't own it, or says she doesn't own it. It's been around seventeen years since old Lucky Haggarty cashed his chips, but there the mine sits."

Romney grunted. "You know more than I do," he said.

"I know that the mine was shut down suddenly after Haggarty died; that there were no problems with water, gases, lawsuits, or anything else. That in all probability there's a fortune in quartz gold still in there, but no one has touched it or reopened the place, even though there are now smelters and rail lines not far away in Ely. And I know that the firm paying the

100

taxes is called Western Holdings, and it has an office here in the Folger Building, but no one is ever in it."

Romney lifted a brass spittoon from the floor and shot a brown gob into it. Then he placed a dose of snuff under his tongue. "Haggarty used to come in here all the time. He always wanted something. Mostly to plug the Alice. I didn't mind. There's never been a mine like it. Haggarty claimed it would be good for ten million of bullion. By the time he croaked he'd pulled over five out of it. He had some smart brain-whackers in there figuring out the geology, and they pretty much agreed there was a lot of gold lying around."

"It's dead as a doornail now, Mr. Romney."

"I'm Con, dammit."

"Con, sure. I looked it over. The shaft's blocked. Not a cave-in either. It's been blown shut. There's a drain at the base that I thought was an adit, but it's not; it's a cave, a water-cut crevice that connects to the works. And it has a grille in front of it."

"Someone's protecting that five million, Jones."

"You know anything about the grave there? Polished marble headstone, not a word on it."

"Jones, I sit at a desk in the hinterlands of San Francisco."

"I thought maybe it was Lucky Haggarty's grave."

"He could be buried on Mount Everest for all I care. In fact, if I know Haggarty, he'd consider that peak to be his private property, a cut above everyone else. Pay a dozen Sherpas to haul him up there. He'd want it to be Mount Haggarty, tallest place on earth." He grinned. "Think how it'd be, Jones. Someday some crazy European will get the notion to climb Everest, and get up an expedition, and hire guides, and train for the thin air, and then climb up, and pant his way to the top of the entire world, and there by God is Haggarty on ice."

Hannibal sighed. He wanted fact, not legend.

"You knew him?"

"Hell, yes."

"What was he like?"

Romney lifted his spittoon and fired again. "Depends on when you're talking about. Beginning, middle, end. There were about three Haggartys I know of, and maybe a few more out in the bushes."

"You have time?"

"Jones, I can talk about Lucky Haggarty two hours straight and never run out of juice. First time I saw Harold Haggarty was before he owned the Alice. He'd bring in corporate news for the company he worked for, you know, dividends, prospects, etc."

"What company?"

"Western Holdings. Big mining outfit."

That jolted Hannibal.

"I'd call him starchy. Big eyeglasses. Black hair combed back with a little hair cream to hold it down. Liquid eyes, his gaze bouncing around like he didn't want to miss anything even when he was talking to me. A paid man, you know. Competent with numbers. Never cussed. Started a family with Faye.

"Then he saw his chance, bought the Alice from a prospector who couldn't figure how to turn a remote mine into a winner. Fast as he got it up and running, Haggarty began to change. All those churchy things, they disappeared. Now it was small-stakes poker, an occasional big bet on other property. Then he met Belle. Mrs. Brandy. She was eighteen."

"She was married?"

"Why not, eh?"

"Is she alive?"

"Full of vinegar."

"I'd like to interview her."

Romney laughed. "You don't interview Belle Brandy. You don't get past her door."

"She's here?"

"Nob Hill."

"Does she own the Alice?"

"No one owns the Alice. That's the whole point, Jones. By the time old Lucky was seeing the sunset, he fixed it that way. He turned into a whimsical and malicious old devil, enjoying the sight of people panting for money. Let 'em suffer. Five million underground! Shut her down and watch the circus! Who'd there be now? Faye, his wife after a fashion; Maxwell, his son, still alive then, but dead now; Belle Brandy; maybe a few others. There were rumors, you know. When Faye shut her door, the rumor is that he got himself another family or two or three. Who knows? Maybe Haggartys are all over the place."

"Bigamy?" The thought horrified Hannibal.

"Oh, Jones, you're a purist. He may have started a few families on the side without any formalities. There were rumors of one in Carson City and another around here somewhere. Old Lucky was a busy bee, pollinating the whole wide world. He liked to spread all that gold around."

An hour later Hannibal headed to the St. Francis for a libation and dinner, drunk with improbability. He was now a man of the world.

Chapter 15

There was nothing like a great hotel. Hannibal strolled confidently through the gray marbled lobby, caught an ornate brass-furnished Otis elevator and was dropped off four floors up, let himself into his suite, and doffed his derby. It didn't quite fit his head, but soon it would. It just needed a little shaping. Ah, the pleasures that awaited!

First he would take a hot bath in the claw-foot tub. Then he would dress in his new pin-striped suit and repair to the ground-floor saloon, where he might rub shoulders with cosmopolitans. But no sooner had he unlaced his new shoes than a sharp rap on the door interrupted him. He swiftly tied the laces and answered.

He opened to discover a female. Not just any female, but one of a certain wild intensity rather than beauty. Dark and sloe-eyed, with unruly hair, high cheekbones, chiseled features, a tall and voluptuous figure encased in yellow velvet. She was not young, but age had improved her. If anything, the years had added to her sultriness.

"Well, are you just going to stand there or are you going to invite me in?"

"Ah . . ."

This might be a lady of the night, but it wasn't yet night. He didn't object, but not at five o'clock. A lady of the night should come during the night. And then suddenly he knew who this lady was, knew it without an introduction and without even a physical description.

"Come in, Belle," he said.

She smiled softly, a faint amusement building on those sweet lips, and she entered. "Where's the pith helmet?" she asked.

"Uh, you seem to be keeping track," he said.

"Every step, Jones. You narrowly escaped a rock slide, took a hacksaw with you when you explored the mine's drainage, poked through the Ely newspapers, visited Faye hoping to bed her, rode coach to Reno and then first-class and Pullman to here, tried to seduce the lady in the observation car, would have seduced the Latvians in the dining car if you could, bought a new wardrobe this morning, and here you are."

"How do you know all that?" he asked, shocked to the bone.

"I have some trained ghosts," she said, smiling.

"Snoops, I guess," he said. He didn't enjoy being the

object of so much attention for so long.

"Ghosts," she said. "The Alice has ghosts and they've taken a personal interest in you. A mining engineer. A geologist. Jones, you may have started something after all these years."

He was taking a personal interest in her, but supposed it was folly to pursue it. Here he was, in his early forties, and there she was, in her early fifties. It would never do. But he sort of hoped it might do. She might be fun to ravish, if she didn't ravish him first.

She studied him, even while he studied her. Never had he seen such a woman. She was the Mount Everest of womanhood. She didn't walk; she undulated. Now she circled him, studying him.

"This'll never do," she said. "All this stuff you bought today. You look like a mannequin in a department store window. San Francisco has a hundred thousand men dressed just like you. I prefer you in your geologist clothing. That suits you."

"Ah . . ."

"Well, if you won't change, I'll do it for you. Now stand still. Don't move a muscle."

He stood, astonished, while she helped him out of his black pin-striped suit coat.

"French cuffs!" she exclaimed. "How could you?"

"Those are jade cuff links," he said. "From Gumps."

"You're a mining geologist. You look like a shrimp in French cuffs. And that cravat. My God, Jones, I'll have to get rid of that. I hope you still have the red polka-dot bow tie."

106

"Uh, wrapped up there in that butcher paper."

She swiftly undid the Windsor knot and whipped his silk cravat off his neck. She stared at it, then pitched it on the bed. "You let the store clerk ruin your taste," she said.

She began unbuttoning his new white shirt.

"Stand still, Jones, or I'll never get it off."

"Ah, I don't think . . ."

"What you're really thinking is that you'd like to grab me. Well, you can grab me later. Right now I'm taking you to dinner. We'll knock back a few whiskeys and have a porterhouse and then see. Maybe I'll grab you first. Who knows? We'll get a banquette with a long tablecloth and you can pat my knee. Now hold still."

She swiftly undid his shirt and helped him out of it.

"Jones, before you ever put a store-bought shirt on, you should have it pressed. Look at those shelf wrinkles. Now where's the shirt you began this day with?"

"Ah . . ." He pointed at the neatly wrapped bundle of old clothes.

She extracted it and helped him into it while he stood half paralyzed. She undid his belt and tucked it in and rebuckled his belt.

"There now, the ordeal is over. You weren't assaulted after all."

"Ah . . ."

She picked up the polka-dot red bow tie, wrapped it under his collar, and expertly tied it, smiling at him as she tugged it just so.

"There now, Jones," she said. "Don't you ever wear jade cuff links again. You're a geologist, not a fruit-cake."

She pulled his familiar baggy tweed coat over him, handed him his pith helmet, and nodded toward the door.

He stood there a moment, not quite believing this entire episode, but there she was. She smiled, unbuttoned her yellow velvet suit coat revealing a gorgeous blouse with a neck that plunged ever and ever lower, ushered him out, and closed the door behind.

"I hope you have a key," she said.

He dug into his suit pants and found it. "I do."

"Good. I'd hate to attack you in the lobby, Jones."

They repaired to the saloon, a walnut-paneled affair with plush red leather banquettes. A grease-haired waiter materialized at once.

"Bring him a double gin and bitters, and a glass of Rothschild red for me, my dear," she said. "I want to get him drunk before he says no."

"Very good, madam. Sir, I shall do my best."

Hannibal settled his tailbone into the quilted leather seat and leaned back, assessing this wunderkind of a woman. She seemed to know more about him than he knew about himself, which he found faintly amusing.

"Do you employ ten snitches per square block, or only five?" he asked.

"Ghosts, Jones. The ghosts tell me everything."

"You seem to want something of me."

"Not your body, Jones, your mind."

"You seem to have an appetite for both."

"Your appetites are useful to me, Jones."

"That cuts both ways. May I call you Belle?"

"No, call me Mrs. Brandy. It's more interesting to get into bed with a married woman."

Hannibal had the distinct feeling that he was getting in over his head, and thought he might pack up and repair to Tucson, where he maintained a small cottage surrounded by a live ocotillo fence to keep the cats out. The dead mines around Wickenburg seemed promising. But he didn't know what he would do with his new suit and cravat and bowler. Maybe the famous Arizona sunshine would restore him to his senses.

The grease-haired functionary returned with the booze and put the drinks on the table with trembling hands.

Hannibal decided there was safety in sticking to business.

He lifted his gin and bitters and toasted her. "Cheers, kid."

"That's what a geologist would say," she replied.

"You've bought me a drink and dinner for some purpose."

"Now you're talking. I want you to figure out how I can get the Alice Mine. I want it. I'm an expert gold digger. Harold was easy. I would rub him up and he'd cave in. I'd kiss his cigar-stained lips and he'd smile. I'd toy with his buttons and he'd pull out his wallet. I'd dig into his pockets and he'd dig into me. Whenever I asked, he gave me something. So I asked and asked. Diamonds, emeralds, rubies, pearls, antique furniture, Faberge jewelry, you name it. I never kept it; I sold everything and bought securities, traction companies, streetcar works, coal and gas utilities. That's how I survived, honey, although it never came to much. But the Alice, now that would solve my financial troubles."

"Who owns the Alice Mine?"

"Nobody! That rat left it unowned. I was not mentioned in any will. Some things were privately given to his assorted wives and me, but not the Alice Mine. It sort of disappeared from all the legal records."

"Is that possible?"

"Who knows? But just before he croaked he whispered in my blushing ear that I could have it if I figured out how to get it. That was it! Just figure it out and I could have the richest mine in the world!" She sipped wine. He could not see her lips or throat moving, yet the level of the wine dropped steadily until the goblet was empty. "That dear sweet rat of a Harold. He told everyone that! They could have it if they figured out how to get it. Then he croaked."

"Who's everyone?"

"He told Faye that. I found it out. We don't talk, but I found it out from her maid. And he told his other wives that too."

"Other wives?"

"Other families. Oh, he was a busy, busy man, Jones. He kept one wife in a mansard-roofed cottage a block from the State Prison in Carson City, and the other wife in an Oakland brick pile. Can you imagine it? Oakland! Who would want to live in Oakland? And he told them the same thing. The Alice was theirs if they could figure out how to get it! The rat."

"And no one's figured it out."

"That's right, and that's where you come in."

"Sorry, that's when I'm out the door, Mrs. Brandy."

He felt her hand pat him affectionately on his thigh, under the tablecloth, and changed his mind.

Chapter 16

Oh, what a dinner that was. Porterhouse so tender it melted between his molars. Candied leeks, mushrooms, and carrots. Mashed potatoes dripping in butter and garlic. Spinach and bacon salad. Crème brûlée. All of it washed down with quarts of wine.

Belle set aside business for the more serious business of gourmandizing, but she didn't neglect to pat Hannibal's knee now and then for reassurance. He got into the spirit of things and patted her thigh now and then, enjoying the firmness under that yellow velvet skirt.

After crème Yvette, she got down to business. "You are my salvation," she said. "The last half dozen vanished from sight. I sent them up to the Alice Mine to look around and never heard from them again. They either quit me or croaked."

"Ghosts," he said, not liking what was coming.

"Rivals," she retorted. "There's been a silent war for

the Alice for years and it's time I won."

"How would you win?"

"Dear Lucky told me it's all mine if I know how to take it."

"And that's what he told a few others, I imagine."

"He told everyone! This is his last bet. You can just imagine he's laughing at us."

"And you want me to wander around the Alice and find out why it was closed. Why me?"

"You're the most likely candidate in years, sweetheart."

"Because of my training?"

"Yes. The secret's inside that mine, and you're the one to figure it out."

"Why do you say that?"

"Because no one can get into it. He planned it that way."

"So I'm to find a way in, and look for what?"

She shrugged. "Whatever's interesting."

"And what would be my reward?"

She slid a hand along his leg. "Woowoo," she said.

"Ah, all right, but what else?"

"Nothing else! I'm insulted! Am I not a legend? Won't you remember this the rest of your life?" She patted his knee for emphasis.

"But no cash."

"Of course not! It's mine. There's five million in quartz ore in there, and it belongs to me."

In spite of the winsome rubbing of her beauteous hand along his right pants-leg, he decided not to let sybaritic San Francisco overwhelm him.

"I'm afraid not," he said.

"Are you a regular male?"

"As regular as they come."

She withdrew her hand. For the first time that lovely evening, both of her paws were above the linen. "Half the men in North America would surrender all they own for one hour with me. And you'll have all the hours you want, night and day, mid-afternoon, midnight, on top of a flagpole, out at sea."

It was not an unattractive offer, but he was Welsh, and Welshmen are crazy by definition.

"I'll go in with you fifty-fifty," he said.

Her restless hands froze. "I wouldn't think of it."

"I have no wish to be done in by ghosts," he added.

"You can pay for the dinner," she said.

He saw that coming. "Fifty-fifty," he said churlishly.

"I don't think there are any ghosts at the Alice," she said. "I think there's people who can't figure out how to cash in and want to keep others from cashing in."

"Such as?"

"Juanita or her boys. That's his second family, the one that lives next to the Nevada prison. She and Lucky were married by a Buddhist monk as the sun set over the Pacific. Or Babette and her girls. She's the one in Oakland. His third wife. He married her on top of the Eiffel Tower, a French postal inspector officiating. They met while gambling in Monte Carlo. She threw a chip at him because his cigars were nauseating her."

"Three all at once?"

"At least three that I know of, plus me. But they didn't count. I counted. That's why he lived with me most of the time."

"Did he rotate?"

"He spun like a roulette wheel."

"But he told them all that the Alice could be theirs if they figured out how to get it?"

She pouted.

"I think I should ask for seventy-five percent of it, not half," he said.

"You're awfully tiresome, Jones."

"When I was poking around the mine, someone started a landslide that barely missed me. Someone else tampered with my mules. And a few other things."

"Ten percent," she said. "You get ten percent, but don't ever touch me."

"Fifty."

She slid that languorous hand along his leg again. "Woowoo," she said.

"Ten percent and we touch."

"You're smart after all, Jones. Whatever else happens in your life, you'll remember me. When you're old and toothless and sitting in a wheelchair and some old rummy wheels you around, you'll still remember me. And twenty years from now, if you say you had Mrs. Brandy, everyone at the dinner table will gasp, and every male will envy you. But that's only half of it. Every woman at the table will itch to try you out."

114

He sighed. "I'd settle for a few hundred thousand in gold bullion," he said.

She pouted. Then she patted his knee.

"So we're on a treasure hunt, but we don't know what we're looking for," he said. He was a practical man and intended to get down to brass tacks.

"Oh, yes, we do. Ownership papers. A document saying we're the owner of the Alice."

"Not a will?"

"How should I know? Whatever papers I'd need to be the legal owner."

"I gather there might be half a dozen such documents, and the one who finds them first is the winner."

She stared into the yellow lamplight. "He loved taxidermy. He had lots of stuffed jaguars and mountain sheep and iguanas. I knew exactly where he hid my document. Inside the stuffing. So as soon as poor old Lucky died, I headed for his lodge and tore all his stuffed heads apart. I yanked them off the walls and made a mess. I thought I had it when I pulled a buffalo head open. Lots of paper in there, but no documents. I opened up a stuffed boa constrictor, sure it would be rolled up in there, but there was nothing but a mountain of smelly cotton. I was so blue I almost told them to cremate him."

"What did happen to Lucky?"

"How should I know? They came and got him and carted him away."

"All right. Why do you think this mythical document is around the Alice Mine?"

"Because that would be just like him. Cause as much trouble as he could."

He waited for more, and she finally obliged. "It wouldn't be at Faye's. She'd find it. She's probably stripped that house down to the foundations looking for it. It wasn't in his San Francisco flat. I was the first one in, and I tore it apart. It wouldn't be with his other wives. It wasn't in any bank vault. So it must be at the mine."

"In other words, you haven't the faintest idea whether it's there or in Timbuktu. Or whether any papers exist at all. Why should there be papers giving the mine to anyone?"

"You sure are mean, Jones."

"You don't know for sure whether a deed exists."

She didn't respond, but looked sulky.

"It could be sitting in any lawyer's office," he said.

"I seduced all his lawyers."

"It could be in his accountant's office."

"I slept with all his accountants."

"It could be filed, exactly where it should be, in a probate court."

She stared. "Why didn't I think of that?"

"Probably because you didn't like the looks of the judges."

"I tried," she said.

"I doubt that the document, if it exists, which I also doubt, is anywhere near the Alice," Hannibal said.

"Oh, yes, it is! I wasn't his lover for twenty years without learning a thing or two about him."

"What you know, Faye knows."

She laughed. "Faye is so frostbitten she never learned the first thing about Lucky Haggarty."

"Mrs. Brandy, this is a wild-goose chase."

She slid a hand along his leg. "Call me Belle."

"Ah, Belle, this is foolishness. All you people have been hunting for a document for a quarter of a century and fighting each other and driving away anyone who visits the Alice. The document obviously doesn't exist. If I understand Lucky right, in his old age he got mean and perverse, and loved to make everyone around him miserable. That's all he was doing, making you miserable."

"Then who's paying the taxes on the Alice?"

She patted him affectionately.

"Probably a trust department of a bank," he said.

But it was a good question. The property hadn't reverted to the state of Nevada for some reason.

She looked gorgeous, sitting there in the lamplight of the great restaurant, the most desired and notorious and elegant woman of her day. It scarcely mattered that years had passed. There she was, patting his kneecap and smiling at him.

"We'll go to the Alice together and solve it," she said.

"The ghosts, if that's what we'll call them, will probably do us in. No, thanks, Belle. I'm going to Wickenburg to look at other mining properties."

"But first you're coming to Nob Hill," she said. "So I can show you the sights. Woowoo!"

He succumbed. "All right, show me the sights," he said, summoning the waiter.

"You're an easy conquest," she said. "I thought you'd give me more trouble, being a geologist in a red bow tie and pith helmet and all."

"What has that got to do with it?"

"You're caught," she said, "so lie back and enjoy it."

Chapter 17

He couldn't move. There was a cast-iron stove on top of him. He needed to stretch. He opened his eyes and discovered sunlight streaming through a gauzy curtain. He was somewhere unfamiliar. There really was no stove on him. He tried to rise, but felt such weariness he preferred to lie still. This didn't seem like his St. Francis hotel room. Definitely not.

Then, in a rush, he knew. This was Nob Hill. He struggled to sit up, managed that, and then managed to stand, though he wasn't sure he could stand for more than a few seconds. The walnut clock said ten-thirty. That could not be. He was an early riser, always dressed and sipping Java by seven. But the clock was holding him accountable.

Belle Brandy had brought him here. He saw no sign of her. He didn't want to see any sign of her for fear he would collapse again. He would quietly shave, dress, retreat to his hotel, pack up, and abandon San Francisco to the sybarites. He wanted the stern solitudes of wilderness. He wanted to brew his coffee over a campfire, and eat a handful of raisins for breakfast.

He found an excellent lavatory adjacent to his room, white tile floor, a fine claw-foot tub, bidet, spacious porcelain sink. He discovered shaving gear laid out for him, which was just as well because his was at the hotel. The house stood silent in the sun, clinging to the east side of Nob Hill. He had difficulty lathering his face because his hands trembled and his arms ached. He would need to be extremely careful with that straight-edge. He worked up some lather in the Wedgwood soap mug and then brushed it into his stubble. That part wasn't bad, but he doubted that he could discipline his shaving hand.

He unfolded the straight-edge and tentatively scraped, staying well clear of his jugular in case he had an accident. Pretty soon his arms and hands got into the spirit of the thing, and he completed his toilet with only two nicks, neither of them fatal. He was not sure he could dress, but knew he must if he wished to escape. He discovered that his comfortable trousers were missing and in their place was a brand-new pair of khaki jodhpurs with a fancy flair at the waist and hips, and leg-hugging from the knee down.

He didn't want to wear them. But she had made off with his pants. He searched but they were gone. He struggled into his shirt, somehow controlling his trembling hands, pulled up the loathsome jodhpurs, added his hosiery and shoes, tied his red polka-dot bow tie, donned his tweedy suit coat, found his pith helmet, and was ready for the day. Well, ready, at any rate, to negotiate the stairs and see about some coffee. By the time he reached the bottom of the stairs, he was out of breath. A firm hand on the banister had kept him upright through this perilous descent, and he found himself in a modest foyer, with a parlor to the left and a dining room and kitchen to the right. He turned that way, hoping to discover a means of resuscitating himself. But no sooner did he enter the silent oak-paneled dining room than a maid in starchy black appeared.

"Mrs. Brandy said you'd be eager for coffee. She's out shopping but bids you to wait."

"I'll have some coffee, and then just slip out, thanks," he said. "Catch her some other time."

He was not well and intended to burrow under the covers in the St. Francis and spend the day incommunicado.

The maid returned with a steaming cup of coffee, and he settled into an embroidered dining chair and tried to drink. The cup rattled like a machine gun on the saucer.

"She said you wouldn't want breakfast, but to offer it, Mr. Jones."

"The coffee will do nicely, thank you. And I'll want a few refills."

He managed to lip some without spilling, and eventually downed the cup, which was promptly refilled. The coffee was very good. He would escape. He would abandon San Francisco. He would never, ever return to San Francisco. He would never return to California if he could help it. He would find good prospects elsewhere.

He stood shakily and was prepared to brave the chilly outdoors, ignore the stares at his jodhpurs, and head for the hotel.

It had been an entertaining night, but one he would not want to repeat more than once a decade. He smiled at the starchy maid and made his way toward the front door, but too late. Belle burst in, followed by a hansom cabdriver laden with huge bundles.

"Ah, you're up, Jones," she said while the driver unloaded his bundles and went out for more. "You're not looking well, but of course no man ever does."

"Belle, I'm heading back to the St. Francis. I'll catch that hansom cab. Ah, thank you. I'll be seeing you, I imagine."

"You poor dear," she said. She wrapped him in her arms and squeezed. There was wintergreen on her breath. Her fingers caressed his neck and toyed with his bow tie. The hug galvanized him, and he felt almost human.

"I've bought everything we'll need," she said. "Wall tent for us, a marquee tent and chairs and tables and rug, a few shelters for the staff, a camp stove, kerosene lanterns. I'll bring a few servants to see to our comforts. You won't have to cook for me. I'll bring a chef, a maid, an accountant, and two groundsmen. Maybe I should add a lawyer and a photographer. Oh, they were so nice to me at Dilworth's. They know the outdoor life. Of course, I almost bought out the store. I also got an elephant gun and a shotgun, a good Purdy."

"Ah . . ."

"Don't worry, I'll practice. I stopped at the Central Pacific. We'll catch the Pullman, I got a compartment, and all the stuff will be expressed. I wanted a private car but they charge too much. Once I get the Alice, I'll buy my own private car. It will be modeled on J. P. Morgan's. We can go clear to Ely now and motor in."

"Ah . . ."

"I also bought three more pairs of jodhpurs for you, sky blue, green, and peach. You do look grand in them, Jones."

"I couldn't find my pants."

"I threw them out. But don't worry. I cleaned out the pockets and put everything in your jodhpurs."

"Ah . . ."

She smiled seductively. "I can hardly wait to get you into that Pullman compartment, lover boy. Woowoo!"

"Ah . . ."

"Look at the rug I got for our tent! It's from Brussels."

"Beautiful."

"I also ordered some dynamite for you. It'll be shipped by freight. They wouldn't carry it on the express car. They told me you needed caps and fuse, too, so I've got the whole thing. They were so sweet to me. I just told them we would blow open an old mine and they took it from there. They promised me you would have everything you need to blow the Alice open."

"Ah . . ."

"But don't worry. It'll all be shipped directly to the Alice Mine."

"But Belle, this won't work. I don't want to be observed. I don't want you and your retainers there. It'll attract attention."

"Exactly, dear boy. Let them all see us! It'll draw the rats out of the woodwork. We're going to settle this, once and for all."

"Belle, we haven't come to an agreement. No matter what, I want a piece of the action."

"You got that last night, Jones."

"We're going to have a contract, or I won't go."

She smothered him in her arms and he began to suffocate.

"There's my contract, Jones. My kiss is my bond."

"Look, if I am to go on a wild-goose chase, it will be with you alone, and without all this claptrap. I don't need a chef, maid, butler, and accountant along. This is wilderness we're going to. You have no idea. Just getting food in there would be a tough problem."

"Just leave it to Belle, Jones. You do your little poking around with your little pick hammer, and blow up rock when you see fit, and we'll sit in camp chairs— Oh, I neglected to order camp chairs. I'll remedy that at once. We'll need a dozen. I'll order camp chairs and mosquito netting. Are there wild Indians around there?"

"Just ghosts, Belle. Mean ghosts. I'm sorry, I'm not going. Get some other geologist."

"But Jones! You can't back out. I've already paid you."

"That was pay?"

"Have you ever been better paid?"

He decided not to answer that. Escape was the thing. Retreat to the St. Francis, leave town, become invisible.

He sighed, resignation creeping over his worn face. "All right. You go order what you want, and I'll go rest. We'll meet at the ferry building."

"Ah, now you are showing some sense. The Central Pacific eastbound leaves Oakland at five. I'll pick up a few odds and ends, meet you here at three, and we'll head for the ferry. You sleep, Jones. We'll have a grand time on the express tonight."

"I'm sure we will," he said.

She turned to one of the servants hovering around.

"Keep an eye on him," Belle said.

She sailed out the door, leaving the pungence of wintergreen in her wake. He stared wearily at her as the hansom pulled away from the curb. It would take a twenty-mule team to haul all her junk up to the Alice Mine.

He waited for the madwoman to vanish down the steep grade, and then smiled at the help and repaired to his room. He had little but the clothing on his back and a few dollars in his pocket. It would have to do.

The Brandy manse settled down to midday quiet, and when Hannibal deemed it safe to leave, he slipped down the polished stairs, keeping a sharp eye out for the servants, padded through the silent foyer, clicked open the massive door, and headed into the chill day. The sunlight nearly blinded him. He wanted only to sleep for two or three days.

It wasn't much of a hike to the St. Francis, and there he would change to his spare trousers, pack up, and flee the sybaritic city. But when he arrived at the hotel, his jodhpurs drawing stares, he discovered that he was already packed up and his valise had been picked up. He was adrift in San Francisco in his pith helmet, jodhpurs, red polka-dot bow tie, and baggy tweed coat.

Chapter 18

Hannibal scarcely knew a soul in San Francisco. Only an acquaintance or two. He stood in the lobby of the St. Francis, realizing he was in a pickle. A matron herding two small children entered, eyed him, and herded the children toward the elevators, shielding them from the awful sight.

Romney. His only hope. He stood straight, pushed through the door into the chill air, and headed east across Union Square, drawing stares. The pith helmet was all right, and the red polka-dot bow tie was all right, but the jodhpurs were a novelty in the city on the bay. But he was resolute. He was a renowned mining geologist and engineer, and he would not let stares and snide comments deter him. He hiked toward the editorial chambers of the *San Francisco Exchange*, and finally plunged through the battered door. Two reporters were torturing typing machines, cigarette smoke curling upward from weeds burning on the lip of ancient desks.

He found Constantine Romney hunched over copy, his green eyeshade over his hoary locks. Romney refused to look up; this was an ancient ploy of editors. Study the copy and let the intruder shift from one foot to the other. But at last he set down his blue pencil and stared, his rheumy gaze absorbing Hannibal's laced shoes, jodhpurs, and on up to the pith helmet.

"I won't ask," he said.

"Romney, I need your help. I've just escaped from a madwoman."

"I see," said Romney.

"I need to borrow a little cash. I don't have any. She got it. I'm good for it; I'll repay you in a few days."

"She got it?"

"She took my pants."

"I won't ask about that either."

"I need to buy some pants, and a coach ticket to Ely, where my duds are stored, and I'll need enough for a meal or two."

"You need pants," he said. "I suppose you do."

"I'll have a check in the mail to you day after tomorrow. From the Ely bank. With interest. I need fifty dollars. Sixty would be better."

Romney settled into his squeaking swivel chair. "Is there a good story in it? A scoop?"

Hannibal sighed. "Later. You'll be the first."

"Should I ask about this madwoman?"

"I can't say, but you'd know her name at once."

"Belle Brandy. She'd steal your pants, all right. She could steal mine, but it wouldn't do any good anymore."

"Now you know why I'm desperate."

A feline smile widened Romney's cigar-stained lips. "It's the Alice," he said. "She's finally found some sucker. Congratulations."

"Not me. I am heading for Wickenburg, Arizona, as fast as I can."

"Without your pants."

Hannibal could not imagine anything he could say, so he removed his pith helmet and stood there, like a beseeching dog.

Romney wheezed cheerfully, found a key upon his massive person, and unlocked a drawer. Within was a small black cash box, from which he extracted three twenties and laid them on the desk. Then he replaced the box and locked the drawer.

Green money never looked so good to Hannibal. It sat there, atop a typed story about the price of Java coffee beans after a drought. Hannibal was tempted to reach, but disciplined his itchy fingers.

"What is Mrs. Brandy up to?" Romney asked.

"A grand encampment at the Alice Mine, servants and all, while her rat terrier, Jones, hunts for ownership papers."

Romney's grin widened. He handed Hannibal the three twenties. "Buy some pants," he said. "Try John's

Clothiers, half a block south. They will dispose of the jodhpurs if you wish." He cocked a questioning eyebrow.

"I wish," Hannibal said, and turned to leave.

"Oh, Jones, I charge interest."

Hannibal paused.

"A story. The whole shebang. Hot tips. Before anyone else gets it. The mysterious Alice Mine."

"You've got it."

Romney wheezed happily and returned to his blue-penciling.

Hannibal stepped into the cold street. Immediately, seven pedestrians gawked. He pushed past them and their rude stares, and trotted directly to the clothier's, where he purchased some brown twill trousers suitable for fieldwork.

"I'll wear them," he told the clerk.

"I was guessing you would, sir. I shall wrap the stylish ones."

"You can throw them out."

"We'd prefer to let you do it, sir."

He left with a clothing carton under his arm, made his way to the ferry terminal, purchased passage to Oakland, purchased coach fare to Cobre, on the Central Pacific, where he could catch a stage to Ely.

An hour later he was sitting in an ancient coach in the eastbound local. Free at last. The Alice Mine was but a memory. Faye Haggarty was dimming in his mind. Belle Brandy was but an ache in his midsection and in a month he'd get past it. He counted himself lucky to have escaped. But he was free. Let her take her circus to the Alice; he wouldn't be there. In Ely, he would sell the pack mules, collect his gear, close his account at the Stockmen and Miners Bank, and slide out of there. He might be riding a local, but he would certainly arrive there before Belle did, given the logistical problems of transporting her entire circus to the mine. He smiled. She was right. He had been well paid. He had never had such a night.

The train rattled through the California hinterlands, past Sacramento, into the oak-studded foothills, and then into darkness as night caught up with it. He settled into the hard wicker seat, offended by the hammering the ancient coach did to his tailbone. Coal smoke eddied through the coach, and the air was alternately icy and warm, depending on when the doors were left open. But that was a small price to pay for freedom from Belle.

After a miserable, hot, cold, smoky, and bone-rattling night squirming on the wicker seat, he arrived in Reno, and decided to switch to the eastbound express that would arrive two hours later. All he wanted was a plush maroon coach seat so he could doze across Nevada. He exchanged tickets, settled into a hard bench, and waited for the sleek coaches to pull in.

The train glided in to the station smack on the hour, bell clanging, steam hissing, the lacquered maroon coaches slowing to a halt. This one had two express cars, two coaches, a Pullman, diner, and observation car. Hannibal sighed. The rest of the journey would be comfortable. In a final cloud of steam, the conductor and brakemen opened doors and dropped steel step stools to the platform.

"Ah, there you are, Jones. I knew we'd catch up," said Belle.

There she was, taking the air on the platform.

He surveyed her. She was smiling voluptuously, her familiar curves encased in red velvet this day, her lips rouged, her gaze knowing. He felt an ancient stirring and fought it back.

"Belle, you can go to the Alice if you want. I'm not going. Good luck," he said.

She smothered him with a hug, a vast, cheerful squeeze, and he felt himself wavering.

"Just for a day, Jones," she said. "You come up to the Alice and show us how to get into it, and then leave."

"No, you can hire any experienced miner to show you how to open that shaft."

"Come along. We'll talk about it. The conductor's waving us on."

Hannibal went along reluctantly, a man walking to his execution. Well, what did it matter? They would part at Ely. He would head for Arizona.

"I'm forward on the coach," he said, hoping to escape her.

"That's fine, Jones. The servants are up there."

Astonishingly, she let him go. He boarded and walked forward. She boarded and headed rearward.

He thought maybe he could jump off at the last

second, but what was the point? He'd finish his business in Ely and abandon her. He soon dozed in the plush seat, lulled by the smooth hum of the coach, and next he knew, the conductor was shaking him awake.

"Cobre," he said.

There was Belle, standing on the gravel, watching expressmen unload a mountain of goods from the express car. Amazingly, a freight outfit was loading the goods into mule-drawn wagons. The unfinished Northern Nevada Railroad had not yet reached Ely, but that had obviously not fazed Belle. A wire or two was all it took.

Hannibal soon found himself sitting opposite Belle in a sturdy old Concord that was weaving and rocking its way south through an arid land. She smiled benignly. Her dark-haired maid, manly chef, and two Orientals were also aboard, the handymen riding the roof. The boot of the coach was jammed with her valises.

He tried not to think about what lay beneath that lush red velvet, and focused on the spare scenery. He had been a little stupid, but firmness would prevail. There was no way on earth that Belle Brandy could lure him up there and put him to work digging into a dead mine, all on a hunch or two.

They reached Ely about midnight. Hannibal's bones ached. Stagecoach travel was a misery the world could do without, and soon would do without. The desert night had lowered, driving down the temperature in the unheated coach, and the cold, cramped ride drained the last of his energy.

"Don't worry, Jones. I have a room for us in the Nevada Hotel," Belle said.

The thought panicked Hannibal. "Never! Not now!" he cried. The servants smiled cheerfully. One of them, the chef, a man with a formidable walrus mustache, looked like a duke.

But by the time they stepped out of the coach into a cold black night, Hannibal was ready for any bed, anywhere, any place. Wearily he followed along in her wake, like a rowboat towed by a frigate. The Nevada Hotel was as good a refuge as any. It loomed across the street from the coach stop, a two-story frame structure lit by a single oil lamp.

He intended to sleep. This night he would enjoy a small victory. Nothing she could do would keep him awake.

Chapter 19

He was right. Nothing stopped him from collapsing into the creaking four-poster and then into oblivion. If Belle had slid in beside him, he didn't know it. Bright sunlight awakened him. He had no idea what the hour was. He peered about at the unfamiliar room with tatty brown wallpaper and machine-made lace curtains and varnished pine woodwork. The only familiar thing was Belle, standing there in the luscious altogether, tickling his nose with a turkey feather.

"No!" he yelled.

"Relax, Jones, everything's taken care of. I wired sixty dollars to Romney, so you're all square."

He bolted straight up. "How . . . ?"

She smiled. "Don't worry your head about it. Do you want to get up—or not?"

"I'm getting out of here," he bawled, and bounded out of bed.

His smallclothes were all laid out. He leapt into them, found his shirt, and started a hunt for his new brown twill pants. A cold chill ran through him. The jodhpurs lay innocently over a chair back.

"I want my pants right now," he said, ransacking the room. There were no pants anywhere, including her duffel, which exuded the fragrance of jasmine.

"You look so grand in khaki jodhpurs, Jones. I want a portrait of you in those jodhpurs, that shirt and baggy tweed coat, the red bow tie, and the pith helmet. You look just like a sahib keeping rein on the natives. I'm going to give you a gold-capped ebony swagger stick for your birthday next week. If there are ghosts at the Alice, your jodhpurs will fend them off."

"That's the most lunatic thing that ever issued from your mouth," he replied.

Her response was to kiss him warmly.

"That's the craziest thing that issues from my mouth," she said softly. "Do you like being crazy?"

He ignored her warm, smooth, honeyed flesh and tied his red polka-dot bow tie, getting it wrong and having to redo it. That had never happened to him. He always tied it right. This woman was giving him rubber fingers. How did she know his birthday was coming? She probably had a dozen detectives pawing through his entire life.

He was going to have to escape all over again.

"For your information, I'm closing my accounts and business arrangements in Ely and taking the next coach out," he said.

"Oh, that's all taken care of, Jones."

"What do you mean by that?"

"I closed your bank account. I've got your mules tied at the hitch rail. We'll need them. They're loaded with your prospecting gear, and I have ten more mules loaded with the rest of it. And a sweet little burro named Pancho will carry the dynamite."

He yanked on the jodhpurs and bolted out the door, straight toward the hitch rail. There was his gear, all right, perched on his mules. He opened one of the panniers, found his clothing, and hunted for pants. He could find none except two more pairs of jodhpurs. She had stolen all his pants. All the trousers he possessed. He didn't have a pair of pants to his name. She was some kind of fiend. What sort of woman would steal pants?

It was then he realized he was up against some sort of mad genius of a woman. If she was this willful, then what must Lucky Haggarty have been like? He dug around for some money, and realized she had that too. But maybe he could charge it, bill it to his Tucson address. He stormed down Campton Street until he came to the Jacobin Clothier, barged in, selected some

134

gray twill trousers, and corralled a clerk.

"I want this billed to my Tucson address," he said.

"We can't do that, sir. Cash only."

"I'm good for it."

The man shook his head dolefully, and furtively examined the jodhpurs. Hannibal abandoned his efforts to find pants and headed for the telegraph office.

"Was a wire sent earlier to Constantine Romney in San Francisco?" he asked.

The wire man pulled a stack of flimsies off a spindle and thumbed through them, licking his thumb. "Not that I can see," the telegraph man said.

"How about the *San Francisco Exchange*? Sixty dollars?"

"I'm not allowed to share confidential information," the telegraph man said, tugging on his green eyeshade.

Hannibal grunted some sort of thanks and stormed toward the Stockmen and Miners Bank. He waited impatiently while a wiry granny deposited thirty-seven Indian-head pennies, a dime, and a liberty-head nickel, but finally he corralled the cashier, who studied his stern ledgers.

"Yes, Mr. Jones, at your request we closed the account. Mrs. Jones has the cash. Let's see now, it was three hundred and twenty-seven and change . . . seven cents."

"But she wasn't authorized. . . ."

"Why, we checked. She showed us your bank book."

Within its yellow pages, the tellers had recorded each transaction in India ink. And now she had it in her wicked little hands.

Theft.

Hannibal sailed straight for the hotel. He was going to turn her upside down and shake his money out of her pockets, and then turn her over to the sheriff and press charges. He exploded into the hotel, and into the room, and there she was, fully attired now in white cotton with blue honeysuckle crawling over it. She was twirling a white parasol with tassels.

"Oh, there you are, Jones. I forgot to give you your money. It was three hundred and twenty-seven, I believe." She laid some fifties and twenties and fives and ones in his palm. "Now, then, sweetheart, let's start. We have a long road ahead of us."

"You have a long road. I don't. I'm catching a stage for Salt Lake."

"In jodhpurs?"

She had him there, but he thought he could endure 150 miles of stagecoach travel just to escape. And now that he had cash, he could buy trousers from the Mormons, assuming they would let him into their mercantiles dressed like a Pakistani swashbuckler.

He barreled out of the hotel, retrieved his mules, and headed for the Kinnear and Brothers Stage Lines offices, located in the front of a tonsorial parlor so that a passenger could get shaved and shorn while waiting for the coach. There he discovered a coach had left for Salt Lake that very morning, and the next twice-weekly stage would be leaving on Friday.

"We'll sell you passage now, and you can count on a seat," the clerk said.

"I'll think about it."

Hannibal headed into the street, returned to the Jacobin Clothier, bought gray and brown twill trousers, put on the grays, left the jodhpurs in the dressing room, and headed into daylight. He was a free man with cash in his pockets, his gear loaded on his mules, and no one hindering him.

He needed to come to some decisions, and fast. He could head north to the railroad, or west by stage to Carson City. He really didn't want to go either direction. But maybe he could hide out. Belle Brandy would swiftly tire of the expedition and head back to San Francisco. Then he could sell his mules, head for Salt Lake, and then to Arizona. But hide where, and how long?

He opened a pannier and withdrew his field notes and maps and studied the White Pine mining district. There were abandoned mines all over the district, a dozen within thirty or forty miles of Ely. None of them had particularly interested him, but now he thought he might probe one or two while he waited for the manic Brandy woman to head back to Nob Hill. There were several abandoned mining camps nearby, such as Ward, Osceola, and Taylor. All gold. The defunct Pinochle Mine had intrigued him once, and now he would visit it. Spend a few days. Return to a safe and quiet and empty Ely, and head south.

He headed for the White Pine Market, and purchased some camp grub from a standard list he had long ago memorized, loaded it carefully on his mules, balancing the weight properly, and then headed out. This time he would walk into the Duck Creek Range where the Pinochle, once a fine gold-producer, had slumbered in exhaustion for three decades.

It was a grand day. A few puffball clouds scudded across a vast sky, driven by brisk winds. Ely fell away and the lonesome road coiled across the empty Steptoe Valley. His pith helmet sheltered him from the blistering sun. A mile or so east of Ely, the road divided. He would, of course, turn left, head for the Pinochle. The right fork would take him where he didn't want to go, toward that rough silent country where the Alice Mine slumbered in deep quietness, all but forgotten.

He was done with that, thank heaven. He remembered Faye Haggarty, with the porcelain face and austere manner. She had resolved his amorousness with a dash of cold water. He thought of Belle, and the night she had dragged him, uncomplaining, up Nob Hill and into her arms. The memories were delicious. Woowoo! She had purred and sighed the whole while. She had vanished behind an elegant red Chinese screen, and when she rounded the screen wearing a sultry smile and a little white silk robe, his life was forever changed. Lucky Haggarty was a thousand times luckier than anyone had ever imagined. He could scarcely imagine Lucky Haggarty straying from

Belle, but the more the Alice Mine heaped gold bullion into Haggarty's lap, the more sybaritic was his life.

Now he trotted down the empty road, his thoughts saturated with Belle. Belle's lips, Belle's sighs. Belle's wintergreen flavor. There had never been a night like it, or a woman like her.

He reached the fork, the place to turn left and head for the Pinochle Mine, the place to resume his fine career as a geologist and mining engineer, the place to establish his independence and manhood, the place to retreat for a few days from the clutches of Belle Brandy.

He remembered Belle and turned right. He didn't know why. He just did. The road ahead led to the Alice Mine, and to Belle.

Chapter 20

They were there, waiting for him. He marveled at it.

All the previous day he had walked resolutely into the Shell Creek Range, through a lonely silence and bright light that made his eyes hurt. The naked land evoked melancholia in him. He was on a sad journey, all because of mankind's greed for gold. As austere as these slopes were, they were at least not despoiled until gold-grubbers tore the earth and rock apart, and left rural hellholes in their wake. He had camped at a small seep, put his reliable mules on good grass, and weathered an icy night wrapped in his bedroll.

In the morning he had downed some raisins and coffee, carefully shaved off his cheek-stubble with his straight-edge, gotten into his gray twill pants, blue shirt, red bow tie, baggy jacket, and white pith helmet. He was especially grateful for the pith helmet, which shaded his face and spared his eyes from perpetual squint in that glaring land.

He encountered no trouble at all, and proceeded the next day up a precipitous trail toward the Alice Mine, enjoying the solitude. As far as he could fathom, the Alice was twenty-five or twenty-eight miles from any other habitation. He spotted not so much as a buzzard in the bold blue firmament. The breeze quieted, and now not even a whisper broke the silence of his solitude. As he climbed, the heat lessened, and eventually he spotted black pines clothing distant ridges. The Alice was about five thousand feet higher than Ely; almost a vertical mile. He cherished the hike, buoyed along by his own solitude. He was his own man. He had an independent spirit. He was a man of reputation and ability and integrity.

Thus, when he topped the last brushy incline and walked out on the high plateau where the ancient mine slumbered in the afternoon sun, he was in fine fettle, the geologist and mining engineer, comfortable in the lonely wastes of the remote West, performing one last examination of a legendary mine, more for his own sake than for the sake of any of Haggarty's mad crowd.

The Alice sagged in the sun, its ancient buildings

bleached almost white, the forbidding red cliffs looming over it, as always. But here was something new. A city of bright tents. Actually, four or five, but their gaudy color made them seem a whole metropolis. There was a ruby-colored wall tent, an open-sided marquee tent with gold and blue awning stripes, two more ordinary wall tents, but smaller and dyed an odd green.

"Oh, there you are," Belle said. "I was just telling Colonel Rathke we should wait a little while more."

"Who's Colonel Rathke?"

"My chef, Jones. From the staff of Czar Alexander. He was with us on the stagecoach. Come along now. We'll get you into your jodhpurs and we'll have tea and tarts. It's four, you know. I always enjoy high tea."

Hannibal stared. There, under the blue-and-gold-striped marquee tent, was a dining table, lavender, green, blue, star-spangled camp chairs, a pink chaise lounge, a pewter ice service for champagne, and a brazier.

"Belle, I have to care for my mules, unpack. . . ."

"That's all taken care of, dear. Yin and Yang are doing it."

He turned, discovering two tall, wiry Chinese in black mandarin silks, leading his mules away. His packsaddles and gear rested on the barren clay. He stared at them, at her, at a raven-haired maid in black with starched white collar and cuffs. He started to lift one of his packs, but Belle stayed him.

"Leave that for Yin and Yang," she said. "You're

late. I was expecting you an hour ago. Now come in and wash up."

"What do you mean, expecting me?"

She patted him on the shoulder.

"I didn't know I was coming here," he said. "I was going somewhere else."

She kissed him on the cheek. "Woowoo," she said.

She led him into the huge ruby silk wall tent. Within was a yellow and sky-blue Brussels carpet, huge double brass bed, more camp chairs, a dry sink with washbasin and pitcher, a sheet-metal bathtub, a portable bidet . . . and his khaki jodhpurs lying on the bed. Sunlight filtered redly through the silk tent walls.

"Belle . . . how did you get here so fast?"

"Money talks, Jones. The world salutes double eagles. Now we'll get washed up. You may put on your jodhpurs, which you carelessly left behind you in the Jacobin Clothier. Here, I'll help you."

She began yanking at his belt and buttons.

"I'll do it!"

"Poor dear," she said. "Oolong tea will freshen you right up. And the colonel made some raspberry tarts and some cherry tarts. I guess he was thinking of me."

She began tugging at his twill pants.

"I'll do it," he rasped.

She sighed. "You're just cheating me out of a little pleasure," she said, watching him wrestle out of his twills and into the khakis.

For a moment he thought not at all about high tea. He thought about nothing but red-lit Belle, standing there in stylish safari garb, her concession to Nevada wilderness. She grinned sweetly. "Let's go eat tarts," she said.

"You took the thought out of my head," he replied.

He plunged through the silk door into the white light, and settled in a lavender camp chair under the awning roof. She joined him. The stern maid swiftly poured steaming tea into blue Wedgwood cups.

He sipped. Never before had he sipped oolong at a defunct mine. Never had he been billeted in a gaudy silk tent with a wild woman at a defunct mine. Never had a woman tried to pull his pants off and pull on jodhpurs.

It dawned on him that this was all a game. She couldn't be serious. There was nothing serious about all these high-priced garden tents and servants and fancy camp life. This was nothing but a little outing. Nothing but a whim. A serious effort to locate missing documents, establish ownership, open up the blocked mine shaft, explore the decaying buildings, would have been conducted in utter secrecy. He relaxed a little. Outings didn't really mesh with his puritanical work ethic or habits, but he could enjoy the fun for a day or two. She'd get bored and pull out the moment a bug bit her.

He sipped, downed luscious tarts, admired the breeze, and peered upward along those ominous red ridges that guarded this plateau. Even as he gazed idly at those towering cliffs, a small landslide clattered down the slope, red rock bouncing and clattering until it dropped in a heap near the Alice mine shaft.

"Ghosts," she said.

Hannibal wasn't so sure. With a practiced eye he surveyed the tent city, found that the servants' tents were too close to the cliff, too close to the mine and decaying buildings, vulnerable to anything that tumbled down those cliffs.

"Belle, have your servants move those tents to the edge of this flat, and just as far away from the cliffs as possible."

Something in his tone caught her attention. She nodded, rose, talked what sounded like Swahili to Colonel Rathke and Yin and Yang, pointed to the towering red rock above, and they nodded. Moments later, the Chinese were pulling up stakes and moving tents and gear outward, away from the haunted mine, and closer to the lip of the plateau.

And just in time. Even as they tugged the colonel's tent away, a deluge of red rock tumbled down from above, peppering the ground around the Alice Mine's shaft and buildings. One boulder was the size of a wagon, and its impact shook the plateau.

"The ghosts," Belle said.

"No, your rivals."

"They don't know we're here."

Hannibal didn't bother to reply. This gaudy caravan had advertised itself from the moment it left Ely. He stared at the sinister cliffs, looking for a flash of movement, but saw nothing. He thought that all it would take to start one of these avalanches was a crowbar and twenty minutes of labor.

Teatime was over. He abandoned his half-sipped tea, the Wedgwood cup, the blue saucer, and headed up the hanging valley. If there was to be a confrontation with Belle's rivals, the sooner the better. He started up the slopes, choosing the same roundabout route he had used during his last visit.

"Where are you going?" Belle cried.

"If there's someone up there, I'll find out," he said.

The colonel rushed up. He might be a chef, but he looked more like a military man with a thick mustache, lean frame, and a commanding air about him. He pointed upward, and Hannibal realized the man had no grasp of English.

Together they rushed the slope, scrambled upward on a narrow game trail until their lungs were pumping and their hearts were thudding. Far below, the women watched, while Yin and Yang set up the tents far from harm's way. At least far enough to be safe from a small rock slide. Hannibal wasn't very sure about it. A man with a few sticks of TNT could blow the whole side of that cliff down and bury the plateau in red rubble.

Neither he nor the colonel was armed, and it was too late to do anything about that. But they pushed on, ever higher, until at last they clambered out on red sandstone rimrock, and heard only the soughing of the wind. They cut along the lip of rock to the point above the Alice Mine, looking for anything that would tell a tale: footprints, tools, debris.

145

But nothing came to eye. Hannibal squinted upward, hoping to catch sight of a retreating figure clambering alpine slopes, dodging through pines, but he saw nothing at all.

The colonel, meanwhile, was studying the spot where the avalanche had started, which was obvious from the newly exposed, unweathered red rock. When Hannibal returned from his quick trip upward, he found the colonel bent over the lip of rimrock. There, if one looked carefully, were the small indentations of a pry bar that had worked its way into a crack and left its mark behind.

"There's our ghost," Hannibal said.

The colonel grinned slightly. He seemed to understand English, even if he did not speak it.

"The guardian of the Alice. Maybe more than one. Whoever they are, I am going to find them," he said.

But he didn't have a notion of what he would do if he did corral a ghost or two. For all he knew, they had a better claim to the Alice Mine than Belle did.

He stood, dusted off his khaki jodhpurs, straightened his pith helmet, and started down the long slope. He and the colonel would return at dusk, and he would find himself billeted in the ruby silk tent.

Woowoo, he thought.

Chapter 21

Hannibal could not move. There was a one-ton ore car on his chest. He had to move. He had to sneeze. He opened his eyes to a sea of red. Sunlight had turned the ruby silk into four red walls. Everything within the tent was red, including Belle, whose peachy flesh reddened nicely in the flood of daylight.

"Poor dear. You slept late," she said.

He sneezed. He discovered his lungs worked. He determined that his arms worked, and then his legs, and he could wiggle his toes and blink his eyes. She was gorgeous.

"I'll dress you," she said.

"I can manage quite well, thank you."

"You're always cheating me out of all the fun."

He sighed, and rolled out of the brass bed, his feet landing gently on the Brussels carpet. He peered about him, absorbing this ruby world inside Belle Brandy's tent. A scorpion lay waiting in a corner, but he decided not to tell her. Let her discover how it is to live in the wild. That was a cruel thought, but he didn't mind. She evoked them.

He dressed himself until it came to the jodhpurs, sky-blue ones this time, while she looked on approvingly.

"Where are my gray pants?" he asked.

"You're blue today, Hannibal."

"You've hidden my gray twill pants."

"For the duration, Jones."

He examined the entire area.

If he hoped to get out and shave and find the great and unappreciated solace of a latrine somewhere, he would have to wear the jodhpurs or nothing. It was not an easy decision. Wearing nothing at all was more appealing than wearing those jodhpurs. But finally he slid on the jodhpurs.

"Here's your red polka-dot bow tie," she said.

"After I shave."

"Oh, Yang is all ready."

"All ready for what?"

"To shave you, Jones."

"I'll shave myself."

"No, you let Yang do it. When you shave yourself, a kiss is an ordeal. You sandpaper my cheeks."

"That's good for you," he said.

"Go fix your chinny-chin-chin," she said.

He saw how it would go and surrendered. He stepped into a beautiful chill morning and found Yang awaiting him under the marquee tent, hot water bubbling over the brazier, a snowy towel over his shoulder. Hannibal settled into the pink chaise lounge, taking care not to wrinkle his sky-blue jodhpurs, and let Yang brush lather into his face and then scrape his beard away. The Chinaman was excellent, and his beard fell away without a tug or nick. Then Yang applied a moist hot towel to Hannibal's smooth face.

"I think I'm a mining geologist and engineer, but I'm not sure anymore," he said. "I might be a cad and a bounder."

Yang smiled and nodded. Hannibal returned to the ruby silk tent and let Belle slip a blue shirt on him, and tie his red polka-dot bow tie.

"You're getting better at it," he said.

148

"I'm good at everything I do," she said. "That's how I got most of Lucky Haggarty's moolah."

"An accomplished gold digger," he said.

She smiled and patted him familiarly. "It wasn't easy. Lucky could be like a wall. You would have been easier."

"That's a compliment, I imagine."

"Faye Haggarty wouldn't think so."

"Speaking of that, Belle, I believe we're here to look for some sort of document, real or imagined, vesting this property in . . . someone. Maybe you. Maybe the first finder."

"Oh, that," she said. "Don't worry about it."

"I do worry about it. That's why I'm here. That's why you, ah, hired me. Because of my expert knowledge of mining."

"No, Jones, I hired you as bait."

"Bait?"

"I'm just joking, sweetheart. Sky-blue jodhpurs. The ghosts will be fascinated."

"I see," he said, but he didn't.

She caught his arm and led him to breakfast. Under the marquee tent Colonel Rathke, in a monogrammed white apron and Cossack hat, had laid a sumptuous feast, presided over by the raven-haired maid in black. Set upon snowy linen was pewter service laden with cantaloupe and honeydew slices, cherries, macadamia nuts, and mangoes. Hannibal swiftly settled in one of the camp chairs, and Belle, perkily dressed in a lavender safari outfit with mother-of-pearl buttons, sat opposite.

149

The maid swiftly produced a whole platter of oysters on the half shell.

"Eat them all, Hannibal," Belle said. "You need them."

Hannibal, remembering his gobbled camp breakfasts of raisins and coffee, marveled. He managed to down an oyster, feeling it slither into his belly, and then examined the quiet and lonely plateau, the sun-gilded mountain ridges, the duns and tans broken by black pine forests on high, and all embraced under a quiet and cloudless sky. He could faintly smell the resins of high-country pine on the breezes eddying down from above. The sun caught the red rimrock around the mining camp and set it afire. An odd thought struck him: This lavish breakfast, in a lavish camp, seemed just right, not out of place.

"Eat the oysters, Jones."

"You have some, Belle."

"I don't need them. You do, poor dear."

Colonel Rathke materialized with a plate of eggs Benedict, asparagus, and red potatoes fried into small salty chunks. He handed the plate to the raven-haired maid, and then patted her derriere familiarly. Hannibal was grateful; the sight of it settled some things that worried him.

"There now, eat up," Belle said, toying with a bowl of shrimp. "You'll be skin and bones before we leave."

"Ah, when are we leaving? Today? Tomorrow?"

"Who knows? It might be months."

"Before winter, I trust."

"Maybe not."

"Well, I don't plan on staying. I'll hunt for this mythical document and leave tomorrow."

"You think so, do you? We're just getting started, Jones."

She was enthusiastically shoveling shrimp, caviar, eggs Benedict, and asparagus into her ruby mouth. Then she dabbed her painted lips with a pink linen napkin.

"It shouldn't take long," he said.

"No one's figured it out in seventeen years," she replied.

Colonel Rathke appeared with a pewter coffeepot, and poured some into a demitasse, and then poured something from a flask into the coffee.

"What's that?" Hannibal asked suspiciously.

"Brandy. In the Brandy residence, we always finish up every meal with brandy."

"I think I'll forgo the honor," he said.

"You didn't finish the oysters."

"I had thirteen."

"Not enough," she said, and patted his knee.

It was time to start work.

"Come along and I'll show you why I'll need manpower and heavy equipment," he said.

"You already have both, Jones."

He ignored her and steered her toward the shaft of the Alice Mine. He kept a sharp eye on the slope above, but saw no avalanche of red rock, so he pulled her into the shaft, which descended on a steep angle until it stopped at the blockage, a mountain of gray rubble from floor to roof.

"There now. It's not so easy to get in there," he said. "I don't know how far back that goes. But you can see that the roof was blown out. It would take a full face crew several days to dig through there. And we'd probably need to put in some rail and bring in a couple of ore cars and a steam winch to haul the cars out. We'd need some timber too, to shore up the collapsed area. It'd take a month or more to get it all together."

His pronouncement didn't faze her a bit. "Lucky always said the Alice Mine had a back door," she said.

"He obviously was talking about that cleft, that fault that carries water out of the mountain and air into the mine," he said.

"No, not that. A back door. A way in and out."

"He said that?"

She shrugged. "He wasn't very sober. He never was, if I could help it. He was always more generous when I poured some brandy into him."

"Is that your real name, Brandy?"

She gazed petulantly at him. "My real name is Fairchild. Randolph Brandy was my husband's name."

"What happened to him?"

"I wore him out."

"Divorce?"

"No, poor dear. He left for Argentina and never returned."

"When did you meet Lucky Haggarty?"

"A week before Randy left."

"What if he returns someday?"

"I'll wear him out again."

Hannibal clasped her arm and started steering her up the steep slope. He didn't much care for going underground without so much as a pick and a candle and some matches, and here they were, forty or fifty yards down the incline.

He heard the roar even before they had gained the mouth of the mine, and knew intuitively what it was. He grabbed Belle Brandy, shoved her against the cold wall of the shaft, and protected her with his own body as a mountain of red rock tumbled down around the mouth of the mine shaft, shooting a choking cloud of red dust into the shaft until they both were coughing.

When at last they could catch their breaths and wipe the tears out of their eyes, they discovered that the shaft was all but sealed. A tiny thread of light filtered through the choking clouds of red dust that still whirled around that small, mean prison.

Chapter 22

They coughed in the dust, which didn't settle, but filled the air of the dark shaft. A little light did spin through at the top of the heap of rock. Air and hope, but for the moment the danger was the choking dust. He pulled her down to the floor and pulled her lavender safari blouse over her nose.

"Breathe through this," he whispered.

He pulled his blue shirt up over his face and then they waited. The dust whirled about, slowly settling, filtering through their clothing. He studied the murky light. There appeared to be a few inches of open space between the rubble and the top of the shaft. But he didn't have a single tool to tear at the rock that choked the shaft. If they were lucky, someone outside would remember that they were here. If not . . .

"Can we get out of here?" Belle whispered.

"Not alone. But I think we'll get help."

"Are we going to die?"

"Not if I can help it."

"How long will we last?"

"Longer than you'll want."

"No water?"

"We have air, and that's important."

"Full of dust."

"Keep breathing through your blouse."

She sat beside him. The dust didn't settle. There was a lot of it, and only a small space between the outside cave-in and the inner one.

He hoped he could crawl up on the heap of red rock and start pulling rock aside with his bare hands. He knew just how futile that would be, unless he got wildly lucky.

The dust did settle after another few minutes. He thought that soon he would climb the rock pile and try shouting. Maybe someone would hear him.

"It sure is slow in here," she said. "Isn't there something to do?"

"Wait."

"Well, I can think of something," she said. Her hands found his blue shirt and started unbuttoning.

"Not now," he said halfheartedly.

"If we're gonna die, we might as well die in style," she said. She had gotten to the lowest button.

He pushed her hands aside. "I'm going to crawl up there and yell," he said.

"I'll make you yell if you want to yell."

"I mean get help."

"A girl can't have a good time around you."

He ignored her and began inching up toward the light, crawling over sharp rubble. He knew the rock would demolish his sky-blue jodhpurs, and that pleased him almost as much as seeing some daylight up there.

Then he heard them outside. "Jones, are you in there? Can you hear us?"

That was a man's voice. Not the colonel's voice and not Yin or Yang's either.

"We're here. We're all right."

"We can't get you out. There's rock tumbling down the cliff every few minutes. But we can get food and water to you, I think."

"Who are you?"

There was no response. But he soon heard the sound of metal clanging over rock, and found a pry bar edging toward him. He took it and pulled it in. Then came a shovel. And a pair of gloves on a stick.

"These'll help," the voice said.

155

"Thank you," Hannibal said. "Please stay close. I may need more."

There wasn't much working room, but a desperate man makes do. Hannibal pried a chunk loose and pulled it into the shaft, then another and another. There were chunks he couldn't move, wedged tight. But he made some progress. If he could clear a foot or fifteen inches, he was pretty sure he and Belle could wriggle out.

He toiled for an hour and then felt worn down, using muscles he wasn't used to working.

"You out there, do you have some water?"

He heard some muffled talk and then the sound of something poking its way through. He found a canteen being shoved and pried in on the end of a stick. He drank deeply and then slid down to the base of the heap and handed it to Belle.

She sipped.

Refreshed, he climbed up the rubble and began prying rock loose. It wasn't easy. He finally came to a huge chunk that wouldn't budge.

"You out there. I need a sledge or a pick," he yelled.

There was only silence. He yelled again, and again, but no one responded. He knew he was exhausted, and slid down to the floor of the shaft for a rest. He had a long way to go and lacked the tools to do it. Maybe they wouldn't make it. He lifted the canteen. It was still three-quarters full, which was good.

He felt Belle's arm around him, and was about to snarl her away, but this time it was different. Her fingers massaged his shoulders and neck. She was quietly helping him all she could.

It would be up to him to free them. He clambered up the mountain of rubble and set to work again. At least the dust had settled. He worked his pry bar under a piece of rubble and lifted it and yanked it free. He loosened another. And a third. He worked steadily, one rock at a time, tossing the freed rock behind him. The little hole grew, and he was heartened by the improvement. He rested again, tried calling again, got no answer, and set to work. He had no way to gauge the time; they had been trapped after a late breakfast, and now the afternoon was well advanced.

His pry bar loosened a key rock, and he finally levered it free and heard it tumble behind him. Other rock fell into the place vacated by the freed one, and these pieces he was able to handle loose, one by one.

He rested twice more, sitting beside Belle, who was silent for a change. Then as they sat there, she brushed a hand through his dusty hair.

"You sit here. I'll do it for a while," she said.

Astonished, he let her. The light tumbling in now gave him a clear view. She clambered up the rock pile, tearing her lavender safari suit, but soon she was prying smaller pieces free, working as methodically as he had, one by one by one. It heartened him. Two people, each resting while the other worked, promised success. By the time she returned to his side, she was winded and worn. But he was ready for another round, and savagely attacked the pile, some frenzy driving

him, and in a half hour he had cleared a passage perhaps a foot or fifteen inches high. Enough for her to
squeeze through; maybe he could too.

He set down the bar and nodded to her.

"Crawl, and try not to dislodge anything. You'll
have to bend around that big rock."

She nodded, squeezed his hand, and slowly worked
her way free. She vanished into sunlight. He followed,
pushing the tools before him, knowing that he would
need them if something collapsed. At one point it was
a scrape, a squeeze around some rock so tight that he
felt utter panic, fear of getting stuck, fear of tons of
rock squeezing down on him. But then he pulled head
and shoulders free and into the light, then suddenly
the rest of him. He was stunned by the brightness. She
stood some distance away, not helping, but watching.

Once he was free, he understood why they all stood
well away. There was a continual rain of red rock off
that bluff far above, each piece a deadly missile. The
ghosts were just as busy as they could be. He gauged
his chances and raced away from the mine head and
reached safety. She was there, sweeping him into her
arms. And so were Colonel Rathke, Yin and Yang, and
the raven-haired maid with the lush figure.

Safe.

"Thank you for helping us," he said to Colonel
Rathke.

But the colonel looked puzzled. He couldn't speak a
word of English. And neither could Yin and Yang. And
it was not the voice of the raven-haired maid he'd

heard, or a woman who had pushed tools through the tiny slot at the top of the rubble. It was an English-speaking male.

"Who gave me tools?" he asked them.

Colonel Rathke, who could at least understand a little English, simply shook his head.

"Someone helped us," Hannibal said. *"Someone who speaks English brought us these tools. They aren't mine. I've never seen them before."*

The colonel summoned a few words: "Big cloud. Red dust. Falling rock. We stay away."

Yin and Yang, whose English was on par with the colonel's, nodded.

"Ghosts," said Belle, and laughed. She turned to the colonel. "You and Yin and Yang start heating up some water. I'm going to have a bath. And so will you, Jones. And then we'll have tea as usual."

She corralled Hannibal and tugged him toward the ruby silk tent.

"You can wash me, and then I'll wash you," she said.

"Ah . . . I think I'll walk down to the creek."

"You sure have a way of spoiling a girl's fun."

"I'll get some fresh duds and clean up down there."

"Your jodhpurs are ruined."

"That's the first good news all day."

She steered him into the silk tent, and they were swiftly bathed in red light. "Just pull that tub out of the corner," she said, pointing to an elaborate tin model. "You can start getting ready. And when the colonel comes with the water, we'll both get in."

"That tub's much too small for two."

"That's the whole point, you ninny."

Hannibal decided that retreat was the better part of valor. He hunted for some fresh clothing in his duffel, found the khaki jodhpurs but not his twill pants, surrendered to his fate, and fled to the little creek that purled out of the rock far below the plateau.

"Coward," she said as he bolted through the ruby silken door.

Chapter 23

He awakened in a red world. The gossamer silk filtered the morning sun and it quivered in every breeze. He did not feel the usual weight on his chest. His limbs worked. He could wiggle his toes. Nothing ached. Somehow everything was different. And then he remembered. She had curled up beside him last night and dropped right to sleep, holding his hand between both of hers. Yesterday's ordeal in the mine had subdued her. He furtively peered at her as she lay there in the hush of dawn. She might be over fifty, but she still had a bright sweet girlishness upon her. Her tawny hair hung loosely, framing a face all the more beautiful in repose.

He liked her. Belle Brandy was improving his life. She might be a gold digger, but she was spreading gold faster than she was finding it. He checked the Brussels carpet for scorpions, found none, and glided out of the double bed, feeling refreshed and ready.

He knew what he would do this day. If Lucky Haggarty had really said there was a back door to the Alice Mine, he intended to find it. He was a geologist; he probably could figure it out. This would not be an easy task. A back door to the Alice could be a mile or two away, high or low, on the other side of the ridge or only a hundred yards from the shaft. There might be no back door at all; Lucky Haggarty had obviously had a way of seeding chaos and falsehood wherever he went, just for the malicious pleasure of it. And yet a back door would be the only feasible way into the Alice Mine. It would take some major expense, heavy equipment and a lot of labor to open up the main shaft.

She was sleeping softly, barely stirring as he collected what he might need to shave down at the little creek purling out of the mountainside below the plateau. He hunted furtively for his pants, not quite daring to dig into her several steamer trunks, but could not find them, so he surrendered, collected the khaki jodhpurs, got partway dressed, and braved the world.

No sooner did he step into the golden morning than her servant was beckoning. Yin, this time. Well, why not? A man could get used to being carefully shaved while lying on a pink chaise lounge under a marquee tent in utter wilderness. In seconds, he felt a hot towel applied to his face, lather being brushed in, and finally the gentle scrape of the straight-edge. Then he was dusted with talcum, sprayed with some scent from an atomizer, which he could do without, and allowed to finish his toilet.

161

This splendid morning Colonel Rathke fed him a breakfast quiche with bacon and Swiss cheese in it, along with fresh apricots, cherries, Kona coffee, English muffins with marmalade, and cream puffs. He ate quietly, enjoying the sublime prospects stretching upward toward distant ridges. Not a living thing inhabited this dawn world apart from himself and Belle's staff. When he was finished, the raven-haired maid presented him with a snowy napkin soaked in hot water, and he dabbed his face clean and wiped his hands. The only thing missing from the idyll was Belle herself, gotten up in her lavender safari clothes and sipping espresso and popping brandied olives into her ruby mouth.

He thought that he could get used to luxury in a hurry.

But he had a task before him, and one that would employ all his skills as a mining geologist. He slipped into the ruby tent intent upon getting his schematic diagram of the mine and his notes from the previous trip, when she smiled at him and reached up for a dawn hug, which he swiftly supplied. Then he sat beside the bed while she caressed his arm.

"You're very beautiful this morning, Belle," he said.

And she was. Her wild dark hair spread out upon the pillow, and her face seemed soft and rested.

"You were asleep before I could molest you," she said.

It wasn't true. She had fallen asleep while he still lay awake, thinking of their narrow escape.

"But I'll make up for it tonight," she added.

"I'm going to hunt for that back door to the Alice," he said.

"And leave me behind?"

"This is dull geology. You'd be bored."

"I'm never bored. I've never been bored one minute of my life. I'll come with you."

The prospect did not displease him, and he wondered at that. He would get a lot less done. But what did it matter? He was here for the amusement of it all. Let her come.

"You can dress me," she said.

"You can manage."

"Coward."

An hour later, they hiked out of the plateau and into the hanging valley above the mine. She wore this fine day a split skirt of softest doeskin, a silky ivory blouse, brown boots, and a flat-crowned black hat. He had stared at her, agog at this new version of Belle, the sublime California lady rather than the queen of San Francisco. He thought it was a practical costume for what lay ahead. He carried a small haversack with his field gear, a pick hammer, some raisins, and water.

Back doors to mines could be anywhere, not even close to the actual diggings. He thought he would start high, and work downslope. He kept a wary eye for ghosts, but none were at hand. He was still haunted by the ghosts who had handed him a pry bar and shovel even while rock and red dust still boiled over the avalanche. It hadn't been any of Belle's staff. But he was certain it hadn't been any supernatural spirits either. Someone, probably more than one, had tried to help him. At Belle's tent he had stored the pry bar and shovel. Their ownership remained unknown. But it wasn't ghost property, that was certain.

He led her up the valley, through deep silence. The steep trail winded them both. It hugged the right-hand cliff under that ominous red rimrock far above, the same stratum that kept tumbling onto the Alice Mine far below. He eyed it uneasily, knowing that an avalanche would trap and kill them. There was no place to hide.

But nothing disturbed the morning. Such ghosts as were hovering about the mountains were guarding the Alice Mine, and not this remote valley that was leading to a distant ridge.

She was game in spite of her age and urban life. But he slowed now and then and occasionally let her catch her breath. It was a rare day, and they might as well enjoy it, even if they were pursuing a chimera.

Above them, the red sandstone petered out abruptly at a side canyon, and across it was an entirely different gray formation.

He pointed upward. "We've come to a fault. The red rock that has been above us all the way stops here. You don't see it anywhere. Some giant force, long ago, shifted the rock here."

"Where did it go, Hannibal?"

"Any direction. Up, down, sideways. It would be interesting to know. It moved a great distance because it's not anywhere in sight, and across there is something very different, that gray stone."

"The gold mine was under that red rock," she said.

"You're right, and it's important."

"So if we find the red rock somewhere, more gold might be under it."

He grinned. "You have the makings of a geologist."

"I'm a gold digger, Jones."

She laughed. He did too. But in fact, her logic had some merit. The quartz seam that the Alice had tapped would probably end here against that gray rock he was hesitant to name until he could get a closer look. But where did it go? A fault could move rock vast distances. It could be a mile straight down. It might have been a mile up and eroded away over aeons. Or it could be any other direction. But it did hold out the slight possibility that there was gold elsewhere, a potential Alice Mine somewhere close.

"Let's go look," he said, turning up the side canyon that erosion had carved out of the fault. Here there was no trail and the path was strewn with red rubble. He eyed the rim above, worried about erosion, both natural and man-made. He felt his heart hammer as he clawed his way upward, helping her along as best he could. She was game, stumbling up behind him, dodging giant boulders, shattered red rock, and finally stunted pines as they gained altitude.

There was none of the gray rock here, the metamorphic rock he thought was a schist or maybe a gneiss, utterly unlike the red sedimentary sandstone above. It never failed to amaze him that the beds of ancient seas could lie atop mountain ranges, as this red rock did.

He helped her up the last steep incline, and then they found themselves on a tree-dotted dome with breath-taking views that pierced scores, maybe hundreds, of miles into white haze.

"Top of the world," he said when he could again talk.

She didn't reply, but was catching her breath.

"All this sedimentary red rock underfoot was once the floor of a sea," he said. "Or at least a giant lake."

She laughed, disbelieving.

"And if I read this right, somewhere deep down is granite, the igneous, crystalline rock with gold-bearing quartz in it that was tapped by the Alice Mine."

She grinned. "If you say so."

"And that granite was tilted by other pressures, what we call tectonic pressures, which is why the shaft of the Alice is an incline, and the gold-bearing strata of the mine are all inclined."

He was in his element, reading the land, enjoying his discoveries, and oddly, she stood there absorbing every word.

"Do you have a field glass?" she asked.

He did, and pulled it out of his haversack. She took it, spun the focus to her needs, and then slowly glassed the world, taking her time, working up and down.

"I don't see it," she said.

"See what?"

"This red rimrock. If I could see it somewhere else, we could go there and look for gold."

He laughed. "You have the right attitude," he said.

She studied the land for what seemed an amazing time, and finally, reluctantly, returned the glass to him.

"It's around here somewhere," she said.

"What is?"

"The back door to the Alice. Lucky talked about the back door. Something unusual about it. But I never sprang the secret out of him. I'd say, 'Lucky, where's the back door? I want to slide in and steal your ore.' And he would just smile. He liked it when I told him I was a gold digger. That was more honest than anything his wives told him. 'Someday,' he said, 'I'll give you the back door.'"

Chapter 24

They settled in a saucer of red rock surrounded by bristlecone pines, under a cloudless blue heaven, with only the soughing of the wind through the pines to disturb the utter stillness.

Their view in three directions ran across counties and states, across ranges and deserts, into the whiteness of the horizon, and into the unknown. It was the loneliest place he had ever been in, in all the lonely corners of the West his vocation had taken him.

He dug into the haversack and extracted a box of raisins and handed them to her.

She smiled and filled her palm with them, and

popped them into her ruby mouth one by one, obviously savoring them. Then she washed these down with a suck from the canteen.

"If you had told me that raisins would make a good meal, I would have laughed at you," she said.

"You're a long way from Nob Hill."

"We're a long way from the tents and the servants," she said.

He thought she was leading to her usual recreation, but she wasn't.

"I like Nob Hill," she said. "I like this too. I've hardly been outside of a city in my life."

"Lucky Haggarty took you places."

"Restaurants, hotels, theaters, saloons, race tracks, yachts, steamships, mineral baths, railroad stations, private Pullman cars, and sometimes hunting lodges so grand you never knew you were in a forest."

"Did you have a good time?"

"I was too busy digging gold out of his pockets to notice."

"You did well."

"I don't have enough. I want ten times more."

"Did you like him?"

"How should I know? I never had a talk with him about anything." She smiled. "Yes, I liked him. We didn't need to talk."

"What are you going to do with the rest of your life?"

"Don't ask, so I won't have to answer."

"I'll ask."

168

"I thought I'd make you a captive. Tie you to Nob Hill with gold and silk and never let you escape."

He smiled. "And what else?"

A fleeting sadness paused and vanished from her eyes. "I don't know," she said.

"It's been many years since Lucky Haggarty died," he said.

"Yes, I was thirty-three."

"So you're fifty now?"

"Not fifty. Never fifty. The clock broke at forty-nine."

She stood suddenly and walked to the rim, where a whole world lay at her feet. "It's not good enough anymore," she said.

"What isn't?"

"Gold."

"You're here to get it if you can."

She brightened. "If I can't find it here, I'll shake it out of your pants pockets, Jones. You're my next Lucky."

"Were you happy with Haggarty?"

"What can I say? He won me at cards at eighteen, and kept me until he croaked."

"And now?"

"You're my last conquest, Jones. You've been too busy looking at rocks to see the wrinkles and the crepe and the corduroy and the crow's-feet."

Hannibal felt embarrassed. He hadn't noticed any of that. She was still glorious.

"Faye Haggarty's a few years older, and looks ten

169

years younger," she said. "She's as beautiful as a woman can be, always was, and still is. He would have gone back to her if he'd stuck around."

"Haggarty seemed to use women as poker chips."

She laughed, something bitter in the undertone. "Faye was his blue chip, all right. Just once. She pretended to hate it. He won and lost me about twenty times, but I didn't mind. I got some variety in my life. I had rendezvous with Russian princes, French mahogany barons, a mango plantation owner, a titled Hungarian, and several shipping magnates, along with several politicians, including a state senator and a sergeant at arms of the House of Representatives who dispensed cash for favors. That was a gem."

He had blundered into something painful to her, and he retreated. "As long as we're up here, I thought maybe we could see what kind of ghosts are floating around. Someone sent a lot of rock down on us, and it keeps happening."

"Sure, Jones, let's have a look. And if there's a back door to the Alice up here, maybe we'll find it."

He shook his head. "Not here," he said. "The geology's wrong."

"That's all right," she said. "I like this place more than anywhere I've ever been."

That startled him. These weren't glorious or scenic mountains like the Sierras. This was mostly spare and arid land, hostile to life. But maybe that's what appealed to her.

They hiked over the roof of the world, actually a

limb of mountain capped with the red-stained sandstone that was visible from the Alice Mine. After a mile or so he came upon familiar ground, where he and the colonel had clambered up a cliff to have a look at the rimrock, and see who or what was bedeviling the camp far below.

Down a vast distance was the mine plateau, with its gaudy tents that were startling to see in a land of dun rock, ochre, brown, gray, and buff. The ruby silk tent glowed and shimmered and looked like a bull's-eye from their aerie, and it was flanked by the blue and gold awning of the marquee tent, and the green tents of the staff.

"Well, you can't miss that," she said beside him.

"The ghosts can't miss it. And with a good bounce, rock from up here could demolish them."

"Are you sure?"

He nodded, and led her along the red rimrock. Great cracks faulted it. Above, cedar and juniper clung to the slopes, along with stunted pines. He paused at a place where a longitudinal crack ran for hundreds of feet, and pointed to it.

"This would require some powder, but some well-placed charges could send this whole thing down the cliff. It could destroy everything on that plateau."

"Ghosts," she said.

There was nothing but the soughing wind working through the juniper.

"Who are the ghosts, Belle?"

"I think Lucky promised the Alice Mine to a dozen

people, and the ghosts are the ones who lurk here keeping it out of the hands of everyone else, even while they hunt for whatever Lucky told them to look for."

"Like you."

"I haven't been here in years."

"If they're not figments of the imagination, they have a camp around here, observation points, and a network of informants. When I came here a few weeks ago they knew it. They tried to scare me off."

"Not scare you off. Kill you, Jones. You're an expert. A mining geologist. You're the one person on earth they fear the most. I have my own informants so I know what happened here. You barely escaped alive. We barely escaped alive yesterday. There's millions of unmined ore in there, and there's people ready to kill for it. But they make it look like an accident. A land-slide, a cave-in. They don't want the law around here. They can't find any deed or will or paper, but they can keep others from finding anything."

"Who?"

"Juanita's boys. She's wife number two, in Carson City. She bore two children that I know of, Nero and Attila. They would be men now."

"What about the other one, number three?"

"Babette? In Oakland? Lucky spawned two girls there. They'd be adults too. I've lost track. One is Cleopatra, but I can't remember the other. He must have promised her the mine too."

"So there could be six people ghosting around here, two wives, four children."

"And whoever they hire, Hannibal."

"When I was here before, at least one of the ghosts was friendly. Took care of my mules. Stuck a rose in one's bridle."

"Well, of course. The ghosts are all fighting each other, and maybe one saw an ally when you showed up."

"Do you have informants keeping an eye on all this?"

"Jones, I shell out so much cash for information that the Alice Mine is going to break my bank. It's worth it. Lucky gave it to me. I want it and I'm going to get it. I've spent years on this, quietly hiring just the right people."

"Such as an assayer or two?"

"Yes, but most of my informants are what are called double agents. They tell me what's cooking around here, and then tell the others, and collect three times for every scrap of news they come up with."

He sat down and laughed uneasily. The Alice Mine was, more and more, a sort of carnival. But a deadly one.

He stood suddenly. "Ghosts like these need a place to eat and sleep, and shelter from weather."

She nodded.

He studied the great dome of red rock above them, and headed up the slope, through pygmy pine and juniper. She struggled along behind him.

"Watch the ground," he said. "For anything man-made."

They gained the ridgetop after a five-hundred-foot climb that left them winded. From here the plateau with the Alice Mine on it was not visible, but one could see a vast country rolling away in all directions. He continued down the far side, following the path of least resistance, and suddenly was rewarded.

There, in a deep hollow of red rock, a shallow cave actually, was a campsite. There was a bedroll neatly tied up and stowed out of the weather, a sheet-metal camp stove, some other items wrapped in oilcloth and tied tightly, and a one-gallon canteen. He lifted the canteen. It was full.

Fifty yards away, tucked into a niche of rock, was a wooden chest. He carefully opened it and found fresh DuPont Hercules dynamite and a coil of Bickford fuse. Around a bend of rock he found the fulminate-of-mercury fuses, kept separately for safety's sake. Whoever kept this camp knew all about mining.

Chapter 25

One ghost anyway. There might well be a few more campsites hidden in the area. Hannibal circled through the brush hunting for a pen, but found no evidence of livestock anywhere. No enclosure, no hay, no grain, no manure. He didn't expect any. The footing there was treacherous, all rock and no soil. But it paid to look. Whoever came here brought supplies on his back.

He returned to the campsite and weighed the propriety of opening that oilskin bundle. He decided he would. Whoever was camping here had not hesitated to murder or injure him or at least scare him off. While Belle watched, he undid the oilskin and found a medium-sized sweater and an India-rubber slicker that could fit most adults, bad-weather gear. He had hoped to find some shoes or boots, but found none. Whoever kept this camp knew what would offer no clues.

"Not much to go on," he said. "But I'll keep on looking."

He had spent much of his professional life in wilderness just like this. Sometimes he could read information into what he found. But there was little to be discovered.

One ghost. He thought he might find more. Much of that day had been consumed, so he led Belle down a different path, wanting to cover new ground before they reached the flat. This one largely followed the hogback ridge downward, but it took them farther from the mine.

A half hour of quiet hiking brought them to a place where they could catch one last view of the Alice Mine far below, but only if they abandoned the hogback and worked out to the rimrock lording over that plateau.

"Let's have a look. I want to know every good observation point above our camp," Hannibal said.

"They can have an eyeful of me anytime," she replied. "And closer up if they want."

Belle was running true to form.

He cut off the ridge and descended through a tumble of red rock, boulders, juniper, and stunted pine clinging desperately to arid slopes. But the plateau came into view, and the ruby silk tent, and the ruins of the Alice Mine.

He rounded another house-sized rock and stopped dead.

In front of him was a young man crouched on the rim, peering down on Belle's camp. He heard Hannibal, whirled, and stared, stricken, at Hannibal, and then Belle.

This one was dark-haired and had high cheekbones and brown eyes. He reached for a rifle lying beside him.

"Hold up," Hannibal said, and then tried a shot in the dark. "It's Attila Haggarty, isn't it?"

The young man froze a moment, then swung the rifle toward Hannibal, and then lowered it. But its muzzle was never far from Hannibal and Belle.

"Let's talk," Hannibal said.

"Let's not."

"Come down to the camp with us. We'd enjoy the company."

Something in the young man hardened. "Never. You're trying to steal the mine from us. It's ours."

"Whose?"

"My father gave it to us, and I intend to get it."

"All the more reason to come down to the camp with us. We're looking for the documents. If the mine's yours and we find the papers, you'd be the first to know."

He glared at Belle. "I would no more enter her camp than I would sit down with the devil."

"What about Faye?" Belle said. "What about Babette?"

"My father gave the mine to us."

He said it with such finality that Hannibal knew it was dogma. Juanita's family apparently didn't grasp the perverse humor in Lucky Haggarty.

"He gave it to his other wives and Belle, and did it just for the fun of it," Hannibal said. "He liked the thought of a fight."

"That's not true!"

There was such violence and pain in the youth's response that Hannibal knew he and Belle were in mortal peril.

He turned to Belle. "I guess we'd better be on our way."

But even before they could start, the youth rushed past them, stumbling and racing up the trail, rifle in hand, fleeing as fast as he could flee.

Hannibal watched him clamber up the steep trail and finally vanish in some boulders and pygmy pines.

"I don't know whether he was running from us or running from what I told him about his father," Hannibal said.

"We don't even know his name for sure. It might have been the other brother, Nero," she said softly.

"I don't much like the idea of watchdogs armed with good rifles hovering over us night and day," he said. "Ghosts don't need rifles. Observers don't need arms.

The only reason to carry a rifle up there is to hurt or kill."

He hoped she would take the hint. She was in the gunsight.

But she ignored his worries.

"Do you think that was his camp we found?" she asked after a while.

"No. I think that camp is the hideout of an older and more experienced ghost."

"His mother must have her informants. I don't think this place is watched constantly. Only when someone in Ely sends word. Someone like a bartender, or livery operator, or a clerk in the courthouse, or a merchant that sells camp supplies," she said.

It was a good observation. Someone, or two or three someones, tipped Juanita, and she sent her son.

"Maybe all these ghosts will run into each other," he said.

"Maybe they'll form an alliance," she replied.

"That might not be amusing. Avalanches of rock; men with rifles. Belle, it's time to pull back before you're hurt. Or the rest of us are."

"Jones, it's all coming together now. All I have to do is wave a red flag, and the bulls attack me!"

There was a crazy logic in it, like painting a bull's-eye on one's chest to draw everyone out. Obviously, she had thought of it and encouraged it and thought it might resolve the whole issue of ownership. Or at least eliminate a few of the ghosts flitting around up there.

He and Belle negotiated a steep and treacherous grade and arrived suddenly on the plateau. A few hundred yards would take them to the Alice Mine.

"Slow up. I want to look for hidden shafts, back doors," he said.

She seemed bored. "I thought maybe you'd like a little bourbon and branch, and other pleasures."

But he wouldn't budge from the task at hand. He had a good eye for things nature didn't do, such as plug a shaft with rock, or heap brush over a mine head. So he took his time, while she yawned her way toward her tent. But there was nothing. He didn't expect to find anything. He had a sharp eye and had made good use of it his previous trip.

He gave up, and headed round the last bend for the ruby silk tent. Only then did he realize there were visitors in camp. Parked ahead were a surrey drawn by a pair of dappled grays and a farm wagon pulled by a pair of black mules. And under the marquee tent were several women and some men as well.

He headed toward the tent. Belle was right. Her encampment was drawing attention. When he stepped into the tent, he discovered a woman of willowy grace, tall and imperial, dressed in white summer muslin that permitted sunlight to shift seductively through the skirts and petticoats. With her were two younger women, one a copy of the older woman, the other looking very like Lucky Haggarty: dark, square, bold.

And on the wagon sat some men he knew: Walt Cuban and the old rummies from his café, all of them

179

staring at the exotic tents and people on the Alice Mine flat.

"Oh, Jones," said Belle, "meet Babette Haggarty, and her daughters, Cleopatra and Delilah."

So another of Haggarty's wives was on hand. Hannibal admired the old financier's taste in women. Never had a remote western mine seen such pulchritude.

"We've come to make sure that the Alice is not stolen from us," Babette said in a voice so low and dulcet that Hannibal strained to hear her. "Lucky promised it to us. And now all these people are trying to take it."

"He promised it to everyone, dear," Belle said.

"You're making a joke of it! He gave it to me! I wouldn't let him touch me until he did! He swore on a Bible!"

Hannibal thought that was a splendid confession.

"You brought some miners with you," he said, nodding toward the wagon full of old birds.

"I did. They're here to make sure I'm not cheated out of my mine. They've been in my employ for years, and when they learned that the Alice was about to be stolen from me, they wired me."

"You came from Oakland?" Hannibal asked.

"We did. We caught the first express."

"I don't know why any sane person would live in Oakland," Belle said. "It defeats the whole purpose of living."

"We have virtue in Oakland, even if none exists across the bay," Babette said.

"Well, what are you planning on doing here?"

"We're going to make sure you don't steal my mine from me."

"Do you have documents proving ownership?" Hannibal asked.

"They're hidden here. Everyone knows that. We're going to find them."

"And what if they award the mine to someone else? Such as Belle?"

"Belle's not eligible," Babette said. "Only his wife is eligible."

"That narrows it to you, Juanita, Faye, and anyone else who might show up," Hannibal said.

"Sir, your opinion is not wanted," Babette retorted.

She was even prettier angry. Belle was eyeing him coldly. "Join the party," Hannibal said. "Set up camp anywhere, but stay away from the cliffs. Ghosts send rock slides down every now and then."

"We will do just that," she said.

"And join us for beverages," Belle said.

Babette absorbed that, and nodded curtly.

"Meeow, Alice Shmine," Cuban said.

"I hope you brought your teeth," Hannibal said.

"Hoo, hoo, har," Cuban replied.

Chapter 26

Hannibal settled into the pink chaise lounge mostly to watch the show. Colonel Rathke instantly produced an amazing Old Crabtree Tennessee double-distilled hundred-proof bourbon and branch in a tall glass, with cold creek water that was almost as good as real ice. Fifty yards away, the four rummy old miners were setting up Babette Haggarty's camp, which consisted of three puritanical white-wall tents, all in a row. They had followed Hannibal's advice and kept well away from the mine and the rimrock above it.

The Haggarty women vanished into their tents, the girls in one and Babette in the other. Hannibal wondered where and how Lucky Haggarty had found Babette and married her while he was supporting two other wives and a mistress and maybe a few others on the side. She was apparently the youngest of Haggarty's conquests, and probably the prettiest, even more than Faye, if beauty could be measured by a perfect figure and a chiseled face framed by lush brown hair, and an undulating way of walking, which probably was what had caught Lucky's eye. But Babette struck Hannibal as something of a snob, maybe worse than wife number one. He intended to keep his distance.

He sipped his excellent bourbon until the four old miners had finished putting up their camp and caring for their livestock, and Walt Cuban was free. Then Hannibal swiftly walked over to Cuban.

"I want to talk. Come have a drink. Some very good bourbon, my friend. And bring your teeth."

"Schmear oww," Cuban said.

But a moment later the old miner was heading for the marquee tent, and Colonel Rathke was ready with a tumbler of Old Crabtree raising sweat on the sides of the glass.

"(Click) you," Cuban said, eyeing the luxury around him.

"You're going to look after the ladies, right?" Hannibal asked.

"(Click) damned ivories. Yep, for three dollars a (click). And they're mighty (click) to look at."

"I want to know if there's a way into the mine. The shaft's blocked. Like, say, a back door."

"(Click) eleven years in there and never (click) another way in or out, Jones. I oughta know."

"Nothing? No air vent?"

"Just that (click) we tapped into on the third level. Can't squeeze a (click) through there. Pumps some air in."

"No exit? No secret tunnel? No adit? No connecting cave?"

Cuban shook his head. Then he dug in his mouth and extracted the offending ivories and stuffed them into his pocket.

"Damn shmoots. Meow ich better."

"I'd pay you a big bonus if you could show us a way into the mine," Hannibal said.

"Shmeaze no diller."

"Put your teeth in and repeat that, please."

Cuban did, muttering softly. "No way in but the (click) and now there's no way a-tall."

He extracted his molars again and stuffed them away. Hannibal knew he'd seen the last of the store-bought ivories.

That's when Belle appeared, this time in a red turban

and orange velvet caftan with leopard lapels.

"Belle, Mr. Cuban worked in the Alice for eleven years, and he says, adamantly I might add, that there is no back door; there's only the main shaft."

"There's a back door, Jones. Lucky told me so. He was a great one to talk after he wilted. I'd just wait and pretty soon he would tell me his secrets. He told me fifty times there's a back door."

"Shas naga hole." Cuban sucked a mightly draft of the bourbon, smacked his lips, and smiled. "Oya smooch."

"Smooth?"

Cuban nodded.

"Mr. Cuban, this is Belle Brandy, who's employing me to find a way into the Alice. I'm sure she'd like to employ you too. Why don't you put in your teeth and tell her you'd like to work for us?"

"Aga . . ." He glanced fearfully toward those puritanical white tents. At any moment some of those women in white muslin would erupt from them, and there would be trouble.

"Five dollars a day, Mr. Cuban," Belle said. "Plus a bonus or two if you can rise to the occasion."

Cuban shook his head. "Shmeeze bought."

Belle sat down beside him and smiled. "You're a very nice man," she whispered, and patted him on his bony knee. Cuban's leg spasmed.

"Yeah, yeah!" Cuban yelled.

"Walt, sweetheart, where did Lucky hide the papers?"

"Doze dimmy?"

"In the mine. Where would he put papers?" She rubbed his bony thigh for emphasis. His leg jerked upward violently.

But Cuban just shook his head, sipped Old Crabtree, and grinned.

"You take me in there and show me the papers and I'll make you very happy, you sweet old billy goat."

"Haw, hee!"

Hannibal was feeling out of sorts. There was Belle seducing the old goat when she belonged to him, Hannibal Jones.

"Belle, I don't think this is a good idea."

"Mind your manners, Jones." She squeezed his knee. "Walt, dearie, just remember that if there's anything you want, anything at all, just let me know." She patted his thigh for punctuation.

"Woowoo!" Cuban thrust his empty glass in the general direction of Colonel Rathke, who was hovering affably just outside the marquee tent. The colonel took the glass with great dignity, and soon returned with a refill.

"It pains me to think that the mine was given to me and I haven't quite found the key," Belle said. "And now everyone ever connected with Lucky is showing up."

"Woowoo!" yelled Cuban.

Off at the newborn camp of Babette, the other three old miners were staring and glaring.

"Colonel, do take a nice bottle of Old Orchard to

them, with my compliments," Belle said. "And of course invite them to join us."

Colonel Rathke nodded, and again Hannibal sensed that the man understood English perfectly well, even if he did not speak it. But no sooner had the colonel delivered his prize to the rummy old hard-rock miners than the Haggarty women emerged from their tents, peered about, and discovered no one had started preparing their dinner. A sharp command from Babette set the rummies to work.

"Jones, dear, invite them all over for dinner," Belle said.

Hannibal set out across no-man's-land, a thirty-yard wasteland unclaimed by either camp, and approached the Haggarty women, now arrayed in camp chairs and sipping what appeared to be tea.

"Yes?" said Babette sharply.

"Mrs. Brandy invites you and your entourage to join us for cocktails and dinner," Hannibal said.

"And who are you, sir?"

"I'm Hannibal Jones, madam."

"And who is Mrs. Brandy?"

Hannibal sighed, seeing how the game would go. "I'll inform her of your regrets," he said. He turned to leave. The two daughters, who had not risen to greet him, stared up at him, a teacup and saucer resting demurely in their laps.

"Just one moment, Mr. Jones. You are employed by the wrong person, who shall go nameless. I have never spoken her name, not in the twenty-seven years since

I was married in a Unitarian service to Harold Haggarty and have been his widow. There is, you see, the matter of moral and spiritual correctness. If you were a correct man, with correct ideals, pursuing a virtuous agenda, you would be working for me, and not for the woman whose name I shall not mention."

"Ah . . ."

"That is just the answer I expected of you, Mr. Jones. And what a pity. I assure you that even if she should find Mr. Haggarty's will—that's what we're looking for you know, his will—before we do, it would not stand up in court if it should devise the woman whose name I shan't mention as his heir. She has no status whatsoever, and the very fact that she calls herself by her married name, and not the name of my husband, suffices to make my point.

"Now, if you are a gentleman of ethical principles, as my researches into your past have revealed to me, you would seriously consider my offer: I will pay you double what she's paying you. I happen to need a highly competent geologist and mining engineer to resolve the questions arising from Mr. Haggarty's final, and some say incompetent, days, when, as any lawyer knows, he was not of sound mind when he executed certain documents and let it be known to us, and alas, to others, that he was disposing of his property in a most unusual manner.

"Now, if you will weigh my offer, and as your good conscience operates upon your character, you will discover, by tomorrow morning, that my position is not only the correct and ethical one, but the only one, and you will wish to associate yourself with the woman who is truly and honorably the widow, as demonstrated in probate court, of Mr. Haggarty."

That was a mouthful. Hannibal found himself listening to this glacial discourse with fascination, and by its conclusion he had the whole of Babette Haggarty worked out in his mind.

"Mrs. Haggarty, you have the wrong impression," he began. "Mrs. Brandy is not paying me anything of material value. In fact, she insisted on it. She told me that she would keep the entire mine, share nothing of it, if I chose to help her establish ownership."

Babette Haggarty was taken aback. She stared, her lush lips pursed and unpursed. Finally, she ventured a question. "If she is paying you nothing, Mr. Jones, then what is your reward? And how may I improve upon it?"

"Well, Mrs. Haggarty the third, my reward is nothing but good company. It's true I first was drawn to the Alice by its prospects, but now I am simply here to enjoy Mrs. Brandy's company."

Babette Haggarty flushed. "Well, Mr. Jones, then I shall withdraw my offer to double your pay."

Chapter 27

Colonel Rathke's menu that evening was beef medallions, paté de foie gras, candied yams, wilted spinach salad with bacon, asparagus with hollandaise sauce, sugared grapes, crème brûlée, and cream puffs, all washed down with a Philippe de Rothschild vintage 1897 Bordeaux. There were finger bowls, linen napkins, Kona coffee, all served on blue Wedgwood. Hannibal and Belle ate at one table, and at another sat Yin and Yang, while the Raven-Haired Maid, as Hannibal had eventually named her, first served and then ate along with the culinary master from the czar's kitchen.

The scents of a splendid meal drifted to the rival camp, and occasioned glowers from the ladies, and obvious longing from the old geezers. But at least they had the bottle of Old Crabtree with which to amuse themselves that quiet evening.

It was the finest of Nevada evenings. The last of the blue hung over the western horizon, while gentle, dry air comforted and elevated everyone's mood. The quiet ridges caught and held the silence of nature, making the whole world seem peaceful. Early stars winked.

Over in the other camp, after the ancient miners tidied up whatever supper they had prepared for the ladies, the women, still dressed in gauzy white muslin, drifted toward the Alice Mine, there to study the tumbledown barracks, the mine shaft with its massive head frame stabbing the twilight, the half-shattered office, the powder magazine, and the great heaps of tailings.

Hannibal didn't like it. He bolted out of his camp chair, headed for Walt Cuban, and shouted a warning.

"Tell them to stay well away from there!"

Too late. A sudden rumble far above loosed tons of red rock, which careened and bounded down the steep grade with such violence that it shocked the very soul.

The women screamed and fled just as the avalanche of red boulders, shards, gravel, and slabs thundered into the ground twenty or thirty yards to the left of them, shaking the very earth underfoot. Cuban and the other miners yanked and tugged the women to safety, even as the last of the slide dribbled and popped down the slope, throwing rock ahead and behind the escaping party.

Hannibal raced in that direction, along with Colonel Rathke, whose hands were wet with soapsuds. But it appeared that the women were safe, and well away from the spot where tons of rock had almost crushed them to death.

There was nothing to be done.

When Babette approached, she glared at Hannibal and the colonel. "You tried to kill us!" she snapped.

Let her think it. Denials would be fruitless. Argument wouldn't suffice either. Not his warning to set up camp far from that rimrock, not his shout of warning moments before, would alter this woman's mind. He turned abruptly and stalked away, angry at her not only for accusing him, but for wandering close to the Alice after she had been warned.

The girls, Cleopatra and Delilah, didn't seem quite so certain as their mother.

"You, Mr. Jones, have sold your soul!" Babette

added as she swept toward her tent.

Hannibal steamed back to his own camp, irked at the woman.

"Sold your soul, have you?" Belle asked. "Well, it's not your most important part."

It didn't amuse Hannibal. He thought maybe he'd pack his mules and head down the road.

Belle patted his knee. "You need some instruction about Babette," she said. "She's not what she claims to be."

"I don't care what she claims to be. I don't care whether I see her again. In fact, I hope I don't. I think I'll head for Arizona. I have real business there, two or three mines well worth a close look."

"Babette's mother was a Paris courtesan who came to San Francisco to get rich," Belle said. "And she did. Babette was her love child."

Hannibal rose to leave, but Belle patted him on the thigh and smiled.

"Woowoo," she said.

"I'm a slave," he muttered, not liking himself.

"Babette learned her mother's wiles, and that's when she met Lucky. Before long, she had two sweet little girls, both of them Lucky Haggarty's. That's when Babette decided she wished to live a respectable life, so she pushed poor old Lucky into a third marriage. It wasn't before a minister either. It was an ordinary justice of the peace, down in Southern California. She invented the story of the minister. She spent the rest of her life grubbing money out of him, but she wasn't half as good at it as I was. She tried to get it from him by withholding her affections, which is a game I never attempted, not once. Lucky was welcome in my arms any time of day or night. But poor Babette thought she had a lever, and used it until Lucky started laughing. And then she suddenly got respectable. You know, virgin mother of two girls."

Hannibal was thinking he knew more about Lucky's matrimonial habits than he wanted to know. "Belle, you'll want to find someone else to figure out how to get into the Alice Mine. It would cost a small fortune to open up that shaft, and having a mining engineer and geologist around isn't going to help any. There's no back door. The geology doesn't suggest one. So I'll just get out and thank you for your hospitality."

"I'll give you a finder's fee."

But he was sick of her, sick of these people, sick of the chaos Lucky Haggarty left behind him, and especially sick of the damned jodhpurs he was still wearing.

"Where are my pants?"

"Under my portable bidet."

He grunted and headed for the ruby silk tent, while she watched from the marquee tent. For a change, she didn't try to stop him. He found two pairs of his trousers under the bidet, a clever little device that required some preliminary hand-pumping to build up pressure. He swiftly changed into his brown twills, left the offending jodhpurs on the bed, stuffed his few things into the panniers, and headed down the grade to collect his mules.

Yin and Yang were grazing them in the creek bottom, the only grass for miles around. Babette's miners had run their livestock into the high country, where some thin grass carpeted the slopes. His mules were pleased to see him, and grunted happily when he slid halters over their heads and led them up to the ruby tent. It didn't take long to blanket and saddle them and hang the packs, and then he was ready.

He steered toward the marquee tent to say good-bye, managed to shake hands with Colonel Rathke, kiss the Raven-Haired Maid on the cheek, smile uneasily at Belle, and start down the hill. The rival camp was watching all this, interpreting it however they chose, but he didn't care. It wasn't but a moment before he was over the lip of the plateau and they were all out of sight, they and their rivals and the old, tumbled-down Alice Mine. And a few ghosts up high above, who were no doubt watching him leave and enjoying the sight.

He worked down to the little creek, intending to take that way out. He had always followed the road, if the rough trail to the Alice Mine deserved to be called a road, but this time he would follow the creek until it vanished in some sink farther down. It didn't run into any valley he knew of.

The summer sun continued to light the blue sky long after the dinner hour had passed, so he could pick his way along without fumbling through darkness.

Odd about Belle, the way she let him go without a quibble, and nothing more than a wandering hand along a thigh this time.

He followed the tiny flow, barely a foot wide in places, as it purled its way to lower elevations through arid and rocky country. He thought he could make the distant valley before full dark, even though the dying sun was now illumining the west-facing flanks of all the mountains.

That's how he saw the red rimrock high above. He stopped, startled, unsure he was seeing what he saw. Way up a cliff side ran that red sandstone formation that overlooked the Alice Mine. At least he thought it was the same. He detoured closer to the cliff base, and was rewarded by the sight of red fragments from above. He plucked up several and swiftly assured himself that this red stone was identical with the rimrock above the Alice Mine, even though he was now half a mile away and much lower.

A thought crossed his mind; one of those wild, singing intuitions, one of those bull's-eye thoughts one has but once in a lifetime. He was about as far below the red rock above him as the Alice Mine's head frame and shaft were below the rimrock up on the flat. Five hundred feet, he imagined.

He paused, studied the terrain, suddenly filled with wild certitude. He veered away from the little creek until he reached the talus at the foot of the cliff, and then began a slow, methodical hunt for a streak of granite, or some gray quartz ore, or some other sign that would prove that this was a continuation of the formation in which the Alice Mine stood.

He walked softly, suddenly fearful of being

observed, and paused frequently to study the surrounding terrain, high points habituated by ghosts, but all he encountered was deep peace. Whatever ghosts were floating around up there were guarding the Alice Mine, not this empty valley.

For the next half hour, as dusk approached, he searched high and low for the formation he sought, but found nothing. Then, intuitively, he retreated, heading uphill, back toward the Alice, and the cleft that released water from the mountain, and then as the light dimmed, he found it: granite hidden by brush, a seam of quartz, a thick wall of granite underneath.

He scrambled for his pick hammer, climbed a precarious pile of talus, whacked loose a dozen specimens of the quartz. He tucked the ore into his field bag and debated what to do. It was not a good place to camp. He needed daylight. He needed to field-test for gold. That meant hanging about, working as secretly as he could. He decided to head back. The explanation would be simple enough: It was getting dark, and he would leave in the light of the new day.

She would misinterpret it, and respond with a "Woowoo."

And he would explore a bonanza of his own.

Chapter 28

There was an ore car on his chest. He knew if he didn't push it off he would be crushed to death. He forced his eyelids up and discovered a red world.

There was no ore car. He wiggled his toes to make sure they worked, then performed the same test on his fingers, and tried his elbows and knees. He decided not to test any more equipment.

Then he remembered. It had taken her about twenty minutes last night to reduce him to wilted spinach. She had welcomed him effusively and said she was expecting him. When he asked why, she simply said, "Woowoo," and then bestowed a knowing smile on him.

Now she was sitting on the edge of the brass bed, wearing a filmy white chiffon robe, in the red light of the ruby silk, tickling him with her fingers. She was gorgeous, but he was too exhausted even to think about her.

"Time to get up, Jones," she said. "Where did you get the gold?"

"Gold?"

"The quartz from the Alice Mine."

"Quartz?"

"Jones, I lived with Lucky too long not to know the quartz from the Alice. He showed me hundreds of samples. You got a dozen pieces of it."

"You raided my sample bag," he accused.

"Of course I did. I go through all your possessions. I'm a gold digger by profession, Jones. You were asleep, so I checked everything. You've found the back door to the Alice Mine."

"It has no back door," he said.

"Well, whatever you found is mine. I suppose you're

going to do field tests."

"I had that in mind, but not here where everyone will be studying me."

"We'll go to the back door and do it there," she said. "Now get up. Yin is waiting with the razor and Colonel Rathke has breakfast ready."

"I think I'll just pack up and leave," Hannibal said.

"Don't be a spoiled boy."

"I don't like people poking around in my possessions."

"Jones, you're my slave, and I own everything you own. You got well paid last night. Woowoo."

He sighed. He had never been so well paid. He wasn't even sure if he could get out of bed, but he knew he would have to try. He checked the Brussels carpet for scorpions and snakes, saw none, and slid out of the sheets.

Minutes later, he was slumped in the pink chaise lounge while Yin, or was it Yang? lathered his jaws and scraped away. He wore no shirt in order to offend the Haggarty women in the next camp, who were watching with narrowed eyes.

He returned to the ruby silk tent for his pants and found them missing again. The khaki jodhpurs lay on the bed.

"I want my pants," he proclaimed loudly enough so that the Haggarty women might hear it.

"You can't have your pants. I prefer you in jodhpurs and your pith helmet and your little red polka-dot bow tie."

He checked the portable bidet but his pants weren't under there, and he could not find them anywhere else. He suspected Yin or Yang held them. But he was ready for the day, so he clambered into the jodhpurs, despising them more than ever, and soon settled in a purple camp chair under the marquee tent, while Colonel Rathke dished out kippers and fried potatoes and baked celery stalks in an artichoke sauce.

Babette Haggarty squinted at him as he ate.

Belle appeared, wearing a hot pink safari costume that set the Haggarty women to gnashing their teeth. Belle's shirt was opened to the waist, revealing tawny curves.

"Are you wearing that to impress them, or impress me?" Hannibal asked.

"Them."

"That's good. You don't need to impress me. I'm impressed."

"Well, let's get on with it. How much gold is in that quartz? And where did you get it?"

She stood next to him, letting him admire the view.

"Where are my mules?"

"Right where Yang put them," she said.

He hiked to the lip of the plateau and then down the steep grade to the tiny valley and the cleft where water sprang from the mountain, and found his mules standing beside the unmarked grave, rubbing their heads on the polished granite marker with no name or date on it.

He haltered them and led them up the steep slope,

past rock and brush, his heart hammering with the effort. At the ruby silk tent, he threw the blankets and packsaddles over them, drew up the cinches, and lowered the panniers into place. In short order he had his bedroll, field kit, clothing except for his pants, and tools aboard the yawning mules.

Belle watched cheerfully.

"Where are my samples?" he asked.

"They're mine, Jones. I should get paid for something, don't you think, a gold digger like me?"

He smiled. Let her have them. He knew where tons more lay hidden.

"Adios, Belle."

"Woowoo," she retorted, and laughed.

His knees went weak.

"I'd better come along and prop you up," she said.

"Not unless you intend to follow me to Wickenburg."

She bussed him on the lips.

The women in the rival camp squinted dangerously.

"I'll come along," Belle said. She plucked up a huge picnic basket that Colonel Rathke had prepared, neatly covered with a linen napkin.

"I'm going alone," he said. "You can picnic with Mrs. Haggarty the third."

Belle laughed and tagged along beside the mules.

Hannibal wondered how to get rid of her. He wanted to get out of sight, make some field tests, check his maps to see whether the place had been claimed, and quietly set up claim cairns and markers if it had not been. None of which was possible with Belle Brandy flapping along beside him.

The best tack would be to keep on going until she gave up and returned to camp. And then sneak back. He eyed the Haggarty women, dressed in filmy white muslin, this time without petticoats, the sun gauzing its way through most everything. Plainly, Babette was bringing her own ordnance into combat. The rummy old miners, including Walt Cuban, didn't know which of the women to study the hardest.

Belle noticed. "I told you so," she said.

Hannibal eyed the rimrock, studying it for signs of ghosts, and saw none. But he didn't doubt that other eyes were studying his departure.

"Adios, Belle, and thanks for everything," he said.

"Woowoo."

He tugged the mules off the plateau and down the steep track, which they negotiated with trouble because of the weight of the packs. And there was Belle, cheerfully bringing up the rear. He didn't have the faintest idea how to get free of her, but he imagined walking would do it. He was a hardened outdoorsman; she was merely the woowoo queen of San Francisco, and he knew his strong legs would triumph if he kept a good pace.

He quickened his pace, working restlessly down the steep grade, risking a broken ankle or a lame mule, but the faster he hiked, the more cheerful she became.

"Shall we do field tests now?" she asked. She pulled the linen napkin aside, and there, nestled like eggs, were the samples of quartz ore. "Great lunch, wouldn't you say?"

"Wickenburg," he said. "Keep the ore."

"Jones, you don't understand. Right here in this picnic basket is your field-test kit. I thought you might forget it. Do you know that people who leave something behind are really expressing a desire to return?"

Trapped. He sighed.

"All right," he said. "I'll do the tests."

And get rid of her.

He found a hidden cove in a hillside, set to work with mortar and pestle, lit his spirit lamp, ran some acid tests and other chemical tests, found gold present in impressive quantities as well as silver and traces of copper, and repeated the testing on other samples. The results were the same. After each, he had a tiny button of pure gold.

She watched carefully, learning the processes as he went along.

"Rich ore," he said. "It'd take an assay to put a value per ton on it. The Alice is a good mine."

"It's not from the Alice," she said. "Remember?"

She dug into the wicker picnic basket and produced another of Hannibal's working materials, the map folder. He glared at her, but she ignored it. She dug into the waterproofed folder, extracted a map he had purchased at the Nevada Bureau of Mines, this of the Alice District of White Pine County, and pointed to a standard-sized mining claim labeled, simply, the BD.

"There! That's the Back Door claim, and that's what

you found, and that's going to be mine, all mine!"

He stared at the map, not wanting to believe it.

He packed away his field-testing tools, the spirit lamp and test tubes and stoppered acid bottles.

"I looked while you were asleep and I was pawing through your stuff," she said, an evil grin building on her gorgeous face. "You're out of luck, Jones. You found the Back Door, but it's mine. Lucky said so."

She waved the map as if it were a deed.

"Not yet," he said. "You don't know who owns it, and you don't know where to find the papers for it, and you don't have a will or conveyance."

But she was laughing. "They'll all fight over the Alice, and I might too. But I've got the ace. You're the ace, Jones. Let's go see where that damned Lucky hid the papers."

"I'm off to Wickenburg," he said. "You can find the Back Door yourself."

"Woowoo," she said, patting his thigh dangerously, and pretty soon he was ready to return to the ruby silk tent. He collected the yawning mules, and started uphill.

"I'm a slave," he said.

Chapter 29

Just when Colonel Rathke was clearing off the dinner plates, and Hannibal and Belle were enjoying an aperitif, a great clatter disrupted the evening silence. Over in the other camp, Babette and her daughters leapt to their teeny feet, while the rummy old miners raced to the lip of the plateau to find what the ruckus was all about.

"Company," said Belle.

"Trouble, then," Hannibal said unhappily. He wanted nothing so much as a peaceful evening at the Alice Mine, watching the sun drop below the north-western ridges and the hush of twilight descend on them all. Belle was particularly ravishing this evening, in a translucent white dinner gown held together with a strategic diamond brooch at her bosom. She was sitting in the gold lamé camp chair, and Hannibal thought she looked like Queen Nefertiti. The dress was so successful that Walt Cuban and his rummy old friends kept finding reasons to visit the marquee tent.

But now an uproar shattered the summer's evening.

"I guess I'd better see," he said, eyeing the red rim-rock warily.

"Woowoo," Belle said, patted his knee as a reminder, and followed him.

Below, and toiling up the steep trail to the flat, was a formidable congregation led by an army lieutenant in mustard uniform, wearing a Sam Browne belt and twin sidearms and visored cap. Just behind him was a middle-aged and imperious woman with white hair tinted blue. Just behind her was a heavy army caisson drawn by two plugs, and behind that were half a dozen rough-looking gents, some armed with long sticks, most of them ragged, unshaven, and fierce. And behind them came a huge high-sided freight wagon

203

filled with gear and drawn by an eight-mule team governed by bullwhackers.

"That's Juanita!" Belle whispered. "And that's her son, Nero. He's an artillery lieutenant."

"What about the rest?"

"I don't know, but they give me the shivers."

"Where's Attila Haggarty? Still up on the rimrock?" Hannibal asked.

Haggarty wife number two, Juanita, struggled up the last grade with imperial dignity, her withering glare taking in Belle, Hannibal, Babette and her daughters, and assorted retainers from both camps. Juanita was plainly a formidable woman, a dreadnought of a woman with a military escort.

Nero Haggarty walked with a natural swagger, his arms swinging in bouncy rhythm with his legs, his uniform immaculate even after the long hike from Ely. He had a fine, exuberant sandy-colored walrus mustache and a keen eye for everything on the flat. He eyed the Alice Mine, the ruby silk tent and marquee tent, the puritanical white-walled camp of Babette, and the empty spaces remaining on the plateau.

His gaze lingered long on Hannibal, in his sky-blue jodhpurs, pith helmet, and red polka-dot bow tie. And it was Hannibal he chose to address.

"You, sir, what is your business here?"

It was as if the entire imperial weight of the United States Army lay in that question.

"I'm a mining geologist. And you?"

"My mother and I are the owners of this mine and

this land and that is why we're here."

"You are, I gather, Nero Haggarty?"

"Who else?"

"And your mother is Juanita Haggarty."

"None other."

"Well, I'd advise you to set up your camp as far from that red rimrock as possible. There are frequent avalanches, some of them the work of someone up there."

"Geologist, I will ascertain that without your advice. You are addressing an officer."

"On duty?"

"On leave."

That was a relief. But the relief was momentary.

"I have brought with me some labor," Haggarty said. "In that caisson—condemned surplus property, I might add—is our powder. And those men behind are a face crew, well experienced in removing cave-ins. We are going to blow our way into the Alice, and will thank you to depart before then."

"I see," Hannibal said.

"The face crew are all Wobblies, men I arrested for anarchy, sedition, treason, consorting with subversives, and assorted felonies. Industrial Workers of the World, the IWW radicals, every one of them an experienced miner. Desperate men. Two of them murderers, one an arsonist, and the others desperados of one sort or another perfectly willing to strangle females and geologists. But all of them experienced miners and powder men. I told them I would free them in exchange for a certain favor. They are going to clear passage into the Alice Mine and then guard it against interlopers—such as I see here."

The gaggle of Wobblies topped the lip of the plateau and spread onto the flat, eyeing the Haggarty women and Belle, and the rummy old miners, and Colonel Rathke and the Raven-Haired Maid.

"We are removing you from the property," Lieutenant Haggarty said. "You will all pack up and leave at once."

"Show me your ownership papers first," Belle shot at him.

"The papers don't matter. My mother possesses this mine by dower right."

"So do Faye and Babette," Belle retorted.

Lieutenant Nero Haggarty loomed over her. "My mother and Harold Haggarty were united by no other than the chief justice of the Nevada Supreme Court, and that settles it."

"Not if the marriage was bigamous, Lieutenant," Hannibal said.

"Your opinion was not asked for, geologist. What did you say your name is?"

"I didn't say."

Nero Haggarty waved a riding crop at Hannibal. "Out. Now."

A rumble followed by a deluge of red rock tumbling down from above stopped conversation cold. A few tons of rimrock clattered and bounced its way to the flat, tossing shattered red rock into the old mine buildings and out on the flat. One large rock with saw-toothed edges landed a few feet from the lieutenant. Hannibal saw a faint cloud of dark powder smoke drift away. Some ghost.

"You were saying?"

The creaking ore wagon and mule team had reached the plateau, along with the Wobblies, who glared darkly at the ruby silk tent and awning-striped marquee tent, and all the rest. They were hungry men with fire in their eye.

"I could use a geologist. You'll work for me, not her."

"I work for myself. She hasn't paid me a dime. And I will continue to work for myself."

"For what?"

"An interest in the Alice."

"Forget it, geologist." He turned to his Wobblies. "Make camp over there," he said, pointing a swagger stick at the sole remaining safe area on the flat.

The Wobblies drove the ore wagon and mule team past Babette's camp, past Belle's camp, and began settling themselves on bare turf well removed from the brooding red cliff above.

But then the lieutenant changed his mind. "Make camp later. Right now, get up on the rim and get hold of whoever's up there and bring him down here. Fast. I'll put him in irons. That was no natural avalanche. I can smell the cordite."

The weary Wobblies stared, and Hannibal thought they might turn on Nero Haggarty, but at last they abandoned their camp-tending and began a slow climb up the valley, one that would eventually take them to the red rimrock above. A mule tender remained behind.

Hannibal took advantage of the break. "You'd better show us your ownership papers, Lieutenant. If the Alice is yours, we'll leave. If it isn't, we'll stay."

"You'll leave because I'll tell you to, and not because of some flimsy sheet of paper."

Oddly, Babette chose that moment to advance her own cause. "Lieutenant, I would like you to meet your half sisters, Cleopatra and Delilah Haggarty," she said. "I am Babette, Lucky Haggarty's third wife, and I believe that is your mother, Juanita. It's a pity Faye isn't here; we could have a family reunion."

Nero started to form a sharp reply, but a soft hand from his mother stayed him. "I am pleased to meet you," Juanita said. "I've often wondered what Harold found in you, and now I know. And you too, Mrs. Brandy. I presume that's who you are?"

Belle nodded.

"Harold had marvelous taste in women," Juanita said.

"But Mother, these are impostors."

"We are three women Harold loved, and there is a fourth."

"I'll drive them off and we'll bust into the Alice at dawn and it'll be over with."

"No, Nero. I should like to meet them. And we'll all see about the missing deeds or will, or whatever

Lucky left us, if he left us anything. Maybe there'll be one winner and many losers. Maybe we'll all share."

"Share! I didn't assemble my platoon and come here to share!" Lieutenant Haggarty snapped.

But the words rising from Juanita's soft throat were filled with such imperial power that they settled the matter then and there.

Hannibal knew they would be staying. He suddenly realized that Juanita Haggarty was an exceptional woman, as were all Haggarty's wives and his mistress. Lucky Haggarty had chosen well. Every one of them was not merely a raving beauty, but willful, strong, and probably dangerous.

There were introductions, and then Belle invited the whole family to her marquee tent for "whatever Colonel Rathke, recently in the czar's service, can whip up."

It amazed Hannibal. War had been turned into peace, all by the formidable Juanita, who was actually surveying Belle's accommodations with relish.

"Nero, I should like a red silk tent. Please send for one," she said. "I shall want it by tomorrow."

"But Mother . . ."

"Or the next day at the worst."

"But that's not possible."

"Nero, my dear, all things are possible to a Haggarty. No excuses. I did not raise you to be a pussy."

Juanita turned to Belle. "I can see why Lucky kept you," she said, and winked.

Chapter 30

Colonel Rathke soon had an improvised repast spread before the company, including shrimp bisque, bamboo heart salad topped with saffron and morels in mayonnaise laced with grated lemon rind, candied sweet potatoes, curried chicken on a bed of wild rice and leeks, and cream puffs or cheesecake, all washed down with abundant Philippe de Rothschild vintage '94.

The Raven-Haired Maid soon had orange Japanese lanterns hanging from the marquee tent, and these cast a cheery glow over the ensemble. The buttery light had a way of probing through Belle's translucent gown, as well as Babette's, which Hannibal didn't mind at all. He rather wished Juanita might have dressed for the party, but her camp was not yet made, with the Wobblies chasing ghosts up on the rimrock.

Belle signaled the maid. "Please take quarts of Old Crab Orchard to the servants," she said. "And ask Yin and Yang to help them make camp."

The maid hurried off and soon was transporting two bottles, one to the rummy miners, and the other to the mule skinner in the new camp.

"I have the most marvelous Celestials," Belle said. "I wouldn't trade them for the Alice."

There was a moment of reverent silence. It was a compliment of such magnitude that none of the others could imagine it.

"I have them shave my legs once a month," Belle added.

"I am very envious," Babette said.

Lieutenant Haggarty settled into the gold-flecked green camp chair and improved his mood with a few quarts of the Bordeaux as well as handfuls of macadamia nuts. His primary occupation was the detailed study of Babette and Belle, who were soon engaged in lively conversation with his mother. It was plain that Juanita had a bad case of camp-envy, and wanted her equipage upgraded to Belle's level as fast as the lieutenant could arrange it.

"Ah, Lieutenant," Hannibal ventured, "just what's in that caisson?"

"Oh, a good shot or two, geologist. A thousand sticks of Dupont Hercules dynamite."

"And what's in that case strapped to the tongue?"

"Oh, five hundred mercury fulminate caps, I believe."

Hannibal went pale. "Ah, Lieutenant, I think you might consider removing the caps to a point at least three hundred yards from the dynamite. And then gently, of course, driving the caisson away from the rimrock."

"Oh, pshaw, geologist, if you were in the army, you wouldn't fuss so."

"The name is Jones, sir, Hannibal Jones."

"Now there's a capital army name. Hannibal. Old Hannibal gave the Romans a run for their money, crossing the Alps with elephants and all. You should've enlisted."

"Ah, Lieutenant, would you mind if I were to carry the caps to a safe distance?"

"My word, but you're a ninny, Jones. Very well, we'll do it directly."

Hannibal and the lieutenant retreated into the dark, reached the caisson, unstrapped the case of caps, and Hannibal gingerly carried the heavy case down the grim grade until the dynamite was out of blast range.

"How about here?"

"Good enough, old sport."

No sooner did they reach the plateau than another, smaller, avalanche clattered down, some of the red rock bouncing cheerfully off the caisson.

"Hmm, I see what you mean, Jones. I'll have my man put the plugs on and drag it off."

"I think the two of us might manage it, sir."

"Well, tallyho, then."

Between them, they rolled the caisson fifty yards, and then returned to the marquee tent.

"What were you boys up to?" asked Juanita.

"Just a little housekeeping, Mother."

The ladies were enjoying Colonel Rathke's impromptu, and Hannibal marveled that they could look so naked even while clothed. It was a trick of the rich. Put the upper class together at a party, and they all looked naked. He thought he wouldn't mind being rich. Of course, none of these people were *rich* rich, which was why they all wanted the Alice Mine. But they weren't exactly starving. Old Lucky Haggarty was the fountain of all this wealth and cheerful living, and Hannibal silently saluted the old rogue.

"Where did you get that chef?" Juanita asked Belle.

"Colonel Rathke? I stole him."

"I'll buy him. Would a thousand dollars do?"

"No, but I'll lend him to you for parties."

"Oh, Belle, how sweet. Now, where did you get this fine geologist?"

"I seduced him. He's come in handy and he costs nothing."

"I might want to borrow him too."

"I'll lease him out. It's pure profit."

"Does he always wear jodhpurs? They're so dear."

"I prefer him without pants," Belle said.

"And a pith helmet! And a bow tie! He reminds me of Teddy Roosevelt."

Hannibal listened amiably from the star-spangled blue camp chair. Good old Belle. He sipped the Bordeaux, content with the world. A fat orange moon topped the distant ridges and threw pale light over the quiet mountains. When had life ever been better?

Nero Haggarty's attention shifted to Cleopatra and Delilah, whom he studied discreetly.

"It's a pity they're my half sisters," he said to Hannibal.

"Toughest of luck, old boy."

"Do you suppose we could pretend they aren't?"

"Give it a try," Hannibal said. "They don't acknowledge your patrimony, and you don't acknowledge theirs, so for all practical purposes you're not related."

"Capital, Jones. I knew you were good for something."

The lieutenant shifted his green camp chair over to the young ladies, and began patting knees, and they responded toothily.

Hannibal settled back in his camp chair to watch the bobbing Japanese lanterns and the rising moon, but a commotion out in the darkness interrupted his reveries. He saw a body of ghostly men straggle across the flat, pass the Alice Mine, and work resolutely toward the marquee tent.

"Here come your Wobblies," he said to Lieutenant Haggarty.

"Why, so they are," Haggarty said, patting female knees and rising to meet his seditionists.

The Wobblies filtered in, a sudden shock of dark raggedness in the midst of all the opulence. And they had a prisoner, Attila Haggarty, the lieutenant's brother, whose hands were stoutly tied behind him.

Nero and Juanita stared.

"Attila, where have you been?" Juanita demanded.

"Doing just what you asked. Keeping an eye on all these interlopers. These people you're now trafficking with."

"Let him go at once," she said.

Nero sprang to work, pulled out a jackknife, and slashed through the cord. Attila rubbed his wrists sullenly.

A darkness stole through the assembled guests.

"Please join us, Attila," Juanita said.

"Never," the young man replied with a savageness that took the breath right out of Hannibal. "You sent

214

me here. I've spent days and weeks, in heat and cold and wind and rain. I've let you know whenever anyone's come. Now I'm caught by your men and you're eating at the table of our enemies."

"Attila . . ." his mother said softly.

"Your avalanches could have blown us up. Almost hit my caisson," Nero said.

"Not mine. Someone else's," Attila shot back.

There was obvious malice between the two brothers.

"Oh, pshaw, don't deny it," Nero said.

Attila bulled into his brother and knocked the lieutenant flat, hammering him a few times as he toppled.

"Now, boys," Juanita said.

Belle stood swiftly and addressed the sullen Wobblies. "Gents, I'll have a meal for you directly. You'll find your camp going up over there, and after you wash up, we'll have a nice dinner waiting for you."

"We'll cook our own grub. Not this fancy stuff. Real food," one of the Wobblies said, acid-voiced. "Not made by slaves. Not rich men's garbage."

The six of them whirled toward the rising new camp.

Nero stood and dusted off his uniform, paying special attention to his epaulets and getting his Sam Browne belt just so.

"I spend weeks looking after your interests, living any way I can, protecting our mine, and what do I find? This!" Attila snapped.

Juanita rose imperiously. "Attila, you go wash up and join us. I will then introduce you to your half sis-

215

ters and your father's other companions. They are here for the same reason. We will find out who owns the Alice."

"Never," he said, and bolted into the darkness.

The evening's idyll had ended.

Hannibal watched the young man vanish into the shadows. He didn't like it. Up high, somewhere, Attila had a rifle, and down here on the flat was a caisson loaded with dynamite, some very vulnerable Haggartys, and assorted innocent and hardworking staff, including the Wobblies themselves.

"Do you suppose I could borrow your portable bathtub, Belle?" Babette asked.

"Oh, you have a tub? I should like to use it after you, Babette," Juanita said.

"Help yourself," Belle said. "And I have a portable bidet if it appeals to you. I'll have Yin and Yang bring them to you."

"Oh, it's a dream. A bidet!"

"That's where she hid my pants," Hannibal said.

"I knew when I first saw you I'd like you, Mr. Jones," Juanita said.

Hannibal watched Yin and Yang tote the tin tub and the bidet out of the ruby tent and into the night.

The Raven-Haired Maid extinguished the Japanese lanterns. A sudden darkness engulfed the plateau.

"Woowoo," said Belle.

216

Chapter 31

The red light pried Hannibal's eyes open. He wondered whether he could get up. The only equipment functioning this morning was his heart and lungs. He got no responses from his toes, fingers, elbows, or other parts. A melancholia filtered through him: He was facing a cruel dilemma and one he could not escape. He would either flee from Belle or else spend the rest of his days in a wheelchair.

The awful thought galvanized him, and he sprang from bed, remembering to check for scorpions and snakes only after his bare feet hit the Brussels carpet. But everything was just fine. He began his morning ablutions and discovered his brown twill pants lying on the bed. A great wonder spread through him. The jodhpurs had been banished! He eagerly tugged on his britches, headed out to the marquee tent, and settled into the pink chaise lounge. His barber this morning would be Yang, who swiftly brushed lather into his beard and scraped his cheeks and jaws until they were as smooth as baby flesh. A steaming hot towel applied over his face completed the task.

Yang volunteered, with pantomime, to brush Hannibal's teeth, but Hannibal declined. That was too effete for his tastes.

"Thank you, Mr. Yang. You are a genius," Hannibal said.

In short order, Hannibal settled into a camp chair

made from grizzly-bear hide and ermine, and enjoyed Colonel Rathke's repast: bacon, turkey breast, corn casserole rolled into tortillas, pickled herring, eggs Benedict with asparagus, and cream puffs for dessert.

He sat back in his camp chair, sipping Java, observing the fevered activity around the head frame of the Alice Mine, where Lieutenant Haggarty and his Wobblies were hard at work, or at least the Wobblies were. They had drawn the big freight wagon close and were wheelbarrowing rock into it as fast as they could muck it from the huge pile of red sandstone that blocked the shaft.

Hannibal glanced up at the rimrock above, but saw no signs of any ghost at work there. He didn't doubt that another avalanche was forthcoming. The lieutenant had been duly warned, so the excavation being done under the brooding cliffs above was entirely his risk. And that of his Wobbly miners.

Maybe when Hannibal had enough Java in his blood to counter the weakness of limb still afflicting him, he would go supervise. That's what his credentials were for. Save lives, save energy. It was plain, as Hannibal watched from across the plateau, that the son of Lucky Haggarty was going to burrow into that mine and nothing would stop him. Maybe he would find the papers bequeathing the mine to his mother; maybe not. Hannibal bet that not a single paper would be found in the depths of the old Alice Mine, and quite possibly Lucky Haggarty had never bequeathed the Alice to anyone at all.

218

Hannibal returned to the ruby silk tent to complete his toilet, and was busily tying his red polka-dot bow tie when Belle swirled through the door. This bright summer's morning she was wearing a white safari outfit with gold epaulets, gold hash stripes on the sleeves, navy-blue cravat, a facsimile Congressional Medal of Honor pinned to her white bosom, blue watershot silk sash, straw boater, and red kid-leather boots. She looked dashing, rather like a navy officer in summer dress.

"Good," she said. "We're going to the Back Door and hunt for papers."

So it was that Hannibal's day was prescribed. He didn't mind. The sooner this mad crew discovered there were no wills or deeds or anything else that might establish ownership of a remote mine in a wilderness, the sooner he could return to serious business.

"Is that why I'm wearing pants this morning?"

"We're going incognito," she said. "Away from prying eyes. They won't notice anyone in pants. Jodhpurs would give us away. You know where the Back Door is, so you'll lead the way."

"I see."

She pressed the pith helmet onto his locks, and then handed him a wicker picnic basket. They marched off the plateau under the squint of Babette, Cleopatra, and Delilah along with their rummy old miners in one camp, and Juanita and her servants in the new camp that had risen in the dusk.

"I think they are watching us," Hannibal said.

"We're going on a picnic," Belle said. She patted his arm. "Woowoo."

"You are demanding the impossible," he retorted.

"Woowoo," she said, patting him on the pith helmet.

But soon they were alone. Hannibal checked for observers, using his field glasses, looking for a glimpse of a ghost, or a retainer, anything that might be a sign that they were being followed. But he saw only a sleeping and arid range of mountains under an anonymous blue sky.

The descent was steep, and he handed her down some of the rougher spots in the trail. He did not have his map folder, but thought he could find the claim without difficulty. The Back Door was shown as patented private property on the map, which meant there would be corner markers, and some discovery work that was needed to prove up a claim. Swiftly they descended into a brushy basin. He continued down a game trail, and hit the tiny creek issuing from the cleft in the mountain.

A great peace pervaded that corner of the world. The creek burbled through the iron grille set in the rock. Some of the livestock from the camps grazed there, though the grass was all but gone. The mysterious grave with the unmarked headstone rested on its small flat. It was covered with horse manure.

The foot-wide creek tumbled down a slope and into a choked valley, an exotic streak of green in a brown and gray land. Hannibal found a narrow trail, and they

220

continued into this hushed Eden. They were getting close to the Back Door. High above, on the cliff, he spotted the red rimrock. That was the clue. A corner cairn was another. Loose rock had been piled into a pyramid perhaps five feet high. They had reached the Back Door.

"Here's a corner of it," he said. "From now on, look for anything disturbed or out of place. We don't even know if this was Lucky Haggarty's property, but if we find a discovery cairn, there should be a claim tucked into it."

"It doesn't seem like much of a claim," she said.

He pointed up high. "See that red sandstone? The stratum high up? That's the same stratum that lies above the Alice Mine."

She peered upward, excitement building in her face. "We're here! This is it!"

"I don't know what's here," he said cautiously. "But now we'll look hard."

They did look hard. But all they saw was anonymous rock, undisturbed. Ahead somewhere the quartz seam outcropped, and he was anxious to find the place where he had chipped samples. But there was no sign of a discovery cairn or mine shaft as they worked through talus, around giant rock slides, through thorny brush.

He plunged through the rough country and she followed gamely, sometimes releasing her white skirts from stickers. For an hour they toiled along the foot of the cliff, finding nothing that signaled a claim or human presence. The day was growing hotter fast.

Then suddenly they pierced into a tiny rocky flat surrounded by brush, an arid Nevada version of a glade. It was heaven. The sun had not yet found this corner of the canyon, and its coolness soothed Hannibal.

"We can take a break," he said. "Somewhere ahead is where I found the quartz seam."

He expected her to make a beeline forward, but she didn't, and he realized he had worn her out. They had spent the morning clambering over loose rock and working around choked gullies and thickets of desert brush. It had been hard work.

"Time to rest," she said. She unfolded a blanket and sat on it, invited him to join her. A peace pervaded this sweet corner of the world. They had found a secret heaven.

"I like it here," she said. "I like all of this so much better than San Francisco. I could spend the rest of my life out in the country, looking for gold."

"Most gold isn't found in pleasant places," he replied. "Hot, dry, miserable, windy, remote places, or cold, icy, snowy, steep places."

She found his hand and took it. "It's you I'm talking about, Jones. Just being with you, hunting gold."

A strange warmth suffused him. "Belle . . . I'm glad you're here, with me."

"I brought some lunch. Maybe it's not noon but I'm ready for it."

"Sure, let's eat."

She pulled opened her wicker basket and pulled out a wedge of Swiss cheese, an unbroken loaf, and two bottles of sarsaparilla. That surprised him. He thought there would be a lunch to rival one at Delmonico's.

She was oddly subdued, almost shy, as she broke bread and cheese and handed him pieces, which he ate with relish. He uncorked the two brown bottles, and they sipped. The sun found their bower after crossing a ridge high above, and bathed them in warmth. He noticed a few crow's-feet around her eyes. No wonder she was tired, he thought. She was a decade older and not used to crawling through mountain wilds.

She kept peering at him, something liquid and warm in her eyes, but she didn't say anything. After they had eaten, she pulled his pith helmet off his head and tugged him down upon the blanket. Then she nestled her head in the hollow of his shoulder, and he enjoyed that. Her head belonged there, fitted there.

But her decorations were stabbing him.

"Your Congressional Medal of Honor is stabbing me," he said.

"Oh!"

She sat up, unpinned the chest decoration, pitched it into the brush, and nestled into the compass of his arm and shoulder once again.

He felt her slide into sleep, and soon she was in her own quiet world, while he rested there, enjoying her closeness. She lay there inert for a while, and then opened her eyes.

"Ready for more hunting?" he asked.

"No," she replied. "We can do that tomorrow."

He marveled. The gold digger was content just as she was.

Chapter 32

When Hannibal and Belle returned to the Alice Mine, they found the Wobblies hard at work removing the massive heap of red rock that blocked the shaft. Lieutenant Haggarty was supervising. The haggard Wobblies were mucking sandstone into wheelbarrows and hauling the rock to the perimeter of the flat and dumping it. It was a slow process, and they had moved only a few cubic yards of it.

"Jones, I'm going to bathe," Belle said. "Send the colonel to my tent with hot water."

Hannibal managed to convey the message to the ubiquitous colonel as well as Yin and Yang, who began heating water on the brazier.

Hannibal headed for the Alice Mine, but was intercepted by the lieutenant.

"This is our show, geologist. We're going in, and whatever we find in there is ours. You may watch from a distance. But my mother and I will not be euchred out of our inheritance."

"You have a long way to go, Lieutenant. When you clear this mountain of red rock, you'll find another major blockage down the shaft a way. That one's granite rubble."

"I have my Wobblies," he replied.

Indeed he did, though they didn't seem to be toiling hard. It would take days to clear away the red rock that had fallen from the rims above, and a week or two to pierce past the second blockage.

"Now you'd better stand back. We're going to blow the pile of rock to kingdom come in a bit."

"What have you in mind?"

Haggarty pointed. "Right there. These Wobblies are all experienced hard-rock men, and they're loading a charge."

"Mind if I look?"

"Of course I mind. This is our show."

But Hannibal ignored the lieutenant and edged forward. What he saw shocked him. The Wobblies, perhaps with malice aforethought, were loading dozens of sticks, all capped and fused, into a pocket facing out upon the flat. Hannibal swiftly counted forty sticks of Dupont, enough to blow away every tent on the flat.

He hurried back to the lieutenant. "Are you trying to kill yourself, your mother, and the rest of us?" he asked.

"Oh, pshaw, Jones, you worry too much."

"There's at least forty sticks. And they're in the wrong place. They'll not only blow away every one of us, which is what your seditionists want, but they'll blow that red rock into the shaft. You want to kill your mother? And yourself?"

"Ah . . ."

"Your Wobblies are about set. They'll be ready as

soon as they fuse the charge."

"Jones, you've spoiled my afternoon."

Nonetheless, Haggarty hurried to the Wobblies, waving his automatic pistol.

"Here now," he said. "We're not going to do that. We're going to set the charge on the other side of this rock pile. One of you'll crawl over the rubble and into the shaft. We're going to blow the rock out, not in."

The Wobblies stood slowly. It was plain to Hannibal that they were all considering a rush upon their captor. They had the dynamite and the fuses in hand, and in a few moments could blow every Haggarty relative to bits.

One of them smirked slightly.

"You, Gillis, you crawl over this rubble, into the shaft, and set up the charge in there," ordered Haggarty. "You, Maginnis, hand Gillis the bundled charges, carefully now."

The Wobblies eyed Haggarty's automatic pistols, and slowly surrendered. Gillis smirked and slowly crawled over the rubble and into the shaft, through the same opening that Hannibal had pried open so he and Belle could escape days earlier. Maginnis gingerly crawled up the heap of red rubble, dynamite in hand, and handed capped bundles of the giant powder to Gillis.

"Blow her sky-high," Maginnis said. "Blow them damned capitalists to kingdom come. Hey, Lieutenant, if I toss this bundle, you want to catch it?"

"That's a good way to commit suicide, Maginnis," Haggarty replied.

"That's fine if I take a few plutocrats with me," Maginnis said, and Hannibal believed him.

The Wobbly waved the fused bundle around a few times, terrifying spectators, and then carefully handed it to Gillis, whose upthrust hands took the bundle tenderly.

Hannibal edged backward fast.

A half hour later, the Wobblies had moved all the dynamite to the inner side of the red rubble, and a long fuse snaked out of the opening.

"All right, you Wobblies, you step back. I'll light it," the lieutenant said.

The Wobblies leered and retreated.

It wasn't what Hannibal would have preferred, but it would do. The Wobblies needed watching.

"I would advise that you remove yourself and everyone else from this flat," he told the lieutenant. "Including your mother."

"Jones, I'm an artillery man."

There was no arguing with that. The lieutenant was plainly annoyed at being found wanting.

"If you won't tell them, I will," Hannibal said.

The Wobblies stared sullenly fifty yards away.

Hannibal retreated hastily across the wasteland around the Alice. He found Colonel Rathke. "I'd advise you to get away, far away, fast, and tell Yin and Yang," he said.

The colonel understood, and acted at once.

Hannibal found Babette, her girls, and the rummy old miners watching.

"Get as far away as you can," he said. "There's forty sticks of Dupont in there."

"Oh, what a show!" Babette said. "I'll just watch, thank you."

"You've been warned," Hannibal said.

"Aeoww, meeth loops!" said Walt Cuban, dancing madly about.

Whatever that meant.

Hannibal was heading for Belle's ruby silk tent when he saw the lieutenant lean over, strike a lucifer on his sole, and hold the wooden match to the fuse until at last it sputtered to life.

No time.

Hannibal hit the ground and clasped his pith helmet tightly over his head. Colonel Rathke did likewise. Yin and Yang fled toward the rim of the flat. The rummy miners slowly caved to earth. Cleopatra and Delilah burst out of their tent to get a better look.

The blast was actually a series of thumps that shook the earth under Hannibal and shot red rock shrapnel in every direction from the shaft. Some boiled high and slowly settled to earth. The three deafening blasts were followed by a roar and rattle as rock sailed high, but fell short of the encampments. A great gust of hot air smacked Hannibal, knocked Babette's girls to the ground, and blew away the walls of the ruby silk tent.

Belle squealed and stood up in her tin bathtub, water rivering off her.

Juanita poked her head out of her tent, observed the

228

wall of dust rising from the shaft, and stepped into the sudden quiet.

Belle stood stock-still, a pink marble Venus.

"She's beautiful. Why wasn't I born with a body like that?" Juanita said, staring at Belle.

"That's why she was Lucky's mistress," Babette said in awe.

Belle stood tall, smiling sweetly, covering nothing.

The Wobblies clambered up to the flat, and stared.

The rummy old miners snickered and guffawed.

"Madam, you're disturbing my men," Lieutenant Haggarty said.

From the ground, Hannibal stared upward at Belle, admiring her all the more because everyone on the flat was admiring her. But Colonel Rathke spoiled the moment, gently walking over to the tent and tugging the loosened ruby silk wall panel downward, so that the vision of Venus vanished from view. It was as if a light went out on the flat of the Alice Mine.

"No wonder Lucky kept her," Juanita said.

"Wives could never compete," Babette whispered. "Not with that."

"I suppose Faye was no match for her either," Juanita said.

"Faye's a beautiful woman, but cold. Cold, cold, cold," Babette said.

"Ah, that's it. There's more than beauty to a woman, and Lucky knew it," said Juanita. She turned to her son. "Stop staring."

"Yes, Mother."

"You lucky dog," said Juanita to Hannibal, who was slowly rising to a sitting position. "No wonder you don't cost her a dime. You get paid every night and twice on Sundays. You're getting the best of the bargain."

Hannibal rose to his feet, adjusted his pith helmet, and dusted himself off with elaborate dignity. The wall of the ruby silk tent now curtained all within the tent, including the lush Belle. It had been a glorious moment. Belle rising out of her bath like Venus had triumphed over her rivals, and he, Hannibal Jones, was Belle's very own. It was like having Victoria Regina of England for a mistress, but on second thought he decided that was a bad analogy. Still, he was now an envied man, and that was something to relish.

As the dust around the mine head lifted, Hannibal spotted the wide-open shaft. All that dynamite exploding in the confines of the blocked shaft had driven rock outward like a cannon shot. The Wobblies, deprived of visions of Belle, slipped close to the shaft, studying the dark reaches within.

Hannibal ventured over to the Alice, wondering whether the blast had also opened up the cave-in that still blocked passage, and was soon assured that the shaft remained sealed. Juanita's minions would still have to conquer the next obstacle before they could enter Lucky Haggarty's fabulous mine.

Colonel Rathke busily set camp chairs upright under the marquee tent, and set pheasant and partridge to broiling on the brazier. Belle emerged wearing one of the gauzy white things that made her look half naked.

"Come join me for cocktails," she said to her rivals. "We can watch those wretches muck out all that rock."

Hannibal thought that would make a capital evening, and settled into the gold lamé camp chair, even as the colonel handed him some Old Crab Orchard and branch.

Chapter 33

Colonel Rathke outdid himself, serving a gorgeous repast to Belle and her guests and rivals. On this sweet, quiet evening, as dusk settled over the peaceful ridges and orange light glowed from the Japanese lanterns decorating the marquee tent, the colonel produced quiche Lorraine and a spinach salad with mangoes, guava, kiwi fruit, celery, and crumbled peanut brittle, topped with Baltic caviar, all washed down with gallons of rowdy Chianti.

As a courtesy, Belle sent the Raven-Haired Maid over to the Wobblies with a quart bottle of her special stock, one-hundred-one-proof Bonded Old Gildersleeve, and sent some Guinness ale over to Babette's old miners, who were cooking their own mess.

But it was not a pleasant meal. Lieutenant Haggarty was in a foul mood. Even as he wolfed down quiche under Belle's marquee tent, he informed the assemblage that he alone would venture into the Alice when it was opened, and there would be no witnesses or rivals.

"And what would you do if you found a deed giving the mine to me? Or Babette?" asked Belle.

"Burn it."

"And leave the mine without an owner?"

"I'd rather seal up the Alice forever than have it ripped from my hands."

"Is that what Lucky would wish?"

"Fiddle on that," the lieutenant said, attacking a mango. "I'll find a way. We're going in, and we'll rip up paper if we must, and take it to the courts."

"Well, tomorrow I'm putting my miners to work in the old superintendent's offices," Babette said. "I'll start them digging for a cache of papers in the floor. If you insist on opening the mine without us, I'll insist on controlling the office."

"Pshaw, that's easily taken care of," the lieutenant said. "I'll send the Wobblies. We'll keep an eye on you."

That was the crushing rejoinder. The assemblage under the marquee tent studied the Wobblies, who had gathered around their own campfire a hundred yards off.

"Send one or two my way," said Belle. "I enjoy them wobbly or straight."

Cleopatra and Delilah giggled.

"Save room for crème brûlée," Belle said. "Colonel Rathke specializes in it."

Hannibal marveled at her placidity. Here she was, surrounded by Haggarty's fierce wives, each with a private army. Here she was, listening to threats and

232

declarations, and yet she was furnishing them with gorgeous dinners and evening revels without hearing a thank-you from any of her guests.

"My dear Babette, I've been wondering how it happens that you show up here in this remote place now, after a quarter of a century," Belle said to the third Mrs. Haggarty.

"Simple," said Babette. "It's him. Jones." She pointed at Hannibal. "Everyone know's he's the foremost man in the world on dead mines. If it had been some bearded prospector with a burro, it wouldn't have mattered. Some wandering idiot, nothing would matter. But it was Jones, the man who brings dead mines to life. I heard about it from about ten sources. They said a man with a red polka-dot bow tie was snooping around the Alice. That triggered all the fire-alarm bells, I assure you. I've never worried about a stray thief, or even an occasional mining magnate. But Jones, here. That was different."

"Of course it was Jones," said Juanita. "That set off all the bells. And when Jones visited Faye and she dumped a bucket of water over his head, I knew things were stirring at the Alice."

"How did you know about that?" Hannibal asked.

"Jones, I have squealers and snitches and detectives and paid spies, and half of them spy on Faye, including her maid. It costs me money, but it keeps the Alice safe from interlopers like you."

"So now, because I showed up, you've all decided to settle the issue. What if old Lucky Haggarty decided not to will the mine to anyone at all? Give it to charity? Donate it to the state of Nevada? Or just enjoy the thought of all of you fighting each other for decades, until lawyers have eaten up all you own?"

"Then we'll kill each other until one of us is still standing," said Babette.

"And where's Faye?"

"Lucky's first wife thinks the Alice is properly hers on the basis of being his first wife, and what she calls the bigamous wives don't count even if we got married by archbishops or cardinals or the Dalai Lama, and someday she'll find the will or the deed or whatever, and we can search until doomsday and never find the papers. That's what her lawyer told me," Juanita said.

"She must have her own sources," Hannibal said.

"She does. And she pays them with her favors," Babette said.

Hannibal shrank into his tweedy coat, and was of a mind to slip into the night and never return. Wickenburg was calling. He was currently in a lunatic asylum.

The Raven-Haired Maid cleared the plates and brought the dessert, while Hannibal watched a blue streak of last light slowly fade in the northwest.

That's when a bottle with a flaming rag sailed into the marquee tent, shattered as it hit the carpeted earth, and burst into blue flames, which sprang up just beside Juanita. The hundred-and-one-proof Bonded Gildersleeve flared brightly, with blue flame crawling under the camp table. She rose swiftly, her diaphanous gown ablaze, and then languorously began swatting the small worms of fire that were working through her petticoat and filmy white dress.

"Oh, my," she said, and deftly undid a few buttons until the smoldering dress tumbled to her ankles and she stepped free. She settled into her gold lamé camp chair looking fetching in her white silk camisole. The umber flesh of her bare limbs and curvy shoulders caught Hannibal's eye. Juanita Haggarty was a match for Belle, and now she was proving it with a leisurely pose or two before she settled back into her camp chair.

"Here now! That's my mother!" Lieutenant Haggarty roared, and leapt into the darkness in the general direction of the Wobblies, waving his automatic pistols at them. "I'll put you in the brig forever!"

Colonel Rathke swiftly extinguished the blaze with a sopping dish towel, and began sweeping the charred debris out of way. Then he tucked a linen tablecloth around Juanita, which depressed Hannibal.

The next moments were punctuated with a few shots from the lieutenant's revolver, white lightning in the dark, and then an enormous crack from a stolen stick of Dupont that flashed white and sent a slap of air that almost flattened the tents.

Wild laughter out of the dark.

"Take that, you slimy plutocrat!"

Another stick boomed, a blinding light, a rain of debris over the striped awning of the tent, and a hot thump of percussion that knocked a plate of bonbons onto the carpet.

The lieutenant was caught in a Wobbly war.

Hannibal sat back. If the Wobblies managed to kill Lieutenant Haggarty, the world would be considerably improved.

"Try another shot, Maginnis," yelled Babette. "Blow the lieutenant off the map!"

But Belle was barging into the night.

"Here now," she cried. "If I get the Alice, you all will have your reward."

"I can imagine," said Babette.

High above, in deep dark, an avalanche broke loose and thundered down near the abandoned buildings.

"Oh, this is better than the opera," said Delilah. "I hope someone ravishes me."

Hannibal thought to volunteer, and decided against it. And besides, Belle had ruined him for life. That was the pity of all this. Hannibal knew that he could never be a man again. Belle had wrecked his manhood so entirely, so permanently, that he was doomed to bachelorhood the rest of his days.

He heard considerable yelling out there, and took comfort in the possibility that a few shots, a few sticks of Hercules, and a few avalanches could end his travail, and he could head for Arizona before winter set in.

But there were no more avalanches, no more blasts, and only one or two more shots. Then, out of the gloom, came the Wobblies, hands held high, followed by Belle and the lieutenant, who had an automatic in each hand, the business ends pointed at the Wobblies.

"Colonel Rathke, would you kindly dish out some quiche to these dear fellows?" said Belle.

The czarist chef understood, even if he confessed to no English, and swiftly handed each Wobbly some quiche on Ming-era plates, with Tiffany silver forks to eat it.

"Maginnis, don't try that again," the lieutenant said. "I'll be forced to try you for sedition. And I hand out drumhead justice, mind you."

"Oh, let the dear boy go," said Juanita, who was sitting handsomely in her tablecloth dishabille, sipping a Grand Marnier.

"I won't. I'm putting them in irons," he said. And indeed, one of the lieutenant's teamsters emerged from the dark, dragging several leg irons with him.

"Lock them together," Haggarty demanded, his automatics never wavering from the Wobblies. The teamster did, clasping leg irons that connected one man's right leg to the next man's left leg, until they were all snaked together.

"Dear boy, what if one wants to answer the call of nature?" Juanita asked.

"They'll all have to answer it at the same time," replied Nero Haggarty. "A waterfall."

"That should be entertaining. I do believe I'll stay up and watch."

"You'll sleep safely tonight with the Wobblies tethered," Juanita said. "My son has a knack."

Hannibal sighed.

The Wobblies finished their quiche and the Raven-Haired Maid took their china plates away, along with the Tiffany forks.

"Because you tried to start a revolution with the Bonded Old Gildersleeve instead of enjoying Mrs. Brandy's largesse, you won't get any tomorrow night," Lieutenant Haggarty declared.

"Death to all plutocrats," Maginnis retorted.

The lieutenant sent them back to their own camp.

Hannibal Jones decided it wasn't safe to sleep in Belle's tent and started to slip away.

"Oh, no, you don't, Jones," she said. "You're my slave."

Hannibal agreed.

Chapter 34

Hannibal settled into the pink chaise and submitted himself to Yang's excellent shaving. The talented Yang brushed foaming lather into Hannibal's beard, stropped the straight-edge, skinned away the emerging whiskers, and patted away the residue. When his stubble had been scraped away and his jowls comforted with a moist hot towel and patted with talcum, Hannibal considered himself prepared to face the day, and retreated to the ruby silk tent to tie his bow tie, lace his high-top boots, and climb into his baggy tweed jacket. No one would ever mistake him for an uneducated man.

Belle slept soundly, having chosen to spend the morning abed after exhausting herself trying to awaken ardor in Hannibal, who was beyond ardor and had curled up in a fetal ball. Hannibal completed his toilet with a little witch hazel, and stepped out upon a fine morning. But not a silent one. Nero Haggarty had freed the Wobblies and set them to work, and now they were down in the inclined shaft of the Alice, picking away at the huge cave-in that barred entry. Now and then some mules dragging a wagon laden with rock erupted from the shaft, and the Wobblies emptied it over the side of the flat.

Hannibal finished his Napoleon-brandy-and-mango-juice cocktail, and eggs Benedict smothered in raspberries, provided suavely by Colonel Rathke, and wandered over to see what young Haggarty was about. The lieutenant was supervising the Wobblies, waving his automatic pistols like batons.

"I think, Lieutenant, you would be well advised to examine your cache of dynamite and see if the Wobblies stole much of it. They might yet blow up your mother," Hannibal said. "They might even blow up you."

"If I need advice, geologist, I'll ask for it."

"Just a thought," Hannibal said blandly.

"I'll prove to you that the dynamite case, which has been padlocked from the time we arrived, cannot be breached."

"Except for the sticks they blew off last night," Hannibal added.

"We'll see about that!"

Young Haggarty stormed past the old mine buildings, over the lip of the flat, and down a steep slope until he reached a bower where his powder was stashed. He stuffed his pistols in their holsters, extracted a key, and unlocked the thick brass padlock, which snapped open with a military click.

"There should be forty sticks gone," he said. "What those scoundrels did was slip a couple into their britches. The dynamite's quite secure, I assure you."

But it wasn't. When he lifted the hinged cover up, it was plain that perhaps a quarter of the five hundred sticks of Dupont Hercules had vanished.

"Well, I'll whip their hides until they confess!" he said.

Further exploration revealed that numerous caps were missing, and a whole coil of fuse.

"Someone has nipped enough dynamite to blow us off the flat," Hannibal said.

Lieutenant Haggarty withdrew his automatics, and surveyed the surrounding brush and rock, but spotted no culprits. "He'll be dealing with the artillery," Haggarty said. "Whoever stole that powder was messing with the artillery corps."

"I'd suggest you examine the Wobbly camp," Hannibal said, but he knew intuitively nothing would be found there. This was the work of the ghosts who had haunted the Alice Mine for years.

The army man strode across the flat, dug through the meager possessions of the Wobblies, mostly patched and grimy clothing, found nothing at all, and glared.

"It's not the Wobblies. Someone's stolen my dynamite," he said.

"Maybe your brother?"

"Attila? Never. He would leave a receipt."

"There's maybe a hundred sticks missing. And fuse and caps. Enough to blow you and your mother to smithereens."

"You don't have to keep reminding me, geologist. I think we'll just do a search. Belle's tent, your baggage, the tent of those old miners Babette brought up here, and the tents of the girls."

"I don't think the miners would stash a hundred sticks in the same place as caps and fuse. They didn't live long by taking chances like that."

"Jones, you stick to geology and I'll stick to explosives."

Hannibal sighed. "Start with Belle. Wake her up. Make sure she's not hiding dynamite under the comforter."

Haggarty leered. "I suspect that's exactly what she keeps under the covers."

Hannibal thought of walking toward Wickenburg, Arizona, and never stopping. These ex-wives and mistresses and children of old Lucky Haggarty were all crazy. What manner of sire and lover was he, to leave behind him so odd a bunch?

Nonetheless, the lieutenant pushed straight toward the ruby silk tent, and barged in.

Belle lay abed, awake, reading the Song of Solomon for clues.

"We're looking for dynamite," said the lieutenant.

"Well, my boy, you've come to the right place," she said.

Haggarty poked his pistol here and there, stabbing it into bags and trunks, but failed to uncover the stash.

"Must be over in Babette's camp. I'll run those old rummies clear back to Ely," he said, and pushed his way into the bright morning.

"What was that all about?" she asked Hannibal.

"Someone nipped a hundred sticks of dynamite last night. And it wasn't his Wobblies."

"That sounds like the Fourth of July," she said. "Are you going to be my Fourth of July tonight?"

Hannibal nodded wearily.

"Maybe the whole stratum of red rock above this flat will land on us," he said.

Having said it, he knew what he was about to do. "I'd better take a look."

"No, love. We're going to slip away and visit the Back Door. Just you and me."

"Right now, the lieutenant is rampaging through the other camps, looking for that powder. And if he doesn't find it, that means that someone, somewhere, has enough dynamite to blow everything on this plateau to bits, including you. Here's what you're going to do, Belle. We're going to pull out. We're going to let the colonel and Yin and Yang know, tell them to pack up, load up our wagons with the tents, and get out while we can. This is no longer a party; this is no longer a safe place. And your life is at stake, along with other lives."

She slipped out of bed, wearing her silky gown, and straightened his bow tie.

"If you say so," she said.

"I say so."

She dressed swiftly, startling him by climbing into blue jodhpurs of her own, along with a silky cream-colored blouse, and then they parted the flaps of the ruby silk tent and beheld the lieutenant furiously poking through Babette's tent and belongings, while she and her daughters squawked.

But he found nothing. Her old miners, led by Walt Cuban and equipped with spades and pry bars and wheelbarrows, were poking around in the old mining company office, ripping up plank floors and looking for hidden treasure.

"That's it," said Lieutenant Haggarty. "That Dupont is not on this flat or anywhere close to the Alice Mine."

The lieutenant beelined back to the shaft, where he could supervise the Wobblies.

Hannibal turned to Belle. "All right then, pack up while we can. There may be no time at all. Someone has nipped a lot of dynamite."

"Pull out, Jones? Never!"

"Away from the Alice. Out of harm's way."

"But we've had such a fine party."

"The party's over. Tell Colonel Rathke to pack up."

"He'll be so disappointed."

At least she wasn't resisting.

"There's one last thing I want to do," he said. "I'll be back in two hours."

She patted his cheek and smiled. "I'll be waiting."

He surveyed the flat. Babette's crew was putting her camp back together. Juanita's crew was doing nothing, but the Wobblies were toiling away in the shaft of the Alice Mine, and the old miners were poking holes in the old mine offices, looking for heaven knows what.

Hannibal quietly headed up the canyon, following a trail now familiar to him, and soon was climbing toward the rims, up a steep and perilous trail that threatened to topple him into the valley far below. His heart was soon hammering, and his lungs were pumping violently, but he didn't slow down. He didn't like the thought that lingered in his mind and wouldn't go away, and he knew he was racing against time.

So he clambered over giant red ledges, hung on to juniper brush, lifted himself higher and higher for an hour until at last he topped the red rim far above the plateau where the Alice Mine had slumbered so long. He was utterly out of breath, and sat down on some red sandstone until his lungs stopped heaving. The vista there always had delighted him, as it did now. He could see almost to tomorrow, almost to Arizona. It was so benign there, away from the racket on the flat below, where the Wobblies were doing some serious hard-rock mining. A playful breeze tugged at his baggy tweed coat and mussed his orderly hair.

Then, refreshed, he began patrolling the red rim-rock, many hundreds of feet above the Alice Mine and

244

the antlike figures on the flat. This was a red-rock and juniper country sloping upward from the rim toward distant highlands. He began a quiet tour of the rims, which jutted like a table edge high above the mine. And what he was looking for was fissures, cracks, and he found what he was looking for. There were plenty of such cracks, formed by weathering and settling of the earth, running in all directions. And in one he found a capped bundle of dynamite. A length of Bickford fuse led toward another bundle ten yards away, carefully wedged into another fissure.

He knew at once where the stolen dynamite had gone and what it would be used for, as soon as the "ghost" finished his preparations. There was enough dynamite up here, and enough caps and fuse, to blow the whole red sandstone rim down on the flat, and cover the flat under many feet of rubble, including everyone who happened to be there.

Chapter 35

In fear of his life, Hannibal studied the slopes, looking for whoever was lurking there. But he saw no one. He had only a jackknife, and no way to defend himself. The breeze slid softly through the juniper and the world was as peaceful as a Sabbath.

He edged down to the crack where the charge had been placed, and gently lifted it out. This charge consisted of three red sticks wired tightly together in a triangle. A copper-clad fulminate-of-mercury cap had been poked into the middle. Bickford fuse had been stuffed into the cap, and crimped flat with an ordinary plier.

Hannibal saw at once that this was not the work of experienced miners. Someone else. He tugged at the fuse and it pulled away easily. It ran toward another bundle twenty or thirty feet away. Another fuse had been jammed into the cap there. That was a similar bundle, three sticks wired tightly together with the cap in the middle. He tugged at that fuse and it easily pulled loose.

A veteran powder man would have cut open one of the sticks and inserted the cap into the gelatinous dynamite and bound up the stick. And he would have used a crimping tool to anchor the fuse in the copper cap. And he would have known that he would have to ignite each fuse, and not hope that the blast of one charge would ignite the fuse to the next charge.

Whoever was doing this knew very little about blasting. That meant that Babette's elderly miners, as well as Juanita's angry Wobblies, all experienced men, were not involved in this. All the signs pointed to Attila Haggarty, the sullen youth haunting these rims, rifle in hand, angrily driving people away from the Alice Mine any way he could. And yet . . . his mother and brother were camped below. It didn't make much sense.

But nothing made any sense. Here were Lucky Haggarty's spouses, children, and mistress, archrivals, bent on snatching the Alice Mine from one another, all because the old goat chose to start some mischief among his heirs. And here was someone prowling these lonely wastes bent on destroying them all. How many ghosts were floating around up there?

Angrily, Hannibal pulled the loose fuse out of the first charge and laid it behind a rock, and then did the same with the second charge. He worked carefully along the red rock, locating charges and disarming them, wary of company, his gaze searching through the juniper and boulders above. But he saw no sign of anyone. Even so, sometimes he felt the gaze of someone on him, felt the bore of a rifle aimed at him until his back prickled. It was in him to break and run, scramble away from this aerie while he could, but below were assorted people in mortal danger, unsuspecting people, jaded and innocent, humble and patrician. Hannibal would protect them if he could, and he wondered why he cared. The Wobblies were right: These were corrupt, useless parasites.

Within an hour he had located around twenty charges jammed into cracks in the red rimrock, and then he found no more. That was as far as the pyrotechnic ghost had gotten. They were all constructed in the same fashion. He gingerly disarmed them all, collected the caps, and hid them in a crevice he was sure would elude the ghost. Some of the charges would have misfired if he had done nothing, but he left nothing to chance. He collected the bundled dynamite and slid the Dupont Hercules into another crevice, well out of sight, and sprinkled enough dust and gravel over the dynamite grave to conceal the sticks.

But the ghost still had plenty of waxy red sticks of Dupont, plenty of copper-clad caps, and plenty of fuse. This situation would take plenty of watching. Hannibal slowly descended the rocky path, weary from his exertion, and walked onto the flat. He spotted the lieutenant directing his Wobblies as they dug at the landslide in the inclined shaft, and headed that way.

"I'm busy, Jones," the officer said.

"I found the missing powder."

"Well, bring it in and we'll use it."

"The powder was up on those rims up there, stuck into any crack in the rock that looked like a chance to blow hundreds of tons of red rock down on us."

That finally caught the lieutenant's attention. "Well, bring it all down and I'll keep it under lock."

"Whoever's up there still has some of it."

"Well, I'll take the Wobblies up there and get him."

"It might be your brother."

"Jones, my brother would not blow up me or our mother."

"This will take constant watching, or maybe we can track down whoever's up there."

"No time for that, Jones. We're going to blow out that landslide this afternoon, shore up the shaft if it needs it, and get whatever documents old Lucky left in there."

"That's optimistic."

"Not at all. My Wobblies are expert miners. We're

248

going to blow about thirty sticks straight off, and in a way that'll blow the rock right up the shaft."

"Unless a landslide of red rock lands on you and the Wobblies, blown by someone who wants you dead."

"Jones, you worry too much. You should have joined the army. We get things done, and if we're under fire we get things done faster."

"You're under fire, all right, Lieutenant. Don't say you haven't been warned."

Hannibal stormed away, furious at the bulge-eyed knucklehead. He found Belle sipping espresso under the marquee tent. She had done nothing to move her camp. She looked dashing in her blue jodhpurs. Much to his astonishment, she had acquired a pith helmet and now it perched prettily on her locks. Just as amazingly, she wore a blue shirt and a red bow tie and a tweed jacket.

"You like it?" she said. "I thought you're cute, so I ordered my own. Babette is green with envy."

Hannibal stared, glared, waved his arms, frowned, and finally found words. "I found that whole rim up there charged with the stolen dynamite. It was intended to land on your head," he said.

"But you fixed it, Jones, so it won't."

"Whoever's up there still has enough dynamite to kill you and everyone else."

"All right. We'll move."

"You mean it?"

"You're my hero, Jones. If you say we'll move, then we'll move."

249

"I want you to get off this flat just as fast as possible, Belle."

"Consider it done, sweetie."

She set down her demitasse of espresso and headed toward Colonel Rathke, who listened and nodded. The colonel swiftly dried his hands on his apron, and headed for Yin and Yang and the Raven-Haired Maid.

"We're moving down to that little bower where the water bubbles out of the mountain," she said. "That's such a lovely little valley. And then you won't worry your little old head or talk of going to Wickenburg anymore."

"I'm still heading for Wickenburg, just as soon as you're safe."

She patted his thigh and smiled.

Yin and Yang headed out to get the mules and harness them to the wagons. Colonel Rathke began striking camp. The Raven-Haired Maid dragged the portable bidet and tin bathtub out of the ruby silk tent.

"Have some espresso, Jones," she said.

He sat delicately, his gaze glued to the rimrock high above, planning to drag Belle to safety the instant he heard a crack, a rumble, and saw a wall of red rock descending. But time passed. He sipped the espresso and relaxed in the Nevada sunlight.

After a while, Yin and Yang returned and with much gesturing conveyed something or other to Belle.

"They say they can't find the mules or the wagons," Belle said.

"They've got to be somewhere! I'll go look."

"They say the ghosts took them. They were picketed, but the picket pins were pulled. And the wagons have vanished. And so have the wagons of the rest. The ghosts want us here."

"That was Attila Haggarty's work. I'll find him and fix him," Hannibal snapped.

But there was no place to go. The tents were already on the lip of the flat, as far from the brooding cliffs as they could be.

"We'd better drag things down the hill by hand," he said.

"That's fine, Jones. You carry my bidet."

Hannibal saw at once how this would go. "Do what you will. I'm going to drag my packs down to that spring creek and stay there."

"You mean you're leaving my bed and board?"

"I'm keeping my body in one piece."

"That'll never do," she retorted.

"I'm going to hunt for the mules and wagons. I've some experience with country like this," he said. "They'll head for grass and water."

"The wagons too?"

He ignored her, and collected some halters and lead lines and started down the slope.

"Wait, Jones, I'm going with you," she said.

He didn't want her along, slowing him down. "You stay here and watch the cliffs. Your flapping jodhpurs will catch on every catclaw and thorn along the way."

She grinned, sat down, pulled them off, and put her

shoes back on. What remained was a pair of ivory silk bloomers.

"There, that's better. I know a very nice bower near the Back Door claim where you can show me how much you care."

Babette and Juanita examined the two of them with bright gazes.

"I knew something was up," said Babette.

Hannibal sighed. He had never seen a semidressed lady in public. Actually, she was quite fetching in her ivory bloomers, tweed jacket, red bow tie, and pith helmet, but he wasn't going to say so, especially to her. He was a slave, all right, and all he wanted was an escape to Wickenburg.

Chapter 36

But before they could abandon the Alice Mine flat, an explosion erupted, blowing gray debris from the shaft of the mine. The Wobblies stood at a respectful distance while dust and shattered rock sailed into the sunlight.

Then, even before the dust settled, Lieutenant Haggarty was waving his pistols, driving the coughing Wobblies into the shaft with wheelbarrows and mucking tools. Hannibal watched this frenzied dance, pitying the Wobblies, whose lungs were being ruined by the greed of Juanita's son.

But what lay at the heart of precious metals mining if not greed? At the rate they were going, they'd pierce through that blockage within a day, and then the lieutenant would march into the unsafe bowels of the mine, hunting for deeds, wills, papers that were not there. Lucky Haggarty was not the sort to stuff such things into a sealed mine. That was too easy. Lucky was too much a rogue for that.

"The lieutenant's a driven man, Belle."

"So are we all, Jones."

"And for what? I'll bet Lucky didn't put so much as a streetcar token in there. But wherever he is, he's enjoying the show."

Hannibal eyed the red-rock cliffs nervously, and nodded to Belle. Getting away from that deadly flat was a good idea. And he had draft animals to find, including his own mules, so they could get out of there.

He helped her down a precipitous grade, through brush that snagged her silk bloomers, and soon they were on the path descending to the little creek. That's where he hoped to find his beasts of burden. If the livestock had drifted, they would drift toward water and feed.

Away from the busy flat, the world quieted. Mining is the world's noisiest business. He helped his friend Belle down another steep grade, and then they dropped to the mouth of the tiny creek purling out of a cleft of rock. The sweet hush of nature ruled here. The grass nurtured by the tiny rivulet had been cropped down to the roots by all the livestock, and the little valley was dotted with manure.

Belle headed straight toward that mysterious grave

with the blank headstone and studied it. Hannibal joined her, but the grave yielded no secrets. Here was the anonymous dead, if there was anything at all. Hannibal had the feeling it was intended for someone yet alive, someone whose name would be cut deep into the headstone when the moment came.

"I don't like death. Let's go," she said, leading the way. That was fine with Hannibal. He wanted his mules back. And he wanted to find out where the two or three dozen mules and oxen the various camping parties had employed to come to the Alice Mine were now. Did anyone other than himself grasp what a crisis was in the making?

She pushed out in front of him in her ivory bloomers, tweed jacket, red bow tie, and pith helmet. He felt vaguely flattered that this woman of style and fashion should seek to dress as he did. Had not Libby Custer, wife of the ill-fated George Armstrong Custer, dressed in her own perky blue officer's army uniform when the Seventh Cavalry marched toward the Little Big Horn?

The analogy unsettled him.

They hiked silently down the brush-choked gulch until suddenly they reached the cairn marking a corner of the Back Door claim. She recognized the place and tugged him toward the bower ahead, and when they reached it, she turned and smiled.

"I have to find the mules, Belle."

"Mules are a dime a dozen, Jones. There's only one Belle Brandy."

"Mules are how we get out of here, how we bring in food, supplies, how we leave, how we haul wagons or packs. How we live in a remote place twenty or thirty miles from anything."

She smiled and tugged at his baggy jacket.

"Who needs food?" she said cheerfully, pulling at his bow tie.

"Belle, we're on the Back Door claim. You look for a cairn or a cache while I look for mules."

She brightened. "A gold mine trumps love any time, Jones. You're talking to a gold digger, and not just any gold digger, but the world's most advanced and progressive gold digger with a doctoral degree in extracting gold from any man's pants."

That settled, they worked slowly through difficult country, choked by talus and brush and scrub trees. Belle found no markers, and Hannibal found no mules. Thorns threatened the integrity of Belle's silk bloomers, and she spent minutes untangling herself.

They reached the point where the gold seam outcropped for a few feet, the spot where Hannibal had chipped some samples.

"Here it is, Belle. That's gold-bearing quartz. That's where I found the samples."

"Gold? The real thing?"

"The same. Identical to the quartz in the Alice Mine, but shifted here by a fault and uplift."

"Gold! I want it!"

"Find that alleged will or deed and you've got it."

"Can't we just sneak it out of here?"

Hannibal laughed.

"Jones, you're driving me crazy."

Hannibal afforded himself a smile or two. "You can sit here and fondle the quartz, and I'll go hunting for mules," he replied.

"Maybe I will. I'm glued to this spot. I'm standing next to a bonanza."

"Well, fine, glue yourself to the quartz and I'll look for my mules."

She followed him reluctantly. But there were no mules, no livestock, no evidence of grazing in that rough terrain. He was growing worried. If the oxen and stock for all those camps had been stolen, save only the mules being worked by the Wobblies, they would all be in trouble as soon as supplies ran out.

They reached another corner cairn for the Back Door, and Hannibal had a good idea of how the claim lay. It started in the narrow canyon, vaulted up the cliff, and ended atop the cliff somewhere on benchland above.

"We'll have to search every inch of this before we can say there's no deed or conveyance here," he said. "But later. Right now I want my mules."

"You are single-minded," Belle said grumpily. "There's more to life than mules."

They worked another mile down the draw before Hannibal gave up. If the livestock had been driven down the mountain through that canyon, there would be lots of sign, but he found none.

"I don't know which way they went, but not this way," he said.

256

"You should let the servants hunt them," Belle said. "I didn't put you in jodhpurs to hunt mules."

Hannibal sighed. "Let's go see whether the red cliff has buried the Alice Mine," he replied. "I could use some Old Crab Orchard."

"That's not all I could use," she replied, but he ignored her. Ignoring Belle was the only way to deal with a woman like that, he decided, until she took his hand and squeezed it.

"You're a sweetheart, Jones," she said.

His mind was awhirl: *Why am I a slave to my passions? Why am I not behaving soberly, prudently, rationally? Why have I surrendered my will and well-being to a gold digger? Why has my brain migrated to my pants? Why am I a sucker?* But he had no answers.

They reached the Alice Mine late in the day, and just in time for another whump, as a blast in the shaft shot gray rock and a cloud of dust and debris out upon the flat.

"The Wobblies have been busy," Hannibal said. "That's the second shot in one day."

They found Babette, Juanita, and the girls drinking gin and bitters under the marquee tent and watching the show while the Raven-Haired Maid hovered about, responding to their every whim.

"Where were you?" Babette asked.

"Looking for missing mules," Belle said.

"Well, that's a strange thing to do. Have the servants do it."

"You're dressed like Jones, except for the

257

bloomers," Juanita said. "I must say, Belle, you're full of fun."

"He wouldn't wear bloomers," she replied.

"She hid my pants," he said.

"I think I'll have gin and bitters too." Belle waved at Colonel Rathke, who was hovering about his camp kitchen. "It wards off malaria, you know."

"Yes, that's why we're drinking it. Awful taste, but just the thing for a pestilential wilderness."

"There are no anopheles mosquitos here," Hannibal said.

"It's a wilderness drink, Jones. The British perfected it. That's the rule, you know. Drink gin and bitters and stay healthy. Look at us, blooming out here."

Hannibal gave up his efforts at education, and headed for the Alice Mine, keeping a wary eye on the brooding cliffs topped with red rock that lorded over the flat.

He found Lieutenant Haggarty waving at the Wobblies, urging them to plunge down the shaft and start hauling rock.

"Let the dust settle. It's hard on their lungs," Hannibal said.

"You stay out of it, Jones. What do you know about blasting?"

"How far are you?"

"Maybe we're in. We'll know in a moment."

"They've moved a lot of rock in one day."

"It beats twenty years in the pen for sedition, Jones."

"Not if it kills them."

The lieutenant glared. "This isn't your deal. I don't even want you around. We're going in as soon as there's a way in, and no one but the Wobblies and I will ever see what's in the Alice Mine."

"I hope you'll wait long enough to shore up that cave-in."

"We wait for nothing, Jones."

"Will you get air samples first?"

"My father always said the Alice was well ventilated."

"Will you check the timbering as you explore?"

"It's not going to land on my head, Jones."

"Write your will before you go in, then, Lieutenant."

But young Haggarty was waving his pistols at the Wobblies, and the Wobblies were coughing their way down the shaft.

Chapter 37

Hannibal eagerly awaited the evening's repast under the marquee tent, knowing that Colonel Rathke was the Georges Auguste Escoffier of the American West. His dinner companions this fine Nevada eve would be the ladies alone. Young Haggarty was off at the Alice Mine, waving his pistols at the Wobblies.

Belle seemed to be in a mood. This evening she wore a dress of black brocade, lightened only by a splash of white lace at the cuffs and collar. All she lacked was a doily on her head and she could be Whistler's Mother. She seemed subdued, even if her dinner guests chattered away in their ermine and pearls. Colonel Rathke seemed to be operating at a leisurely pace this soft desert eve.

When the gins and bitters were at last cleared away, the Raven-Haired Maid produced plates of oatmeal and alfalfa sprouts. Hannibal stared, tasted, discovered there was no taste, for the oatmeal lacked even salt and alfalfa sprouts defy the taste glands of the tongue. He stared, bewildered, at Belle.

"We are going to have a night of penance," she said.

"A what?"

"Penance, Jones. We are all greedy, all voluptuaries, all loose, and all the prisoners of lust. So this evening we will eat gruel and alfalfa and say prayers for the soul of the dead, whose great benevolence has blessed each of us."

"But I'm not repenting anything! How about a filet mignon for me?"

"Jones, that's cruel. Eating a Colonel Rathke speciality while the rest of us are doing our duty."

Hannibal subsided. He had been indifferent to food for years, and often swallowed a handful of raisins in lieu of tastier things when he was camping. Still, what Belle was this? And why did her guests smile benignly and nibble at alfalfa?

Alfalfa, of all things. He reserved alfalfa sprouts as a last resort. He would rather eat grasshoppers than alfalfa sprouts. But there he was, stuffing that crisp hairy stuff between his molars, and crunching it down. He studied Belle, as if she were a creature from

260

another planet. He was just growing fond of her, and he had even come to enjoy her little Hannibal Jones costume, with her own itty-bitty bow tie and pith helmet. He studied her, looking for signs of madness, but she spooned oatmeal into her ruby lips and gazed at the serene heavens, as stars popped out of the twilight.

The Alice Mine flat wasn't serene. Over at the mine, the movement of carbide lamps signaled furious activity, which continued nonstop. Hannibal eyed those looming cliffs, wondering when the blast would come that would bury them all under a mountain of red rock. How sad, he thought, to die under a pile of rock while eating oatmeal.

Some strange foreboding lay upon the camp this evening, something felt, something hovering in the background. Probably it had to do with young Haggarty's crew and the bobbing carbide lights over there. Hannibal didn't mind. This wasn't his party.

Then, suddenly, shouting. The Wobblies were exclaiming.

The ladies rushed toward the mine head, with Hannibal not far behind, and were met by Lieutenant Haggarty.

"We're in!" he said. "We pulled some rubble away and a great rush of air met us. We'll have enough cleared away in a few minutes to explore the gold mine."

He waved his pistols dangerously, and Hannibal considered dropping flat to the earth.

"Mother, you'll come with us. I'm leaving two Wobblies here to guard the shaft from intruders. They'll have baseball bats and bullwhips. The mine is ours! The rest of you will be trespassing if you set foot in it."

"That's nice," said Belle.

"There's nothing in there anyway," Hannibal ventured.

"Yes, there is and it's ours."

Hannibal watched, bemused, as the weary Wobblies wheelbarrowed two more loads out of the shaft, and then charged their carbide lamps.

Young Haggarty produced an electric torch, and then he and a nervous Juanita and four Wobblies pierced the shaft, their lights flickering at its mouth. Then all was darkness. Two other Wobblies guarded the mine head in the dark, but Hannibal wasn't inclined to test them, and neither were Babette's rummy old miners.

"Kneef lash ooda da," bellowed Walt Cuban.

"You'll need to put in your ivories if you want me to understand," Hannibal said.

But another rummy filled in. "They need a guide. Someone been in there. Mile or so of drifts and tunnels."

"All four of you know that mine?" Hannibal asked.

"Yep, every corner."

"What's their chances of getting lost?"

Cuban laughed gleefully, and the other rummies explained.

The Wobblies could explore only the top level. Without the cage running up and down the shaft, they couldn't get to the lower ones. The shaft to levels two and three was vertical.

So the search would come to nothing.

There was no point hanging around the mine head under the brow of those black cliffs towering into the night sky, so he urged Belle back to the marquee tent with its cheerful orange Japanese lanterns.

Back at the marquee tent, Belle threw herself into the pink chaise lounge and sulked.

"I'm going to do penance, so don't bring me any apple strudel and sugar-crusted kiwi fruit," she told Colonel Rathke.

"Penance for what?" Hannibal asked.

"For being evil."

Hannibal laughed, which was a mistake.

"You can sleep somewhere else tonight," she said. "I wish to purify myself."

"Woowoo," he said, getting into deeper trouble.

She dabbed tears from her eyes. "You don't know what it's like to be evil," she said. "You have to work at it all the time, or else goodness creeps in."

Babette ordered a double Bonded Old Gildersleeve for herself and Rothschild Bordeaux for her daughters, and waited grimly, a frown corduroying her lovely forehead. Colonel Rathke quietly served her a drink in a cordial glass, and each daughter received her Bordeaux in a goblet.

It was odd, waiting there for young Haggarty to

erupt from the Alice Mine shaft along with his mother and some Wobblies. Fate hinged on this moment, and yet no one seemed very tense. Maybe it was the helplessness. None of them were a match for six tough Wobblies. Lieutenant Haggarty could be doing anything down there. He could be burning Lucky Haggarty's will, forging it, or more likely, finding nothing at all.

Hannibal didn't know where to sleep. If he had found his blasted mules, he would have loaded up his packs and walked out. He had traveled in deep darkness hundreds of times, and a night departure held no menace. But he was stuck, at least until dawn. If worse came to worst, he'd walk back to Ely, carrying what he could and leaving the rest of his gear to fate.

Belle was still leaking tears and staring into the stars.

"Woowoo," he said, trying to cheer her up.

"Jones, this is a sacred moment," she replied.

An hour passed, and then lights bobbed at the Alice Mine shaft, and soon Lieutenant Haggarty and his mother emerged out of the gloom. Hannibal stared. Juanita showed not the slightest sign of having descended into a mine. Her gauzy white gown was just as white now as before.

But both were tight-lipped and morose.

"Nothing there," the lieutenant said. "Not a blasted thing. Bare rock. No papers. No cache." He turned to Hannibal. "You were wrong, Jones. That mine's in perfect shape. Not a rotted timber in it. Dry air. Just like walking down Broadway. Gold glinting at the faces."

Juanita settled grimly into a camp chair. "It was our last hope," she said. "When Lucky died, we hired a detective. He looked everywhere. He tracked down every connection. But he never found a thing."

"Why? What were you looking for?" Belle asked.

"Why?" Juanita struggled with something, and overcame it. "I will tell you. Whenever Lucky and I were . . . intimate, he always poured his heart out to me. Juanita, you're the most beautiful woman in all the world. Juanita, everything I have will be yours. Juanita, my last cent will go to you and you alone. And all these years . . . I've waited for it to come true."

Babette was laughing and not kindly. "Why, that old rogue! He told me the same thing! And at the same moments! And with the same fervor! I thought I was the one and only! And I looked, too, even hiring a court clerk to examine every public document for a clue, for a will, for a hidden asset! It cost me thousands!"

Juanita began to weep. Belle simply smiled familiarly.

The sheer duplicity of Lucky Haggarty lay upon his wives now.

Hannibal turned to the lieutenant. "Did you look in the lower levels?"

"We did. There was a perfectly good iron ladder down the side of the shaft. Nothing, bare rock and square-set timbers, and no sign of anything. It was our last hope."

"That cruel man. He promised me everything and it was all just a joke," Babette said.

Juanita was leaking tears. "All these years, all these years, all the dreaming, the searching, the hoping. Now we don't have any hope left."

"The Alice Mine is full of gold. Plain and obvious," said the lieutenant. "Millions and millions. In plain sight. Thick seams. And no one owns it. If my father were alive, I'd throttle him. I'd turn him over to Congress."

Babette downed her bourbon and branch and thrust her empty glass at Colonel Rathke.

"Damn him, damn him, he was so . . . marvelous in bed," she muttered.

"He never promised me anything," said Belle. "But I got all I could. When he was sleeping—after our intimate moments—I emptied his pockets. But I had my own investigator hunting for Lucky's moolah, only he hid it, damn him."

A strange clatter filled the night. Two people were approaching, one looking like an Indian or a mountain man, dressed in fringed buckskins and moccasins, with long light hair drawn back into a ponytail, and the other—Hannibal knew them both. One was Juanita's other son, Attila Haggarty, and he was carrying a rifle and it was aimed in the general direction of the other person walking ahead of him, who was Faye Haggarty.

Chapter 38

Attila herded Faye into the lantern-lit marquee tent.

"Here's the ghost of the Alice Mine," he said. "I caught her trying to kill my mother and brothers."

Faye might have had a rifle poking her along, but she was utterly in command. She stopped, claimed some turf, and addressed Belle.

"Tell Colonel Rathke I'll have a gin and bitters and dinner," she said.

Belle did.

"And tell this interloper, Jones, to get out of my sight."

Hannibal thought the woman was all the more attractive for disdaining him.

"He is our friend," Belle said.

"This bastard boy caught me trying to kill you," she said.

"She was up there sliding some charged and fused dynamite into cracks right above the Alice mine head," Attila said. "So I told her she wasn't going to start an avalanche on my mother. She could avalanche Nero, but not my mother."

"Now, Attila, put that thing down and have a gin and bitters," Juanita said.

"No one's thanked me for saving any lives or figuring out who's ghosting around here."

"I thank you," said Hannibal.

"You don't count."

"I have no wish to take away your family's wealth. I came here to see how the mine might be put into operation."

"They all say that."

Juanita's dander was up. She stormed at Attila. "Then I'll thank you and tell you to go back up there until you're civil. We are mourning just now. There were no papers in the mine."

"All right, I'm staying." Attila settled into a green and gold camp chair, his rifle bore never far from Faye, who elaborately ignored him.

"A nasty young man, like all bastards," Faye said. "It's a pity you found no papers or wills or deeds. Then I could take them away from you. I'm Lucky's wife. You're all whores of one sort or another."

"I'm glad you figured that out," said Belle. "I'm a gold digger too."

Colonel Rathke appeared with a tall and sweated glass of gin and bitters, which he handed to Faye. She ate delicately, enjoying the sublime food.

Hannibal couldn't get over her beauty. She was the queen of the beauty parade, looking all the more fetching in buckskins and beaded moccasins, her ash-blond hair, tinged with gray, cascading down her slim back.

"I believe you tried to kill us, more than once," Babette said.

Cleopatra and Delilah looked very solemn.

"That's what you get for running around half naked," Faye said. "Tell that cook I want a meal. Let's see. Quiche sounds right and that salad with the mangos and crushed peanut brittle."

Colonel Rathke understood, bowed, and retreated toward the camp kitchen.

"It doesn't matter whether you find a will or a deed. The Alice Mine belongs to me. Any court in the land would give it to Lucky Haggarty's one legitimate wife, as a dowry."

"Oh, shut up," Attila Haggarty snapped.

"We checked every level," Nero said. He had one of his pistols in hand in case he had to shoot Faye or Attila.

"The mine belongs to somebody," Hannibal said. "Some company called Western Holdings pays the taxes regularly. It has an office in San Francisco but the room is empty. Some company pays rent for that office."

"Your advice is not wanted, Jones," said Faye.

Attila downed some booze and stood up. "This woman's a murderer. She tried to dump red rock on everyone here. She nearly blew up that whole cliff. I've been stalking her for days and finally got her. I'll take her to Ely and put her in jail."

"A pack of bigamists and bastard children and Wobblies and old wrecks of miners are going to put me in jail?" Faye smiled so brightly that Hannibal went weak at the knees. "I buy and sell judges," she added.

"Mrs. Haggarty, where are the mules?" Hannibal asked.

"So well hidden you'll never find them. If you live, you'll walk out."

Hannibal addressed them all. "Maybe you should seal the Alice Mine and leave," he said. "Cave in the shaft so gold doesn't walk away and get out. The papers aren't here. None of you owns it."

"Seal the mine, Jones?" yelled Lieutenant Haggarty. "You're daft. There's millions there. The mine is open. I intend to mine it. It belongs to me. I'm the one who opened it. If nobody owns it, it's mine."

"And how many days do you expect to survive?" Faye said.

"To rich old age, madam. Artillerymen might get deaf, but they don't croak."

"You're not going to mine it. I've got my claim and I'll make sure to get it, and if you mine what's not yours, the courts will hear about it in an hour," said Babette.

Belle laughed. "You see? We can't even agree to share it."

"You're not a part of this; you and Jones have nothing to say about it," Juanita said. "Lucky's slut."

"Gold digger," Belle retorted.

"Well, I'm vamoosing as soon as Faye tells me where my mules are," Hannibal said. "There's no secrets in the Alice. There's no reason for a geologist to be here."

"Sorry, Jones. You'll have to walk. That's for trying to seduce me," Faye said.

"Did he succeed?" Belle asked.

"Don't be ridiculous."

"I had to seduce him. He didn't know how to seduce me," Belle said. "Isn't that sad, going through life innocent of what counts?"

"He looked awful in jodhpurs," said Faye. "I thought the British had taken over Nevada."

"That's how I made a slave of him. Jodhpurs do that to a man."

"He'd look better in knickerbockers," Faye said.

"Knickers! Now there's an idea!" Belle said.

"What do I do with her?" asked Attila, waving his rifle at Faye.

"Shoot her if she runs," Juanita said. "She tried to murder us. She dumped a hundred tons of red rock on Jones here, and tried to trap him and Belle in the shaft. Heaven knows how many others she's tried to kill."

"It should be obvious to you that I scared away all sorts of mine-robbers over the years and that I preserved this mine. If I hadn't, it would be a dead mine," Faye said. "Every ounce stolen."

"How many people did you kill? That's what I want to know," Belle said.

Faye stood straight, a faint grim smile playing across her thin lips, and said nothing.

"There have been ghost stories for years," Hannibal said quietly. "Mysterious rock slides, prospectors' mules and gear vanishing, specters in the night."

"Whatever it took," Faye said.

"Including murder?"

Faye's head bobbed. Hannibal marveled at her

271

beauty, the ash-blond hair, the slim figure in the soft buckskins. But this woman had come within an ace of killing him, and more than once.

"Lieutenant Haggarty, I suggest you take her to the authorities in Ely, with a formal complaint signed by those present, and see to it that she's brought to trial," Hannibal said.

"You stay out of it, Jones," Juanita said. "You have absolutely no claim on this mine and it's not your business. This woman will be dealt with by the army."

"I'm on leave, Mother," said Nero. "But I have a little army of my own. Speaking of which . . ." He hastened into the dark, waving his pistols, and soon there rose the sound of complaint, and then all six Wobblies drifted into the lantern light, herded by Lieutenant Haggarty.

They stood in a cluster, sullen and amused at the same time, looking ready to massacre all the plutocrats congregated under the striped awning of the marquee tent.

"Empty your pockets!" the lieutenant bellowed.

"And if we don't?"

"One Wobbly will disappear. Maybe six Wobblies will disappear."

They milled about, and finally Maginnis pulled his pockets free, spilling small rocks onto the clay.

"Highgrading! I knew it!" Haggarty bellowed. "Stealing my ore!"

"It's the people's ore. You don't own it," said one.

"Empty those pockets!"

272

More ore spilled to the ground.

"Drop your pants!" the lieutenant bellowed.

"Really, Nero, is that needed?" Babette asked. "I may have to send my daughters to their tent."

"They'll have rocks in their underdrawers."

"What a marvel," said Belle. "Do you want me to search?"

"You just stand back."

"Don't look," Babette commanded Cleo and Delilah. The girls pretended to look at the Big Dipper.

"You first!" Haggarty bellowed, waving his weapon at a Wobbly.

"The rich not only are parasites, they shame a workingman," the Wobbly said.

He turned his back and slowly lowered his ragged pants, revealing grimy underdrawers.

"Shake that rock loose," Haggarty commanded.

The man gently did, and nothing tumbled out.

Delilah sighed.

One by one the Wobblies did as they were told, but not a single piece of ore fell to the earth. Just as slowly, they drew up their ragged pants and stood there, somehow more dignified than their tormentor.

Hannibal wished he had not witnessed any of it.

Chapter 39

Hannibal dragged himself from the bed, stood on rubbery knees, and wished he had gotten some sleep. Whenever he had tried, Belle had whispered,

"Woowoo," and he knew he was sunk. It would take a month to gain his strength back.

Nonetheless, now she slept, the dawn's light piercing redly through the ruby silk tent. He was not the first up at the Alice Mine. The rattle of ore being shoveled into wheelbarrows disturbed the deep peace of the morning.

He started to dress, intending to wear his pants, but she had hidden them again. She had laid out the brown jodhpurs, which he despised only slightly less than the blue ones. She was reminding him that he was her slave.

But he would have news for her when she woke up. He was heading for the gold mines of Wickenburg, and nothing would stop him. He would try to find his mules, but even if he had to abandon his costly wilderness and geology gear, he would do so if that was how to purchase his freedom from these bizarre relatives of Lucky Haggarty.

He settled into the pink chaise lounge at the marquee tent, and soon enough Yin appeared with a razor, strop, hot water, and a lathering brush and mug. Soon Yin was scraping away the morning beard and applying hot moist towels to Hannibal's face, a pleasure he was reluctant to surrender. But the thought of enduring one more day with these warring heirs of Lucky Haggarty was all it took.

He finished his toilet, and was surprised to find Faye sitting quietly in the marquee tent, awaiting breakfast. Last night Nero Haggarty had put her in irons along with his Wobblies. This morning she wandered freely. Last night the rest were ready to haul her to Ely and charge her with attempted murder. Now she sipped breakfast tea, looking ravishing in her trim buckskins.

"Won't you join me, Mr. Jones?" she said. "I believe Belle's excellent Colonel Rathke can whip up something delicious."

He stared. "Has something changed? I believe last night you hoped I would vanish."

"That was yesterday. This is today."

"He freed you."

"Of course. The lieutenant has his mine and his Wobblies to keep us out of it, and the sooner we leave, the happier he'll be. He suggested I have a bite and depart. He's won, you know. The army won."

"And he didn't mind that you tried to bury him and his mother under tons of rock?"

She smiled. "Not at all. He would cheerfully have done the same to me."

"There will be no need to kill me. I'll be out of here within the hour," Hannibal said acerbically. "You can speed the process along by telling me how to find my mules."

"I think you can find them easily," she said.

"I think I can too. There's water and grass upslope, but only desert and no water downslope."

She smiled. "There. You see? You know how to live in wilderness. But you won't be leaving in an hour. You're still wearing your slave collar."

"My what?"

275

"Jodhpurs, Jones. She took your pants."

"What has that to do with anything?"

"You are so naive about women, Jones."

The colonel arrived mysteriously, carrying two hot plates laden with pumpkin pie topped with green-dyed whipped cream, eggs Benedict dyed pink, and sliced kiwi fruit, served in a hollowed-out grapefruit.

"You see? I'd pay a fortune for him," she said, daintily slicing into the pink eggs Benedict and sliding small bits between her trim lips.

She was trim all over, trim facial lines, trim lips, trim body, he thought. If she had wings on her back she could be Mercury. Utterly unlike Belle, who had voluptuous qualities, or Juanita, who was earthy, or Babette, who was peaches-and-cream feminine.

When she had finished, she dabbed her lips with a linen napkin supplied by the Raven-Haired Maid.

"You have prejudices," she said.

"None that I know of."

"Of course you do. You consider me a blond ice goddess."

"I really . . ."

"Tut-tut, Jones. I am the iceberg. I lost Lucky Haggarty because I lack the warmth, and shall we say, the amorousness, of his other women. That's what you think. Admit it."

"Well, I admit it."

"And you're wrong. I have all the warmth and passion of your Belle or his other women. When we first were married, our, shall we say, private lives were more beautiful and joyous than anything I could have imagined in my straitlaced girlhood. That was before Lucky struck it rich, found gold, and got the Alice. I was the happiest of women, with my Lucky to love and comfort each day and night. Are you religious, Mr. Jones?"

"Ah, that's a private matter. My geology leads me to question some things."

"I am. We were married in the Episcopal Church. I remain a member and a believer. I believe I am the only one here who possesses any such beliefs."

Hannibal nodded. He knew of nothing remotely spiritual in Belle, and saw little of it in Juanita or Babette.

"A goodly faith makes the relationship between a husband and a wife all the more beautiful, Mr. Jones. There is a beauty there that your Belle craves, although she doesn't know what she's looking for. Can you not see it in her hungers, in her eyes? I see it."

Hannibal did not dare respond, except with a nod.

"Gold changed everything, Mr. Jones. Gold ate out Lucky's character and left him without a scruple. Gold led him to women. Belle was but one of dozens. Babette and Juanita each answered a need in him, a lust. But still my Lucky came home, and I thought perhaps gold might bring him contentment too, and the pleasures of our hearth. Instead . . . Mr. Jones . . . It brought me a horrible disease he had gotten, and which took almost forever for me to overcome, and

I'm not sure I truly have. Do I shock you? Am I mentioning the unmentionable?"

Hannibal gulped the last of his eggs Benedict and popped the kiwi fruit.

"Poor Mr. Jones. I am leading you where you would not go. You are rather a timid bachelor, I think."

"Ah . . ."

"And the result of this vile disease, Mr. Jones, was to transform me from a loving and eager wife into an iceberg, blond, handsome, demure, and a million miles distant from any male. Does that make sense?"

"Yes, of course."

"Still, when you showed up at my door, I was flattered, even if I dumped a bucket of water over your head."

She laughed suddenly. He had never seen her laugh. There was no bitterness in the laughter, but only affection, and for a moment her iceberg eyes blazed with fire.

She sipped coffee and smiled. "He went his way, and I rarely saw him. My bedroom door was locked. Next thing I knew, he was getting married here, there, everywhere. I'm not even sure if the whole lot's collected here. He may have had a few more wives stashed away somewhere. But this lot is enough. Two spare wives and a mistress. And of these, he loved only Belle. The others he married just for fun. You have to understand that the more gold Lucky had, the more outrageous he became. By the time he was a multiple millionaire, he was truly a scandal."

"Did you like him that way?"

"I adored him always, but I am also a woman of faith, Mr. Jones, and a woman who draws lines. Rules are for our own good, and for our own happiness." She smiled broadly. "I thought to tell you. I'm sure you wanted to know."

"Well, Mrs. Haggarty, I'm not sure I've ever experienced such a confession, or conversation. But I thank you."

"You are too politic, Jones. Now you have an opportunity to tell me about yourself."

"Oh, nothing much to tell. I take pride in one thing, though. I am the foremost mining geologist in the world when it comes to turning dead or dying mines into profitable ventures."

"So I heard from the dozen spies I have in Ely, watching out for my interests. But what of all this? What of Belle?"

"Ah . . ."

"She is a very good lover, Jones. She has reduced you to slavery."

He nodded. He could not escape it. Belle's lips and hands and lush body and enthusiasms had turned him into a lickspittle.

"I will give you some advice, Jones. Be a happy slave. She has done wondrous things to you. The Jones I see now is not the Jones who approached me a while ago. Go bring dead mines to life, and renew yourself in Belle's arms."

Faye amazed him. No woman had ever spoken to

him with such candor. She was a paradox, a woman of faith and yet a woman who did not condemn. Not once in all of this had she condemned Belle or the bigamous wives. In fact, Faye had complimented them in her own way.

"I feel somewhat the boy in your presence," he said. "You are very worldly, and have lived far more than I."

"Then live! You've certainly found someone who will make you happy, and you in turn give something to Belle that she truly needs."

That was ground he was not ready to probe, and he rose suddenly.

"Would you care to walk with me and fetch the livestock?" he asked.

"No, Jones, I had a bad night. That beast put me in irons and I was forced to sleep on a carpet. I hope the Wobblies revolt and seal him in the Alice Mine and blow the shaft shut forever."

Suddenly she was the iceberg again.

"I will tell Belle that you are looking for your mules and that you will be leaving for Wickenburg," she said.

"How did you know I am going to Wickenburg?"

"Ghosts know everything, Jones," she said.

Hannibal pondered that, and what he heard, with skepticism.

"Tell me, Mrs. Haggarty. If you are a woman of faith, why did you try to kill us?"

"I didn't. I've scared a few prospectors off by

sending a few rocks down. I don't have the strength to do much more. No, Mr. Jones. Not I. There's a real ghost haunting the Alice, and I think that ghost is Lucky himself."

Chapter 40

Hannibal collected two halters and lead lines and started up the valley, but Faye caught up with him.

"I changed my mind. Want company?" she asked.

Hannibal agreed. She would lead him to his mules and presumably the rest of the livestock, including Belle's and Babette's animals.

This trail took them away from the plateau and up a long grade toward the high country, which was dotted with bristlecone pine and grasses. Hannibal didn't doubt that his mules were far from the Alice Mine flat, maybe several miles.

As soon as they rounded a bend, the racket from the mining diminished along with the aura of greed and anger.

"The Wobblies are working hard," he said.

"That's because Nero offered them a piece of the mine and supervisory jobs when the mine is started up. I heard him last night. Each gets one percent of the profits and a top position. That's how he turned six anarchists into capitalists. After some ritual complaints about the ways of the world, and some readjustment, they all signed on."

"But the mine's not his."

"Possession is nine-tenths of the law, Jones. I wish I had remembered that. I am Lucky's widow. The Alice belongs to me, papers or not. I simply should have hired a supervisor and crew and started it up again."

"Do you need it?"

"Gold evokes its own lust, Jones. It's not a matter of need. It's a matter of sitting on a gold mine like a fat hen."

They hiked through a peaceful dawn, enjoying the deep silence of the Nevada wilds. The higher they climbed, the closer they came to a moisture zone where the desert gave way to grass and shrubs, and finally to sparse timber. They were climbing a valley that led toward a distant peak.

"I'm familiar with that sentiment," he said.

"Just what exactly do you do around dead mines?"

"I look for ore that was overlooked or processed inefficiently. Some mines have rich tailings, ore that contains more gold or silver or other metals than anyone knew. Others were never properly explored. Modern geology and core drilling enable me to assess them. Other mines were shut because of quarrels or debt, and are still loaded with minerals. I go in, assess the prospects, work out a deal with the owners in which I share my expertise, usually for a share but sometimes for a flat price, and make a comfortable living."

"That's what I found out. You're one of a handful, and the one with the reputation."

"That is true. It's a rare vocation."

"And you wanted a part of the Alice?"

"I want no part of the Alice, but I did want to sell my findings to its owners if I could find them. I came here looking for opportunities, but all that is over. I want only to remove myself from eastern Nevada."

"If I get the Alice Mine, I'll hire you," she said.

They toiled up a steep grade and she led him into a mile-long side canyon. At its highest point he could make out the animals, quietly grazing in the early sunlight.

"Thank you," he said.

"For dumping water on your head, or for refusing your advances?"

"For not putting me in jodhpurs."

They struggled up the talus-strewn grade, passed a hidden spring not visible from below that seeped water into a tiny hollow of rock, and finally reached a smooth grassy basin where a dozen mules and horses and a few oxen slept or grazed. He saw his two mules at once. They were staring at him, their big ears rotated straight toward him.

He had no trouble approaching one and haltering it, and handed the lead line to Faye. In another minute he had the second mule haltered, and they began the long trek down to the Alice Mine, each leading one of his mules. He was elated. Within the hour he would be heading for Ely.

"There wasn't any grass left down there near that spring below the mine," he said. "You did us a favor putting the stock up here."

"I didn't do it; the ghost of the Alice did it."

"I don't happen to believe in ghosts."

"There's one around here. I think it's Lucky. That's his grave, you know, down there next to the little stream that pops out of the mountain."

"No, I don't know, and I can't imagine it. How do you know?"

"I just do. You can't be married to a man for a lifetime and not know."

"It has no marker. It's an empty stone. It's a grave site waiting for someone."

"That's just the way Lucky Haggarty would want it. A prank to the last gasp."

"He was a joker?"

"A practical joker. And those are mean people, Jones. You know what practical jokers do? They humiliate others. That's Lucky. After he got rich from the Alice and a dozen other gold mines, people were always trying to pry money loose from him, and the more they tried, the worse he became. He got mean. He enjoyed their groveling. Their begging and whining. He devised all sorts of humiliating things and made them do it. Did a woman want his cash? He'd make her spend a night in a bordello before he'd unloose a dime. Did a man try to pry something loose? Lucky would make him volunteer his wife. Nasty man, Lucky. But the awful thing is, Jones, that I loved him. Never stopped. To this very moment I grieve for him and weep because I lost him."

They negotiated a perilous stretch of trail silently,

and found the climate had changed when they reached the bottom. It was desert again, sere, brooding, and getting hot.

Hannibal marveled. The more he heard about Haggarty, the more appalled he was. The gold magnate seemed to operate outside of moral or any other sort of law, and yet women adored him. His wives and mistress loved him and fiercely defended him.

A half hour later, they reached the Alice Mine. The flat hummed with life. Various breakfasters occupied the marquee tent. Babette's rummy old miners had joined forces with the Wobblies and were cleaning out the shaft. Colonel Rathke was serving up crèpes suzette with sliced mangos. Babette and her girls were dressed in white gauze that was pierced by the morning sun. And Belle was having her feet massaged by the Raven-Haired Maid, while sipping espresso.

"There you are, Jones," she said. "If you're going to go, I'll give you your pants back."

"He should be in knickers," Babette said. "And some argyle socks. They'd be just right, don't you think?"

Hannibal ignored them and headed for the ruby silk tent, determined to load up and get out. He picketed the mules and went in. But sure enough, lying on the bed inside were his trousers. That made his first order of business getting rid of the jodhpurs now and forever, and if he had any sense he would carry them out to Colonel Rathke's cook fire and burn them.

He tugged savagely at his belt and undid his shoes,

and then yanked his jodhpurs off, good riddance, gone forever, this was over, he was free!

Then she slipped the ruby door aside and stood there, watching him. She was particularly beautiful this morning, aglow with life.

"I prefer you with your pants off, Jones," Belle said.

He ignored her, and tugged his own blessed brown twills up his legs. He turned away from her to button up.

"I'll miss you," she said.

It was the way she said it that surprised him.

He tied his shoelaces and slid the belt through its loops. His two packsaddles and packs lay in a corner.

"Thank you," he said neutrally.

"Faye took you to the mules. Is my stock up there too?"

"Yes, in a side canyon about two miles up the valley. And so is Babette's stock. They're on good grass and water. Yin or Yang could find them easily."

"What did Faye say?"

"She said she's not the ghost of the Alice Mine. There's a real ghost. And she said that's Lucky's grave down in the gully where the creek comes out of the mountain."

"Lucky's?"

"That what Faye thinks. She has no proof. She said it's because she's known him all her life and that's what she thinks."

"But why there?"

"Who knows?"

"Did she say why there's no name on the stone?"

"Another of Lucky's jokes."

"Maybe Lucky wanted to be anonymous."

"Maybe it's not Lucky at all," Hannibal said.

He found a brush and headed into the sunlight and brushed the mules down, and then he hoisted a pack-saddle over each, and cinched them tight. She watched, a strange resignation on her face. He glanced at her covertly, and found sadness written all over her. Was this Belle?

"What are you going to do?" he asked.

"I don't know."

"Why are you staying here? The lieutenant commandeered the mine, and your chances of snatching it from him are about zero. He simply walked in and took it. Not a bad idea, after all the hunting for a will or deed or papers."

"I don't know, Jones. I'm staying because I like it here. You made me feel at home in the wilderness. I've never had such a good time. That's because of you."

He hoisted the panniers to the packsaddle and buckled them down, and then loaded the second pack. And then he was done. He was free. He even possessed his pants. He had all his mining and geology and camping paraphernalia. He could escape. He could reach Ely by midnight. He could leave for Arizona tomorrow.

And she was crying.

Chapter 41

Belle's tears soaked his blue shirt. She held him fiercely, knocking his pith helmet askew and deranging his red polka-dot bow tie. He didn't know what to do except wait her out, so he held her quietly, while red light streamed through the walls of the ruby silk tent.

Then she quieted and smiled. "Woowoo," she said.

He felt his knees go wobbly, but then he recovered his stern resolve and stood stiffly, waiting for the crisis to pass. With a free hand, he adjusted his pith helmet until its latitude and longitude matched his cranium's.

That's when Faye arrived.

"Hello," she said. "May I?"

Without waiting, she pushed through the ruby silk door, and instantly backed away.

"I'm sorry. I'll leave you to your entertainments. I was looking for a shovel, and Jones has one on his pack mule."

"A shovel?" he asked.

"I know where Lucky hid the papers. I'm sure of it. I've known him forever, and I know how his mind worked. I need a shovel."

"But there are lots of shovels."

"No. The Wobblies have theirs and they snatched every spade in Juanita's camp. The old miners have all of Babette's. Someone has all of yours. Except for Jones's here."

"Madam, I'm on my way to Ely."

"But I know where the papers are. It came to me. Of course! I said to myself. That's Lucky for you."

"Where?" asked Belle.

"In his grave."

Belle recoiled. "Grave! Dig him up? Look for papers on his . . . body? Surely you wouldn't! It's disgusting. I respect the dead. And who would put a will or ownership papers into a coffin? No, Faye."

"I haven't the slightest scruple about digging him up," Faye replied. She eyed Belle. "I have some scruples you don't have, and you have one that I don't have. So if Mr. Jones will lend me the shovel . . ."

"Madam, please inquire among the other camps," Hannibal said.

"I have. No luck. But the idea titillates."

Hannibal could see what was coming. For one thing, he was not about to wander toward Ely until someone had excavated old Lucky Haggarty's coffin, opened it, and hunted for documents that would not be there. And then everyone would stand around, pretending not to be ashamed of their greed and rapacity, and he might flee down the trail, late in the afternoon. It was not a pleasing prospect.

"How do you know they're there?" he asked.

"Mr. Jones, how does your body know that Belle is embracing you?" Faye replied.

It wasn't logic, but it was persuasive.

"It isn't right," he said.

"That's what Lucky counted on."

289

"We're not grave robbers."

"That's just what Lucky wanted us to think."

"I respect the dead."

"Lucky has kept himself alive in this camp, at this old mine, because he wanted to keep himself alive."

"If we open that coffin, we'll all be horrified. Madam, bodies don't, well, survive. . . ."

"Jones, you let me dig. You can come and wring your hands if you want. I'm going to get my inheritance. I have dower rights, if nothing else, being his one and only true wife."

Belle's mood changed. "Come along, Jones. You can do our worrying and hand-wringing for us."

"I can also lead my mules toward Ely and get free," he said.

"And then you'd never know," Belle said.

She had him there.

"Woowoo," she said, and elbowed him.

That did it. He settled his helmet and emerged into morning light, undid the shovel from one of the packs, and handed it to Faye.

A remarkable parade followed. First Hannibal leading his laden mules, then Belle, then Faye waving the shovel, then Juanita, then Babette along with Cleopatra and Delilah, then Colonel Rathke, Yin and Yang, and the Raven-Haired Maid. Over at the shaft of the Alice Mine, Wobblies and rummy old miners stared, until Lieutenant Haggarty, waving his pistols, put them back to work on the rock pile.

Hannibal was not enjoying himself. He had gotten

free, gotten packed, put on his pith helmet, and was ready to bolt for Ely when this miserable crew conspired to keep him on hand a few hours longer. Well, they would get what they deserved. He would not dig, nor would he lift the casket if there was one down there, nor would he open it, nor would he look in. Let them gasp and fall back and slam it shut, and ashamedly pile clay over it again. Then he would retrieve his handy spade, buckle it onto his packs, and start for Ely, and no woowoos would stop him or even slow him down.

That decided, he worked his way down the terrific grade below the flat, through prickly brush, tugging the balky mules through nettles, descending two hundred feet until at last he burst into that narrow gulch where the little rivulet popped out of the mountain, ran in the open for a few hundred yards, and then vanished into the earth.

There indeed was the grave, its mysterious headstone poking upward, nameless and anonymous. Horse and mule droppings littered the site. A gentle mound announced the presence of something down below, four or five feet.

"Well, there he is," said Belle. "You were right, Faye. The moment you said it, I knew you had it. Lucky had himself carted out here and planted."

"He always liked a ride," Faye said dryly.

Faye did not hesitate. She stabbed the spade into the clay, and tried to shove it into the ground with her moccasin-covered feet, only to find that moccasins weren't the footwear of choice for all of this.

The rest, having descended into the gulch, surrounded the grave, staring solemnly at it, unsure about any of this.

"Jones, you dig," Faye said, handing him his spade.

"Ah, perhaps Colonel Rathke . . ."

But the colonel bowed from the waist, a deep, gracious, and absolutely meaningful bow, and declined.

Hannibal thrust the spade at Juanita, at Babette, at the girls, and finally at Attila, who brought up the rear.

"You're a Haggarty; you may have the honor of disinterring your father," Hannibal said.

"I'm here for the show. It's a joke, Jones. They've all ganged up on you."

"I fear you're right, young man. So you can dig, and find nothing, and end this charade."

But Attila smiled and shook his head.

There it was, a grave unlike any other in the ruins of the Alice Mine. They waited. Hannibal stood stock still, shovel in hand, pith helmet, red bow tie, baggy tweed jacket, genuine pants. They waited. He waited. They sighed. He sighed.

Then, seeing as how this vulturish crowd could not be dispatched with a stake through its heart, he began to dig. Daintily, of course. A little bit, a small clod, a carefully measured bite of soil, so slowly that they began standing on one foot and then the other, and he heard a dozen silent protests. But he did not hurry. He had found a fine new tactic, watchful waiting, slow, slow, slow.

292

"Good Lord, Jones, hand it to me," Belle said.

He did, standing at attention like a minuteman.

She hacked away enthusiastically, and when she tired she handed the shovel to Faye, who smiled and handed it to Juanita, who dug a little and handed it to Babette, who took two bites and handed it to her girls, who giggled and passed it back to Jones.

This passing the buck was getting him nowhere, so he decided to get it done and get out. Wickenburg beckoned. The desert heat was building, so he doffed his baggy tweed coat and handed it to Belle, took a firm grip on the spade, and began chewing up ground in earnest. Once he had broken through the hard surface, the interior clay sliced up easier, and he made steady progress. But digging a grave is no small project, and he toiled for what seemed a long time even to dig down a couple of feet.

He paused to rest. "There, now. Nothing here," he said, wiping his brow. He had a considerable congregation to preach to, and they stared solemnly.

"Two feet more, Jones, and we'll believe you," Belle said.

"I'm a geologist, not a grave robber," Hannibal muttered, but he dug again, shovelful by shovelful, heaping yellow clay up, biting farther into the solemn earth. He confined himself to a simple hole near the headstone, and didn't attempt to strip away soil the length of a coffin. He'd show them a thing or two, namely that nothing was there, and then he'd be on his way to Ely, free at last of this mad clan.

"There, now, deep enough," he said, leaning on his shovel. He was hot and tired.

"One more foot," Faye said. "Lucky would make it hard, not easy."

"All right, all right!" Hannibal said, his patience gone. He slammed the spade into the soil, and hit something. A thump. He jabbed it again, and hit the obstacle again. Another thump. He carefully dug down and exposed a horizontal surface, shiny even when fouled with dirt.

"Aiee!" exclaimed Babette.

Hannibal had enough of shoveling and jammed the spade at Attila, who took it this time, almost feverishly, and began whaling away at the overburden. He was half berserk, chopping out huge chunks of earth, baring more and more of the shining dark surface, half mad, while the spectators stood silently, each a prisoner of private thoughts.

Then Attila cleaned off the last of the burden and began working around the edges of what was obviously a handsome casket, so someone could lift the lid.

That's when his brother, Lieutenant Nero Haggarty, arrived with his six Wobblies and four rummy old miners, including Walt Cuban.

"A joke," said Lieutenant Haggarty.

"You just be quiet," said his mother sharply. "And take off your hat. This is a sacred moment."

At last Attila was ready to pry open the lid.

Chapter 42

The lid didn't budge. Attila tugged and yanked down there, but nothing happened.

The heirs of Lucky Haggarty, arrayed around the hole, stood silently, mesmerized by what lay in that pit. They knew nothing. It might or might not be Haggarty in there. The mystery of the Alice might or might not be resolved. They might or might not inherit the most valuable gold mine in the country.

Maybe, maybe not.

And behind the presumptive heirs stood the rest of that odd collection, including the sharp-eyed Wobblies, the old miners, Yin and Yang, Colonel Rathke, the Raven-Haired Maid, and a few stray teamsters. There was not a soul left on the flat where the Alice Mine buildings stood.

Attila tugged again, and was again thwarted. He peered up at the assemblage angrily.

"Maybe you can do better?" he snapped.

No one replied.

Hannibal imagined he was the only one present not really affected by the spectacle. His mules were packed and waiting, yawning in the afternoon desert heat. He would satisfy his curiosity and then head for Ely.

"You'll have to lift it out of there," said Lieutenant Haggarty, but he did not offer help.

Attila glared. He spotted a corner of the lid still buried

under soil, and spaded the overburden away, tossing it upward angrily so that it landed at the feet of his rivals. Then he jammed the spade into the clay, grasped the lid at the lower end of the coffin, and yanked.

This time, with a great screeching, it pulled loose an inch. He yanked again, and with a howl the lid popped free. Attila grasped both sides of it, and yanked again, and this time the lid flew upward, almost knocking Attila backward.

The mob rushed forward and peered down. There indeed lay Lucky Haggarty. He peered up at them from bright green eyes, shining in the sun. A sly smile wreathed his face. His flesh was an odd color, leathery yellow. His hair was neatly combed. And in his hands, which lay upon his breast over a black pin-striped suit, was an oilcloth portfolio. The papers! The secret of the Alice Mine!

Cleopatra peered down upon her father and shrieked in contralto tones. Delilah studied her father and shrieked louder in soprano ranges. The daughters began a shrieking contest, each outshrieking the other.

Belle clasped Hannibal's arm. "That's him! Those eyes! He's watching us, the old dog!"

"Glass eyes. That's not the work of a mortician. That's the work of a taxidermist," Hannibal said.

"Yes!" cried Belle. "He had himself taxidermied! He always admired trophy taxidermy!"

Faye peered down and smiled bitterly. "You're right. That's nothing but cured hide and green glass eyes. Damn him."

Juanita groaned and sighed.

Babette peered at her husband, or at least at the man she had married, and sobbed.

The Wobblies and miners crowded forward. Walt Cuban began to babble.

Attila recovered his balance and started to reach for the oilcloth portfolio.

"Don't you dare touch that, you thief," snapped Faye.

"Hand it to me," Lieutenant Haggarty said.

"Oh, no! You'll keep what you want and hide the rest from us!" cried Babette.

Hannibal marveled. They could not even agree on who should look at the papers in the old rogue's hand.

"Do something," Belle said, squeezing Hannibal's arm.

"Ah, since I am the least involved, being about to depart, why not let me open the portfolio?" he said softly.

Oddly, no one objected. Instead, assorted pairs of eyes riveted him. Out of the silence he knew he was elected. He sank to his knees and gingerly reached downward into that box, grasped the portfolio, and tugged. Those ancient hands didn't surrender it. He tugged again, and this time it jerked free and Lucky Haggarty's stiff hands flopped uselessly on his pin-striped suit.

"You steal those and I'll hang you on the spot," snapped Lieutenant Haggarty.

Belle laughed.

Hannibal unfolded the flap, found a sheaf of manila envelopes within, and carefully withdrew them. They were in perfect condition, well protected from moisture and rot and bugs. There appeared to be several documents, each one carefully labeled and in an envelope. One was addressed to Faye.

"This is labeled Faye Haggarty," he said, and handed it up to her.

The next was labeled Juanita Haggarty, and he handed it to Juanita. The next was labeled Babette Haggarty, and he handed the manila envelope to her.

There were three other manila envelopes. "Is there a Kathleen Haggarty?" Hannibal asked, and met only silence. "How about a Mary Haggarty or a Margaret Haggarty?"

Belle laughed. "More wives than anyone knew about! Or another of Lucky's rotten jokes."

No one else laughed. Belle saw that was the last of the envelopes, and there was none for her. She stood silently, her body taut. Hannibal pitied her.

"I propose that each recipient read the contents aloud," Hannibal said, enjoying his role as major-domo. "Starting with Faye. That way you will all know exactly what lies in each paper."

Down in the coffin, the taxidermist's version of Lucky Haggarty gazed upward cheerfully through green glass eyes.

Lieutenant Haggarty slid one of his automatic pistols from its sheath and waved it. "This'll keep the proceedings honest," he said.

Faye studied the lieutenant. "If you plan to shoot, be about it. Otherwise, put it away. I won't read until you do."

The young lieutenant slowly slid the .45 automatic into its holster, and substituted a haughty glare.

Faye smiled in her odd way. Hannibal thought she was the only woman on earth who smiled by turning her lips downward.

She withdrew the document.

"It's a will," she said. "Signed by Harold Haggarty, and witnessed by three people."

They waited in deep silence.

"I, Harold Haggarty, being of sound mind, will and bequeath to my beloved wife Faye Haggarty the Alice Mine in its entirety, for her sole and exclusive use and enjoyment."

The silence was brutal.

"Should she enter into any combination with any person or entity or corporation to exploit or profit from the Alice Mine, the sole ownership of said mine will immediately and irrevocably pass from Faye Haggarty and be vested in the San Mateo, California, Home for Wayward Girls."

Faye smiled again. "There. I have it. You may all leave now."

Hannibal spotted some long faces and steely glares around that grave, and could almost read Lieutenant Haggarty's mind. The young man was on the brink of ripping the will out of Faye's hands and burning it.

But the gazes shifted to Juanita, who withdrew the

contents of her envelope.

"It is also a will," she said, "signed by Lucky and witnessed by three people."

She began softly. "I, Harold Haggarty, being of sound mind, will and bequeath to my beloved wife Juanita Haggarty the Alice Mine in its entirety, for her sole and exclusive use and enjoyment.

"Should she enter into any combination with any person, entity, or corporation to exploit or profit from the Alice Mine, the sole ownership of said mine will immediately and irrevocably pass from Juanita Haggarty and be vested in the Prohibition Party of California."

A grim silence ensued.

All except for Belle, who began whooping. No one else dared to laugh. They glared at one another, each knowing exactly what lay ahead when Babette read.

Babette swiftly busted open the envelope, her gaze devouring chunks of text, and she focused at last upon the last. "If I combine with anyone to mine the Alice, it goes to the Skull and Bones Society of Yale University," she said.

Belle laughed. The rest glared solemnly, registering all of this.

Lucky was having his fun, even after years in the grave. And the Alice Mine belonged to no one. He had given it exclusively to each of those clamoring for it, and forbidden them to combine or work on shares.

"These wills are all frauds," Lieutenant Haggarty declared. "It's mine by right of possession."

"See how far you get when I file this in court," Faye said.

"And when we file ours," Babette said. "And the sheriff shows up and pinches you."

"Maybe this is a joke, and there's a real will," Juanita said. "What do those other wills say?"

Hannibal studied them. "They're the same, except for the recipients if the will's terms are violated."

Belle sat down, laughing.

"It's not funny," Babette said.

"Go on up to the marquee tent," she said. "I'll ask Colonel Rathke to pour tea and serve up some tarts."

"You keep out of this. You didn't get a will," Babette said. "You're not even included. He included only his legitimate wives."

"Legitimate!" snapped Faye. "Bigamous! Illegal! You have no standing at all, and the courts know it. The courts will throw out all your claims and give the Alice to me. I'm his one and only wife."

"After fifty years of litigation," Belle said, obviously enjoying herself.

Hannibal collected his spade, eyed Lucky Haggarty, whose bright green eyes and smirky smile brightened the afternoon.

"Somebody should bury Lucky," he said, but no one did, and no one cared.

The Haggarty heirs were studying their wills and weighing their options.

Chapter 43

The desert heat was piercing even this shadowed gulch. The combatants stared at one another. No words were necessary. They all knew this would end in the courts, and there would be appeals, and none of them would see the end of it in their lifetimes. And there, smiling winsomely up at them, was the author of it all.

Attila Haggarty glared down at his father, and then spat. The gesture didn't earn him a single condemnation. The Haggarty wives and children despised Lucky, and Attila had merely done what the rest were thinking. Cleopatra picked up a rock and threw it at Lucky, but her aim was bad and it tumbled to rest outside the coffin. Babette picked up a bigger one, and this time the rock smashed into Lucky's pin-striped pants, right where the legs joined.

Hannibal wondered just how far the taxidermist had gone in his preservation of Lucky's hide, but he did not voice his curiosity.

Babette's rock rested heavily on Lucky's groin.

"That's where all the trouble started," Belle said.

For a response, Babette heaved another missile, this one a clod of clay.

Hannibal foresaw an aerial bombardment, and put a stop to it. He tugged the heavy lid over Lucky, even as chunks of earth and rock showered down on the coffin. The taxidermied sire was safe, more or less.

When Lucky's grinning, glass-eyed face vanished, so did the bombardment.

"Back to work," Lieutenant Haggarty said to the Wobblies.

"Back to work! It ain't your mine!" retorted one.

"Back to work or it'll be fifty years in the pen for sedition."

"I'll take the pen. I quit. Seditionists, they're the only sane people here."

"You'll work!"

"I quit. Haul me away."

That obviously posed a dilemma for Nero Haggarty. Take the man away and someone else might grab the Alice. And all the rest might ditch him too. Hannibal relished it, and secretly admired the brave Wobbly.

"March," Haggarty said, waving his automatic pistol.

They did, slowly maneuvering on the steep grade to the flat. The rummy old miners followed, enjoying the sight. The women, glaring at one another, followed, and then Colonel Rathke, Yin and Yang, and the Raven-Haired Maid.

"Put on some tea, Colonel," said Belle.

Colonel Rathke turned and bowed, and proceeded up the slope.

That's when the roar shook the very earth. One moment, it was a quiet desert afternoon in the fast-nesses of Nevada. The next moment, Hannibal's ears were greeted with an incredible thunder, a rumble that seemed to rise right out of the rock, through his feet, and into his body.

Belle reached for him, frightened. The roar didn't subside for another minute or so, and then at last quiet resumed. But as the first of the party reached the lip of the flat high above, there were shouts. Something large had happened. A huge orange cloud boiled into the blue. An occasional rattle disturbed the peace.

"I know what that was," he said to Belle. "By some miracle, we all were here."

He worked his way up the precipitous grade, helping her along until they too topped out on the mining flat. A sea of shattered red rock had engulfed the Alice Mine shaft and the adjacent mine buildings. Dust still lifted from it. The whole lip of rimrock, far above, had given in and tumbled down upon the Alice, burying it in eighty or a hundred feet of rubble.

Yet not a stone had reached the several encampments on the outer edge of the flat. The marquee tent stood bravely, dusted in red but otherwise intact. The remaining tents had acquired a coating of red dust, but stood unharmed. The Alice Mine and its shaft lay under tens of thousands of tons of rock that tumbled like a waterfall over the flat.

Hannibal pulled off his pith helmet in sheer reverence. Never had he experienced such a rock slide. He looked upward, and found the skyline changed. No longer did rimrock brood over the Alice Mine and the flat. The very rock he had walked upon up there days earlier now lay shattered in a gigantic heap.

"I told you there was still a ghost up there," said Faye, wiping red dust off of her face. "He's there! It's

Lucky, getting even for tossing dirt on him."

Belle clutched Hannibal's arm and stared mutely.

"My mine!" yelled the lieutenant.

"What mine?" snarled the Wobbly named Maginnis. "We're pulling out."

"You can't! I'll have you for sedition."

"We did what you wanted. We cleaned out the shaft. Now we're going. Unless you plan to welsh on the deal."

Walt Cuban danced a little jig, muttering things that only a set of teeth could translate into English.

"The Alice is mine, and I'll file the will in probate," said Faye.

"Oh, no, you won't! It's ours!" cried Juanita.

"I plan to hire Snidely, Parsons, and Malone, and you know what that means," said Babette. "It means the Alice will be ours."

"All my sentry work for nothing," Attila grumbled. "For years I've patrolled this place, driving out everyone. And all I did was waste ten years."

"It's not wasted, my boy. We're going to prove to a court that it's ours, and then we'll mine it," Juanita said.

Colonel Rathke was dusting off the pink chaise in the marquee tent, and the other camp furniture as well, and cleaning the dust out of his camp kitchen, while the Raven-Haired Maid feather-dusted everything in sight. Yin and Yang cleaned tents, straightened equipment, gathered firewood, and poured out dust-coated drinking water. Camp life was about to resume.

"We shall have tea shortly," Belle proclaimed.

But her rivals ignored her. It was a strange thing. She wasn't included in Lucky's malevolent joke, but they scarcely noticed. They knew only that she wasn't a rival. But it was she who was offering them hospitality, some good tea while they all studied the monstrous heap of red rock that nearly engulfed the flat.

She turned to Hannibal. "Woowoo," she said, and winked.

He could not fathom her.

In short order, Colonel Rathke had tea and crumpets, along with some cream puffs and brandied cherries ready for any takers. The camp table shone, all red dust had vanished from the chairs, and the world at Alice Mine flats had returned to normal.

Except for the geography.

And there was no sign of guests. Indeed, Babette's four old miners were harnessing livestock and breaking camp. The Wobblies had picked up their miserable possessions and vanished. The Haggarty brothers were breaking up Juanita's camp and preparing to leave. And Faye was quietly hiking up the valley, probably to her campsite high above, and maybe to her home in Ely after that.

It was an oddly sad moment. Rivals they might all be, but bound by blood and other ties, and somehow all connected to old Lucky.

"It doesn't look like we'll have guests," Belle said.

It took an hour or two for the livestock to be collected and harnessed, and the camps to be broken down and loaded, but by dusk the last of Lucky's wives had vanished down the long grade, and only Belle's entourage and camp remained. The day was all but spent. A strange and unaccustomed silence fell over the mournful flat.

Hannibal remembered his loaded mules, and thought maybe to stay one last night, mostly to help Belle. It was all over anyway. He slid and slipped down the slope to the hidden gulch where the creek ran, noted the still-open grave, untied his mules, and led them up the slope. At the ruby silk tent he unloaded their packs and turned them over to Yin and Yang.

"Woowoo," said Belle.

Hannibal wasn't in a woowoo mood, and ignored her.

"Your lover's grave is still open. I suppose I should shovel the dirt and seal it," he said.

"I'll come with you," she said. "We must hurry before dark."

So they hiked down the slope in dusk and Hannibal shoveled the yellow clay over the silent coffin. Belle sat nearby, watching, and he knew from the cast of her face that her thoughts were with Lucky, and that the gold digger loved her man and was grieving.

By the time they returned to the camp, it was full dark, but the Raven-Haired Maid had bravely lit some Japanese lanterns and a fine liverwurst, bacon, and yams dinner, sauteed by Colonel Rathke, awaited them, along with some young and robust Beaujolais.

Belle summoned Yin and Yang and invited them all to feast at her table, which they all did in deep silence. Somehow a chapter had ended, and the story too. What possible story was left? Tomorrow they too would break camp and head for Ely, and he would say his good-byes and start for the mines at Wickenburg.

It was the sweetest of nights, with bold stars, a soft summer's breeze, and the wilds friendly and welcoming. The servants retreated to their tents after clearing away the dishes, leaving only Belle and Hannibal enjoying the summer's night.

Belle stepped away from the marquee tent, raised her arms, and addressed the ghost. "Thank you, Lucky," she said.

"For what?" Hannibal asked, after she returned.

"I didn't receive a will giving me the Alice," she said. "They liked that. I was excluded. Lucky had nothing to offer his gold digger." She laughed cheerfully. "But I won."

"Won?"

"Those were mean wills, intended to torment his assorted wives. He even threw in a few ringers just to torment them all the more, wills to wives that didn't exist. Except me. He didn't give me any grief. That's why I loved him, and still do."

"Maybe he had something else in mind," Hannibal offered.

"Woowoo," she said, and tugged him out of his chair and dragged him to the ruby silk tent.

Chapter 44

Sometime in the middle of the night, Belle jammed an elbow into Hannibal.

"Wake up. I've got it. I figured out Lucky."

Hannibal slowly surfaced from some subterranean place, but he was too limp to rise from that brass bed.

"I feel like a wet noodle," he said.

"And you made love like one. I don't know about you, Jones."

But she had sprung up and lit a lantern, and was dancing about in something diaphanous.

"Get dressed," she said. "We're going down to Lucky's grave."

He yawned. "It can wait," he said. "And besides, nothing's there."

"You don't know Lucky," she retorted, tossing his underdrawers, undershirt, blue shirt, bow tie, and pants in his direction.

"What time is it?" he asked.

"Time to get rich."

He pulled out his pocket watch. "It's two-thirty."

"We're rich, Jones."

"Whatever it is, it can wait."

"No, we're going to do this right now."

He noted that she was industriously sliding into clothing, this time her mimicking little Jones costume, with its blue shirt and red bow tie and tweedy old jacket.

"You've got to wear what I do," she said. "For luck."

"I thought you figured it out."

"We need luck too."

There was no escape. Colonel Rathke, Yin and Yang, and the maid slept soundly in their tents. He slowly slid his varicosed ankles toward the Brussels carpet, avoiding scorpions, and managed to dress himself without assistance, though his knees buckled.

She found the acetylene lantern, tossed in some carbide, waited a moment for the gas to generate, and then lit it with a lucifer. There was a satisfying whoosh, and the ruby walls of the tent glowed redly.

"This is some sort of plot to keep me from leaving tomorrow," he said.

"No, Jones. You sometimes have nothing but bone between your ears. We're rich."

He ignored her, much the safest thing to do. But eventually he was dressed, the red polka-dot bow tie was strangling him, and he wore his baggy tweed jacket and pith helmet.

"Now bring your shovel and come with me," she said, plunging fearlessly into the lonely night. The lantern bobbed, casting weird light around odd shadows.

"I'm tired of shoveling."

"Well, I'm the gold digger. It's exhilarating, digging for gold. You'll get used to it."

He plucked his shovel from the pack, and wearily followed her as she hiked through the gloom to the steep trail down to the rivulet and the grave.

"Not again," he said, but followed meekly, because he couldn't think of any reason not to follow, except that he yearned to climb back into his bed and draw up the comforter and drop into deep sleep.

The steep slope was appalling at night and he feared he'd break an ankle. But Belle barged ahead, oblivious of danger. Then, at last, they dropped into the little gulch and heard the rivulet twittering through the darkness. She headed straight to the grave.

"Dig," she said.

"Dig? Dig him out?"

"Dig."

"But I thought we were going to look for a cache somewhere."

"Dig. We missed it. Lucky's last joke."

"This is madness. I'm going back to bed."

"It's the will giving me the Back Door claim."

Hannibal glared. He refused to unearth poor Lucky Haggarty again, and leaned on his shovel. "I think something upset your tummy," he said.

"The only thing that would ever upset my tummy would be a baby, and it's too late for that. Now dig, Jones."

He was feeling stubborn. "You'd better tell me what this is about."

"Lucky always wore trapdoor union suits in the winter. Only he always called them back-door union suits. It was a joke. That's where he hid his will for me."

"You wouldn't!"

"I would. He wanted me to."

"You wouldn't desecrate the grave or the dead."

"Jones, that's not Lucky. That's nothing but his hide, some glass eyeballs, and a lot of cotton stuffing."

"But Belle . . ."

"If you won't, I will, Jones."

"I'll dig, but I refuse to touch him."

She sighed. "When he lived, I left no Haggarty corner untouched. Leave it to me."

Hannibal saw he was losing the contest. Well, he'd close his mind and thoughts to this, dig as a slave might dig, and flee for Wickenburg at dawn. Slowly he lifted the loose clay away, once again.

"I can't do this. It's wrong. It's . . . obscene."

"That's our Lucky," she retorted.

There was no arguing with her on that point.

He slowly shoveled, wondering what madness possessed him, and why he rhythmically lifted spadeful after spadeful and tossed it aside. The acetylene lamp hissed softly and tossed florid light over the macabre scene. He wondered what a spectator might think, seeing two grave robbers clawing away in the small hours of the night.

Wearily, he worked his way down to the coffin until it thumped under his shovel, and then spent another twenty minutes lifting the treacherous disturbed earth out of there. He had reached the point where he despised her, loathed Haggarty, scorned the whole clan, and hated himself for being used.

Then, finally, he had the clay scraped away from the lid. She lifted the lamp and held it over the hole while he reached down and tugged. The cover didn't come loose easily, and he had to pry with his spade, but at last it was loose and he wrestled it up to the surface.

She held the lamp over the opened coffin. There, just as before, rested Lucky in his pin-striped suit, his green eyes bright, a naughty smile on his lips. Only the portfolio was missing.

"All right, hold the lantern. I'm going down there," she said.

"This isn't right, Belle."

"Woowoo," she said, and laughed.

He did as bid, closed his eyes, but then peeked as she lowered herself into that ghastly pit. She knelt, a knee on each side of the coffin, and rolled Lucky once or twice. Then her hand crept around Lucky, under the seat of his pants.

Hannibal closed his eyes. He refused to look.

She squealed. Then, triumphantly, she pulled out a small oilcloth portfolio that had been resting under Lucky's back door.

"Woowoo!" she said.

A moment later she was crawling out, clutching the portfolio.

"That old Lucky," she said affectionately.

They sat on the earth while he held the lamp overhead. She tugged the oilcloth open, and extracted some papers.

"I, Harold Haggarty, being of sound mind, will and

bequeath the Back Door claim to my companion Belle Brandy, to have and to hold as she sees fit."

There were no restrictions. The papers included a patented claim, a map, and one other note, handwritten.

"That's his handwriting," she said, and read:

"Dear Belle, this is yours. I have one small request. When you bury me again, please have a stonecutter put my name and the dates of my birth and death on that empty marker. My fun is over. Here's a century note to cover the cost. Love, Lucky."

Belle was weeping softly.

Hannibal let her weep, and sat quietly. Then, when the heavens were lightening in the east, he quietly replaced Lucky's lid and filled up the grave, while she watched mutely.

When he had finished, it was almost dawn.

"Jones, half of this is yours," she said.

"The Back Door is all yours," he replied.

"No, Jones, we're going to share this. We'll start tomorrow by filing this and hiring a crew."

He didn't really want it. He didn't want anything to do with Lucky Haggarty.

He liked the new day. "I have a better idea," he said. "I want you to come to Wickenburg. You and the colonel, and Yin and Yang, and the beautiful maid, and set up shop with me while I see about some old mines."

"Oh, Jones, I thought you'd never ask."

"Well, I'm asking."

"I'd love nothing better!"

"I thought you might."

"Jones, I'm a gold digger. You mine gold, and I'll mine you."

"I'll save out a little for a ring, if you want."

"A ring? A slave collar?"

"We can be slaves together, Belle."

"Not a bad idea, Jones, woowoo!"

"You have to promise me one thing, Belle: no jodhpurs."

"How about knickers?"

"Only on Sundays, Belle."

"With brown and cream and green argyle socks and a set of golf clubs. I'm for it, Jones."

They stood side by side at Lucky Haggarty's grave, holding hands and paying their respects to the old rogue.

"You're a rascal, Lucky," she said.

A wind came up and blew red dust about, and then subsided.

"I'll take care of the marker as soon as we reach Ely," she said.

High above, a single stone dropped from the Back Door claim and tumbled down the cliff, landing not far from where they stood. And then some clouds played with the moon.

Epilogue

Hannibal Jones and Belle Brandy were married by the Ely justice of the peace, Judge Ray Beam, and lived happily ever after. They considered themselves especially blessed because they were too old to have children. Hannibal always said he preferred rocks to babies; no rock ever wet a diaper. He became the most eminent mining geologist in the world, known for his uncanny ability to locate ore-bearing seams that a fault or several faults had shifted far from the original mine. He brought so many dead mines back to life that envious colleagues accused him of possessing sinister powers and communing with spirits.

Wherever he went after that, no matter whether it was the Sonoran desert or a Montana gulch or some wild corner of Nevada, he would show up with his entire entourage, ·consisting of his wife, Colonel Rathke, Yin and Yang, and one or another striking maid who changed the bedsheets and washed underwear. Where other mining prospectors cooked beans, had no baths for weeks at a time, and loved their burros more than they loved people, Hannibal Jones lived in high style wherever he was, ably assisted by his wife and servants. They were always the soul of hospitality, even to Haggarty's three widows.

His first name gradually disappeared. Belle always addressed him as Jones. He became known across the continent as Jones the Geologist, and whenever mining companies had a particularly difficult problem to solve, they wired Jones, who had offices in Reno, Bisbee, and Singapore. He grew a full but carefully trimmed beard, having surrendered his straight-edge and strop forever. Belle liked the beard and said it tickled her nose. In time the beard turned iron gray, making Jones all the more formidable-looking, and he was much photographed.

He died in 1937 and *Life* magazine called him "the man who made the twentieth century possible." Belle was featured in a sidebar that said that under every great man there is a great woman. When asked to explain what she meant to Hannibal, she mystified the interviewer by saying only, "Woowoo."

In time, Yin and Yang left to go into the hashish business, but were replaced by two Armenians who were graduated with high honors from a domestic sciences academy in Turkestan. And one day Colonel Rathke gave notice, having accepted the position of chief steward with the Maharaja of Calcutta. He explained gently that he was to receive an annual wage of ten pounds of gem-quality emeralds, payable each year upon Buddha's birthday. That was a sad day, but Belle hired an apprentice of Escoffier named Jean Baptiste Lourdes to cook, and the meals were as fine as ever.

The ruby silk tent wore out in time, but was replaced by several of other hues, at first a royal purple silk tent. But the one they favored the most was a leopard-skin silk tent, although a zebra-striped one was a close second.

They grew moderately rich. The Back Door was never the success that the Alice Mine had been, but it earned them a tidy sum, and Jones and Belle owned it all. There was a court fight over it that consumed several years, because the wives insisted Haggarty was not of sound mind when he willed it to Belle, but the judge found just the opposite to be true; Haggarty was never of sounder mind than when he willed that property to her. So Belle and Hannibal were free to enter a partnership with an experienced mining firm located in Butte, Montana, and before the ore ran out, they had gotten four hundred thousand out of it, which they shrewdly invested in streetcar companies and golf courses.

Lucky Haggarty became even more famous after death than he was during his lifetime. He attracted the attention of professors and reformers, who collectively deemed him the most horrible American of the nineteenth century. The reformers used him as the ultimate bad example, and the reason why there should be stricter laws and more control of business. By the mid-twentieth century, there was a formidable bibliography associated with Haggarty, including three biographies, twelve monographs, forty-seven learned articles, twenty-seven magazine pieces, and eighty-nine socialist tracts. He was also the featured subject in a pictorial book of American robber barons and their families, with a foreword by Warren G. Harding.

The Alice Mine was never reopened. It lay buried under a mountain of lawsuits as the wives and their heirs, and finally assorted holding companies and banks, fought to gain title and access to it. The ghosts of the Alice rained rock on anyone who approached it, always finding more red sandstone to pelt at visitors. In time the whole flat was buried in red rubble, and one could no longer tell there had ever been a mine there. In spite of file cabinets and drawers filled with court records, the Alice Mine gradually faded from memory, and along with it the estimated five million dollars of ore still underground.

Belle and Hannibal retired in 1923, moved to a cliff-side casa at Cobo San Lucas, Baja California, Mexico, and engaged a mariachi band to serenade them every night after they had their fill of margaritas and enchiladas. The band always ended the serenade with Jones's favorite, "La Cucaracha."

"Woowoo," they said, when the band quit playing, and patted each other on the knee.

Center Point Publishing
600 Brooks Road ● PO Box 1
Thorndike ME 04986-0001 USA

(207) 568-3717

US & Canada:
1 800 929-9108